Siena

HELEN EVE

MACMILLAN

First published 2015 by Macmillan Children's Books
an imprint of Pan Macmillan
a division of Macmillan Publishers Limited
20 New Wharf Road, London N1 9RR
Associated companies throughout the world
www.panmacmillan.com

ISBN 978-1-4472-4850-7

A CIP catalogue record for this book is available from
the British Library.

Printed and bound by CPI Group (UK) Ltd, Croydon CR0 4YY

'She left the web, she left the loom,
She made three paces thro' the room,
She saw the water-lily bloom,
She saw the helmet and the plume,
She look'd down to Camelot.
Out flew the web and floated wide;
The mirror crack'd from side to side;
'The curse is come upon me,' cried
The Lady of Shalott.'

Alfred, Lord Tennyson, *The Lady of Shalott*

Prologue

Romy Dyer

It might be trial by school cafeteria, but it's no less horrifying than a courtroom. I shrink into my seat, scratching the oak table as if I can eradicate not only the spikily engraved *R* that marks my place, but myself along with it.

The Starlets are crying, their voices hoarse from shock and sleeplessness.

'She didn't scream.' Libby clutches her stomach with both hands, almost doubled over with the effort of breathing. 'She never made a sound.'

'That proves nothing,' Madison says as she reaches out to wipe Libby's eyes. I think this is supposed to be a kind gesture but she succeeds only in smearing mascara across her cheeks. 'She didn't have time to scream. It happened so quickly . . . everything changed just like *that*.'

She leans against Libby as if comforted by the rhythm of her hysterics.

Cassidy's luminous green eyes shine with tears and something like hope. She traces the engraved *C* that marks her own place frenziedly back and forth. 'Do you mean . . . she didn't have time to realize what was happening to her?'

I want someone to tell Cassidy that *yes*, Siena had no idea what she was falling towards, or how it would feel to hit it, or even that she was falling at all. I want someone to tell her that this is all a mistake, and that Siena isn't dead, and that we aren't ruined so badly that we might as well join her wherever she is now.

'Don't be stupid.' Cassidy has a way of making people want to protect her, but Phoebe is immune to it. 'Of course she knew. She knew *everything*.'

Then I'm crying too, in a way I have no power to stop. I put my hands over my face to shut out Phoebe's pale, set features, but in the darkness I see only Siena, and I jerk them away again.

Phoebe stares me out. 'Stop feeling sorry for yourself. We aren't fooled. We all know *exactly* how you felt about Siena. How you feel about us all, for that matter.'

I tip back my head as if it will stop my tears from falling, looking beyond the Starlets across the cafeteria. This is an orientation day for the incoming Shells, the twelve-year-olds who will join Temperley High School next term, and right now our housemistress Mrs Denbigh is walking the new students through the French windows in formation. My vision clears, and, one by one, the Starlets follow my gaze as a tiny aurora appears between the curtains, her blonde hair a blazing halo in the July sun.

I stand abruptly, my chair crashing over as I run out of the door, my shoes burning and jarring me with every step. I kick them off and run faster barefoot, my breath coming in sobs and gasps and howls.

In my dreams I chase a sunbeam that haunts my endless nights. Often I wake as it melts into snow, or disappears beyond a pink horizon where rabbits play at dusk, but now it transforms before me into a golden rope woven with flowers and leaves and stars. It shimmers out of reach, a fathomless mirage that I would chase forever more without ever wishing to escape.

And, for the fact that the truth about me and Siena remains as elusive as my sunbeam, I am able to feel thankful.

Chapter One
Six months earlier

Siena Hamilton

'I suppose you've heard?'

Libby has no interest in a world beyond Temperley High, but her knowledge of everything within its stone walls is absolute. She's scrolling rapidly through her phone, checking texts alongside tweets and status updates and missed calls. Frowning, she reaches into her Aspinal satchel to cross-reference her bulging day planner with her online diary, and this hesitation costs her the scoop.

'She's *back*,' interjects Phoebe. This is only a lucky guess: Phoebe might possess a hack's instinct for scandal but she lacks Libby's networking flair.

'Of course she's back.' I say this as if I already knew, because revealing ignorance at this table is as dangerous as wearing last season's Miu Miu. 'It's January. She was always due back after a year.'

'I'm aware of that,' says Phoebe defensively. 'I just hoped she might . . .'

'Take the hint?' Libby pushes her lensless glasses up her nose as she and Phoebe break into identical laughter.

'Have you seen her yet?' Madison abandons the problem sheet she and Cassidy are trying to finish

4

before registration. 'I wonder if Paris has been a good influence, or if she's still the daughter of darkness.'

'Inevitably it's the latter.' Libby straightens her lace Peter Pan collar. 'A daughter of darkness who thinks she can treat *us* any way she wants.'

We stare at the empty place at our round cafeteria table. We each sit before our own engraved initial, united by the six-point star carved deep into the mahogany that represents our identity as Temperley High's premier clique. We haven't had time to redecorate in the past year, so Romy's spiny *R* remains an unfortunate reminder of its erstwhile inhabitant.

'She didn't think she could treat us any way she wanted.' I trace my finger up and down the unclaimed sharp edge. 'It was never about that.'

They exchange glances. 'You're very compassionate, Siena,' says Libby. 'I'm sure I'll never forgive her in the way you have. But then, I *am* the only one of us who carries the physical reminders.'

She gathers her nut-brown hair into a ponytail to showcase the faint scar that runs along her hairline and behind her ear. Apparently it still smarts in cold weather.

I smile. 'Don't worry, Libby. It's not about forgiveness either.'

'Good.' Phoebe twists her own white-blonde braid around her finger as if she can't decide how to continue. She's a picture of innocence, but people should know better than to take her at face value. 'So what will you do about Jack?'

The school football team, the Stripes, are doing a lap of the gloomy pitch as part of their morning practice, and I watch my boyfriend Jack through the window as he pulls into the lead and shows off by running the final steps backwards.

'What do you mean?' I ask. 'Why would I need to do anything about him?'

'You won't, of course.' Libby frowns at Phoebe. 'It's just that . . . you know what Romy's capable of. Maybe she's spent her year at reform school planning revenge.'

As she looks around for support, no one points out that a Parisian private school isn't exactly Pentonville. Cassidy is pale and trembling, and I laugh to break the silence. She has a nervous disposition, and a resurgence of last year's screaming nightmares would draw very unwanted attention to us.

'Like *Carrie*?' I ask.

'Maybe,' counters Libby. 'She could have deadly powers for all we know. When she pushed me, I saw my whole life flash . . .'

As much as we sympathize with Libby, there are times when I think I'd plummet down a ladder myself sooner than hear her recount the incident one more time.

'Don't worry, Siena,' interrupts Madison. 'We totally have your back.'

'Of course, some of us have proven our loyalty

6

more than others,' says Libby, exhibiting her scar once again. Madison has a theory that she highlights it with lip liner on special occasions, but we've never caught her at it.

'You've all proven yourselves sufficiently loyal.' I place my hand in the centre of the table and they pile their own on top.

'Starlets for all time,' we whisper before raising our arms into the air. It's a five-year-old ritual too childish to continue now we're seventeen, but the others cling to it, and who am I to rob them of their comfort blanket?

Jack is still wearing his muddy kit as he pulls up a chair beside me. He displaces Libby, who shifts offendedly a couple of inches, and leans over to kiss me, his lips soft but freezing. I press my cheek against his for as long as I can stand it and let him put his cold hands between my knees as I look him over for signs of change after the Christmas holiday. He's reassuringly the same: tall and athletic with messy black hair and a face that always makes him look as if he's up to no good. Usually he's not.

'You're so warm,' he murmurs with a look of concentration as he moves his hand up my leg.

I push him away as Libby makes a disgusted face. 'We're at the *breakfast table*, Jack,' she chides him. 'I'm eating a *granola slice*. Please show some respect for protocol.'

'Sorry,' he says contritely as he turns to his giant cooked breakfast – he's the cafeteria ladies' favourite – and starts to eat. 'Sometimes I just can't help it.'

He whispers into my ear. 'Libby still isn't getting any, then?'

I shake my head, smiling at Libby as she watches us suspiciously.

Phoebe leans forward. 'Jack, did you hear who's coming back this term?'

Jack stops shovelling hash browns into his mouth for half a second and gives her a warning glance. 'What are you planning, Phoebs?'

Phoebe's kitten eyes are round and innocent. 'Nothing,' she says, and it comes out like a mew. Sometimes I think Phoebe is a genius.

'Good,' says Jack. 'Because I think you made your point very clearly last year. The last thing any of you needs is more trouble.'

Madison raises an eyebrow as she tosses the little stars woven into her ash-blonde hair. 'That's a matter of opinion. And, if you remember, Romy created the entire situation by maiming Libby in an attempted murder. Don't put the blame onto us.'

Madison's interjection is helpful as she's the Starlet to whom Jack always refers as *sensible*. Phoebe and I smile at each other as he returns his attention to his fast-increasing cholesterol levels, and then we gather our books as the registration bell clangs.

'Let the fun begin,' Phoebe sings.

'The fun of a new term,' she clarifies as Jack looks at her warningly. 'New lessons, and challenges, and . . . tribulations.'

When they've gone, Jack pulls me down onto his lap and wraps his arms tightly around me.

'Don't get mud on me,' I say, trying to twist away. 'Or egg yolk.'

He kisses me, and, in case he's thinking about anything – or anyone – other than me, I don't stop him until Mrs Denbigh blows her whistle from the teachers' table. 'Two feet on the floor, Siena,' she shouts. 'Both hands where I can see them, Jack.'

'I have to go,' I tell him, struggling to my feet as the other Stripes start cat-calling from their own table.

He stands up and lifts my chin so I have to look at him. He gets offended when I talk over his shoulder to my reflection, not understanding that his face could never be as diverting as my own. 'I'm serious,' he says. 'Tell me you don't have anything planned for Romy.'

'I really don't. I have many more important considerations, like whether Bethany's Achilles has healed for the start of netball season . . .'

'How did she tear it again?' he asks mildly.

'She's extremely clumsy. And whether vermilion makes me look jaundiced . . .'

He frowns. 'I'd no idea you had so much on your mind.'

I'm about to elaborate on my complexion concerns when it occurs to me that he might be joking. Incognizant of the commitment involved, he sometimes treats the responsibilities of Starlet membership as trivial.

'*And* the plight of the white rhino, which Libby and I are working tirelessly to rectify,' I say instead.

He laughs as if he can't help himself. 'I wondered what your sponsored bikini car wash was in aid of. What was it about the white rhino's plight in particular that touched you?'

I turn the conversation back. 'Why do you care what we do to Romy, anyway? Is there something you want to tell me?'

My voice is light but he knows I'm serious, and for a second our eyes fix on the empty star point.

'I love *you*, Siena,' he says steadily as he reaches for my hand. 'You and only you. Don't forget it. In fact . . .'

'Yes?' I prompt. Soliciting compliments is some way beneath my dignity, but there's no harm in offering encouragement when he's feeling tongue-tied.

'The next few months will be important for us, if everything goes to plan,' he says. 'I hope this term will be our most exciting ever.'

My heart is beating fast, and I collect myself before I betray my excitement. For a moment I actually wondered if Jack might go down on one knee right here, in the cafeteria. Even though he'd never do anything so indecorous, I breathe an internal sigh of relief at his words, which are his first hint that a marriage proposal is imminent. The end of our schooldays is approaching at speed, and, with no firm reassurance from him about our future, I've even wondered if . . . well, it doesn't matter now.

Supplementary details would be helpful, but the breakfast table, with its debris of muesli and coffee stains and stagnant appetite suppressants, isn't the place to discuss something as romantic as a betrothal. Instead, I put aside my mud-related misgivings, wrap my arms around his shoulders and kiss him hard. There's no harm in a carefully judged public show of togetherness, especially during times of shifting sands. I pull away again as Mrs Denbigh's whistle sounds with increasing shrillness.

'Remain two feet apart,' she bellows. 'Or I fetch my bucket of water.'

I kiss him once on the cheek as I turn to leave, as if I'm branding him. Feeling the buzz of my phone, I retrieve a message from Libby.

Are you ready for the off?

Even though Jack's gone, I still check that no one's watching before I reply.

I'm always ready.

Chapter Two

Romy

For twelve months I drew and erased chalk marks that counted down weeks and days and minutes. I explained *ceci n'est que temporaire* so often that it became my nickname amongst my classmates. I spent endlessly confusing mornings cramming alongside native French overachievers and diplomats' kids on the Harvard fast track, and endlessly confusing afternoons watching dubbed re-runs of *Gossip Girl* in a Common Room thick with smoke.

I hoped that my enrolment in the French-only quarter of my international school was, as my dad promised, *accidental*; that being reprimanded for tripping over false cognates was good for me; that the Opéra Bastille and the Genevan Model UN Conference and a brutal volleyball championship would be helpful distractions.

But in the end none of this mattered at all, because, while my conscious hours passed as blurrily as the chalk I smudged across the dormitory walls, my never-ending dreams, spiked with Tarot cards and trapdoors and unfathomable amounts of trouble, remain as vividly technicolour today as they did on the day I left.

And just like *that*, in the time it takes to fly from Charles de Gaulle to Heathrow and take a cab down winding, narrow Oxfordshire lanes and a driveway lined with oak trees that conceal the place I hate most in the world, I'm back at Temperley High.

And, as I'd feared on my darkest nights away, nothing has changed in a year except that the Starlets have grown more unified and more powerful and more untouchable. Despite my entirely separate Parisian existence, my new haircut and wardrobe and determinedly laissez-faire attitude, I'm still nothing but an exile; an ex-Starlet whose errors can never be forgotten or forgiven or rectified.

So I stand once again before my erstwhile form group as Mrs Denbigh, sturdier and bushier and more eager than ever for us all to be friends, or at least not kill each other while she's on duty, reintroduces me to the girls who hoped they'd never see me again and the boys who never gave me a second glance.

Why don't they notice you? Siena complained when we were fourteen and she was tired of me encroaching on her time with Jack. I'd warned her that finding me a boyfriend would be an impossible task, and she'd finally started to believe me. *You're a Starlet, for crying out loud*.

I frowned in embarrassment into her ever-present mirror as she pulled my hair out of my face. *I don't care whether boys notice me or not*.

You must care, she said. *What else is there to live for?*

She ran her fingers up and down my back until I twisted away from her. *What are you looking for?*

13

Your re-set switch. It must be here somewhere.

'I expect Romy can teach us all a thing or two about Parisian fashions,' Mrs Denbigh suggests now.

She's trying to help me, but her suggestion elicits nothing but eye-rolling from the back row and a giggle from Phoebe as she whispers something to Madison, hand over her mouth so she can't be lip-read, as she's done ever since we were Shells and they spoke in their own language – devised by Libby and complete with past tenses and prepositions and five synonyms for the concept of *cankles* – as back-up security.

I know better than to reply, and an all-too-familiar lethargy takes me over as I trudge to an empty seat in the second row. I try to make eye contact with several students whom I once believed friends, but under the Starlets' gaze they stare furiously at their desks as if I'm not even there. Allowing myself one backward glance, just to see which guise Siena is wearing today, I'm blindsided and paralysed and jettisoned in the second it takes to do so.

Because Siena at seventeen is more breathtaking than Siena at sixteen, or fifteen, or all the other ages at which her beauty grew in inverse proportion to her niceness, and she's entirely aware of her brilliance. Her eyes are bluer, and larger, and more intense. Her golden hair is still piled up in jewels and leaves and flowers, but I sense that it's grown longer, as if she can't find a stylist worthy of touching it. She's thinner, her cheeks pale and hollow, and she's lounging in her seat, her

14

gazelle limbs carelessly sprung as if at any moment she might uncoil and escape from captivity.

She's smiling at something Libby has said, and I catch the tail end of that smile as she meets my gaze. I can't look away: I'm frozen as she scrawls on her notebook and holds up the page as soon as Mrs Denbigh has turned towards the whiteboard.

She's pierced the paper with earrings shaped like stars, displaying them as if they're in a jeweller's. They wink and dazzle and laugh at me as I read the words beneath them.

> *Clock tower.*
> *Midnight.*
> *Formal dress.*
> *Feel lucky.*

This particular invitation, or threat, or Mayday, depending on your outlook, is directed squarely at me, and, as Mrs Denbigh begins her register at exactly nine o'clock, the ancient clock in the tower strikes like a death knell.

Chapter Three

Siena

Registration, always inconsequential, is especially so today, and Mrs Denbigh's vain attempts to restore peace give us time to evaluate this new incarnation of Romy. Phoebe and Madison giggle, while Libby narrows her eyes and Cassidy shivers like a startled mouse.

We assess the back of her head as she sits down a few rows in front of us.

'She's different,' observes Phoebe after a moment. 'What's happened to her?'

'Her hair has grown back in now she's got rid of those awful purple streaks,' says Madison. 'I can't think why we let her get away with them.'

Romy's long hair, dark brown with auburn lights and a *swish* that she never uses to her advantage, was almost pretty enough to accommodate those heinous streaks, but is considerably improved now. I might even be envious if I weren't blessed with naturally blonde hair, an achievement that can never be surpassed.

'Her clothes are better too.' Madison gives Romy's blue Pilotto dress a grudging once-over. 'That ensemble is quite presentable. At least she's ditched that leather jacket with the peace signs painted on the back.'

'She had to ditch that,' Phoebe says. 'Not even an emo like Romy would tolerate it covered in Libby's blood stains. And no amount of dry cleaning could cleanse *those* memories.'

Madison winces. 'Do you remember her Doc Martens with the multi-coloured laces? Never mind contravening dress code; I'm surprised they were even *legal*. Maybe she got stopped at Customs and had to rethink her life choices before she was allowed to enter the Champs-Élysées.'

Phoebe sniffs indignantly. 'It goes to show that you should always trust your instincts. We should never have let her *near* the Starlet brand.'

Romy is rigid, as if she's listening. This is encouraging: last year one would have thought that our critiques weren't even relevant to her, let alone that she was taking them on board. And she needs to listen, because today we have a special message to impart.

'Let's hope she's had time to rethink her *loyalties*,' I say loudly. 'We might be broad-minded, but we don't have an endless supply of chances.'

'You sound as if you're considering readmitting her,' Phoebe frowns. 'I assume that's just your signature tolerance speaking?'

'Naturally,' I say. 'In case you haven't noticed, the Starlets have evolved seamlessly into a five-piece. All that remains of Romy's legacy is her table engraving, and I think we should leave it there, like a *lest we forget.'*

As Romy flips her hair over her shoulder, her shiny manicure and burnished highlights flame in the sunlight, and from this angle she could be any one of us. She turns awkwardly, as if she's forcing herself to do so, but when she meets my eyes I know she's daring me to engage with her. She makes no sound, but I still hear her voice as plainly as if it were yesterday. It's distorted by choking and sobbing and shock, and it's so much effort for her to force out the words that it's obvious how fervently she means them.

Even if she's completely wrong, not to mention delusional.

Can't you see what's happening? You think she's your friend, and you let her do this?

I stare her out with my blandest expression. It's not as if we're sharing the same memory, after all; she doesn't even know I remember that moment. I offer up the diamond bait when I have her full attention, but her reaction is impossible to decipher.

Our eye contact is severed by chair-scraping as the bell rings and we start to get up.

'Romy, stay behind,' calls Mrs Denbigh.

'What's that about?' asks Libby under her breath.

Madison giggles. 'Romy's starting as she means to go on: in trouble from her very first lesson. Do you think Mrs Denbigh is giving her community service?'

18

I'm cheered by this. 'I hope it's something terrible, like cleaning the Stripes' kits after their summer matches, or dragging the swimming pool for frogs, or missing the Valentine's social with Radley.'

'She should be made to join the Geology Society,' Phoebe adds bitterly. She once had to take minutes at their AGM as a punishment for using their rarest specimen as a pumice stone. 'She'd never survive that.'

'Have you forgotten that she was a member of something far worse?' Libby reminds us. 'G Soc is positively colourful and gregarious next to Student Council.'

A shudder passes right through me at the mention of the Student Council, who meet in an office underneath the back stairs to discuss the library décor and weekend prep sessions and other issues too grey even to contemplate. Members so drab and dismal that they appear to have mouldered from within are seen in public only when they swoop into assembly wearing bat-like scholar's gowns, their skin sallow and their noses beaky, their hair colourless and lank. The culmination of their mediocre membership comes when two of them assume the positions of Head Girl and Boy following an ancient nomination system that no outsiders care to understand or participate in.

'There's no excuse for it,' Libby murmurs each time one of them takes to the microphone with a reedy reminder for us to return our library books

19

on time so we don't deprive others; to keep silent after curfew; and to donate to the bake sale or the art gallery or whichever other unedifying and entirely unaspirational project they're plugging.

'How's it possible to be so unsightly?' Madison comments now with a sense of wonder. 'Are they even mortal?'

'There is something of the netherworld about them,' Libby agrees. 'I worry that if one of them comes too close, their *greyness* might contaminate me like spores.'

'None of them would dare,' says Phoebe. 'They usually sort of flap away when they see us.'

'That's because the celestial light *we* emanate might turn them to dust,' explains Libby. 'But who knows: with any luck, one day we might make them disintegrate altogether.'

'I can't imagine why Romy was permitted to be a Council member,' Phoebe complains. 'What came over us?'

'She duped us,' says Madison. 'We trusted her.'

Libby flips back her hair sadly, showing her silvery scar. 'And look how she repaid us for our trust.'

Chapter Four

Romy

I'm surrounded by Starlets before I can pick up my bag. I know better than to ask for clarification of their note, but their derisive expressions show me that, whatever the purpose of their invitation, it wasn't an overture of friendship.

'How was reform school, Romy?' Phoebe asks, her kittenish appearance always so at odds with her acerbic put-downs. 'I heard that's where you spent last year.'

'How's remedial class, Phoebe?' I ask. 'I expect that's where you spent yours.'

Phoebe mutters something about remedial class and Home Economics class being two different concepts, and I take advantage of the distraction to head for the safety of Mrs Denbigh's desk. I've almost made it when she calls out again.

'Siena, I want you to stay behind as well.'

I groan inwardly, turning around as Siena halts so suddenly that Phoebe almost walks into her. 'Excuse me?' she says blankly.

Libby is immediately by her side, skimming through her day planner and shaking her head regretfully. 'Siena has a packed schedule today, Mrs Denbigh. She doesn't have a window until late this afternoon. Could we perhaps pencil something in during prep?'

'No.' Mrs Denbigh is irritated. 'Whatever Siena's doing, it's less important than this.'

Libby is insulted. 'You aren't suggesting that charity work should take a back seat . . .'

She lets the sentence dangle in the air, and Siena smiles ruefully as she leaves Libby to firm up a more convenient appointment. But Mrs Denbigh, instead of negotiating, sets two chairs in front of her desk and motions me into one.

'Can I find you a stand-in?' Libby offers. 'I could have a less busy student with you in three minutes.'

Mrs Denbigh ignores Libby entirely. '*Now*, Siena,' she barks.

Libby looks startled but quickly regroups. 'I'll handle the schedule, Siena,' she reassures her. 'I can cover for you in this morning's debate, for a start. What is it again? This House believes . . . that crocodile-skin bags can be totally ethical?'

She departs before Siena can reply, talking on her phone at high speed. 'I need to postpone Siena's dress fitting. Something's come up. I *know* . . . it's inopportune. Can we get her in this afternoon? Prep time is fine; I'll finish her English essay and Madison can sit tomorrow's French test for her . . .'

'Ethical crocodile-skin bags?' I mutter when she's gone. 'Is she for real?'

'I was the opposition,' Siena says without looking at me. 'It's called a *debate*.'

22

'Libby can't replace you as the opposition. How can she support animal protection? Skinning giant reptiles must be one of her more humane pastimes.'

I don't expect her to elaborate, but she smiles triumphantly. 'If you must know, the prize is a crocodile-skin tote no matter who wins. Libby, as my *best friend*, will be on the side she's required to represent. As always, that means mine.'

I shrug at her *best friend* jibe. 'It's lucky that you're so replaceable, then. It's lucky that I am, too.'

A memory flashes into my head of me and Siena as bored Fifth Formers, escaping from a tedious, Libby-led, review of the *Starlet Statutes*, via Siena's balcony. Siena followed me down the trellis, wincing as Libby noticed our absence and yelled at us over the ledge: *Siena, you ripped your tights*.

Siena looked fearful, as if this actually mattered, so I pulled at the hole, laddering the tights from ankle to thigh. *Guttersnipe*, screamed Libby. *Siena has a dinner tonight!*

Oh God, Siena groaned. *She's right. My mother is expecting me in an hour*.

Her hair was pulled sideways and I released the pins so that curls fluttered around her face. *Anyone would think you didn't want me to attend this dinner*, she said, trying not to smile. *Don't you know that it's a state occasion? I'm wearing Prada.*

I shrugged. *I'm going riding tonight. Have fun at your dinner*.

I hadn't made it across the paddock before she was beside me, her hair secured in the tights that I'd wrecked beyond repair. *I'm in so much trouble*, she shouted as she took the lead. *You're the worst influence ever*.

Now she checks her flawless reflection before turning her attention to Mrs Denbigh. 'So how can I help?' she asks with a conciliatory smile. 'Is this about what happened between Jack and me in the cafeteria? I've *told* him to take a cold shower before breakfast, but . . .'

I pull a face. 'Please spare us the disgusting details.'

Mrs Denbigh ignores me. 'It's not about that, Siena, although I do live for the day when you and Jack learn to . . . control yourselves.'

Siena pats her already pristine dress. 'I'm in complete control. The boys around me are a different matter: it's unfortunate that their hormones sometimes run away with them.'

'Mrs Denbigh,' I cut in, 'I'm well aware that we're all just bit players in *The Siena Show*, but I haven't finished unpacking yet, and I hoped . . .'

Mrs Denbigh clasps her hands as she looks at us. 'I want to make it clear that last year's events are not forgotten. We may not have resolved them, but, if either of you puts a foot out of line with regard to each other, I *assure* you that we'll reinvestigate.'

Siena frowns. 'The incident in question involved *Libby* and Romy. It had nothing to do with me.'

I expect Mrs Denbigh to take her side, but she

hardly reacts. 'In my experience, Siena, everything has something to do with you.'

Siena smiles graciously at this perceived compliment. 'I'm willing to forgive Romy, and I'd like nothing more than for us to move on as friends.'

I shake my head. 'Forget it, Siena. You've made it clear that you were never truly my friend.'

'It's a shame you couldn't find Romy a *lycée* with a finishing school attached,' she tells Mrs Denbigh sympathetically. 'Such wasted potential.'

Mrs Denbigh starts directing comments to Siena about Temperley High being a home from home; too small a family to form factions that exclude others. Evidently considering this irrelevant to her, Siena searches her bag for face powder. Libby usually holds her mirror for her and she looks momentarily unequal to the task.

'I *completely* agree,' she says, contemplating the compact as if it's a demanding puzzle. 'After all, there's nothing more important than family.'

Chapter Five

Siena

I leave the classroom at speed, but stop short as I almost collide with Jack. He's leaning against a row of lockers and smiling as he always does when he knows I'm keeping a secret.

'What was that about?' he asks. 'Are you in trouble, or was Mrs Denbigh begging you to be Head Girl next year?'

We laugh at the absurdity of this concept, because, aside from being a cadaverous Council clone, our Head Girl is always a scholarship case. Accepting the position is practically a public poverty announcement, like inviting one's contemporaries to throw pennies at them in the corridor. The more uncouth Stripes have been known to anoint the victor thus, but none of the Starlets would ever dream of doing so. There's nothing worse for pulling one's purse out of shape than carrying coins in it.

'What are you doing here?' I ask him. 'Shouldn't you be in Maths by now?'

'Yes, and this is making me late.' He takes my hand and leads me around the corner. 'But I need to see you on your own, and that's not as easy as it sounds.'

He's so earnest – as if we can only meet by formal

appointment – that I almost smile. He should know that, availability allowing, Libby frequently lets him jump the queue.

'What did you need to see me about?' I ask, looking at my watch. If he's quick, I'll only miss the debate's opening arguments.

'I wanted to check you're still on for dinner tonight,' he says. 'You haven't forgotten?'

I maintain a neutral countenance. 'Dinner,' I say reflectively. 'Tonight.'

'My mother's fortieth?' he says. 'You know how emotional she gets around birthdays, and this is a big one. I need the support.'

Libby has standing appointments in my diary for unavoidable commitments such as this, but it's understandable that it's taken second place to the more pressing event we're planning tonight.

I consider the best approach. Jack looks a little upset, so I take his hand and pull him the length of the corridor. Although he looks as if he might resist, he falls into step with me as we cross the courtyard and climb the stairs to his bedroom in Riverside.

'I really am late for Maths,' he says as I shut the door behind us. He no longer sounds very emphatic.

'I know you are,' I say as I unbutton his shirt.

'I wouldn't mind, but it's Applied, which you know is my weakest . . .'

I push him onto the bed and kiss him across his collarbone and down his chest. He inhales sharply, and soon he's stopped talking about Maths. And, more importantly, his mother.

When I stand up to head for the nearest mirror, Jack pulls me back onto the bed.

'I'm out of time,' I say apologetically. 'Maybe we could revisit this later?'

He rolls his eyes. 'I didn't mean that. Can't we just talk for a minute?'

'Of course.' I sit carefully beside him, twisting my hair back into its grips as neatly as I can with only the window as a reflection.

'Your hair looks pretty when it's a mess,' he says, trying to tug it down.

I swipe his hands away before letting him draw me close so that my head rests in the hollow beneath his collar bone. He smells like cinnamon, his bare skin soft and warm, and I almost allow myself to close my eyes and stay there, listening to the rhythm of his heart.

Then my phone vibrates – it's in my bag across the room but I have a sixth sense when I'm needed – and I brush him off. 'What did you want to talk about?'

He doesn't reply until I'm reaching for the door handle. 'Do I take it that dinner's off?'

I shrug. 'Tonight's just crazy for me – you know what the start of term is like. Libby will reschedule for next week.'

'It won't be my mother's birthday next week.'

I blow him a kiss as I open the door. 'You should

have cleared it with Libby first. You know I have a bad memory for details.'

He mumbles something that sounds like *I did*, but I'm already too far away to return for clarification. Certainly time spent with Jack's mother is intensely precious to me, but I tactfully steer clear of her when her birthday is imminent, just as I do my own mother. Proximity to the youthfully exuberant can only serve to intensify the agony of the ageing process.

I arrive in the Common Room to find the Starlets in our favourite seats. The popular sofas are positioned underneath a large mural depicting *vanity*, and no one else, other than our opposite numbers in the Stripes, ever dares sit here. The debate is over, and, judging by the prominence with which she's displayed a pink crocodile-skin bag on the table, I guess Libby won for me. She's unequalled at eliciting a swift denouement to any problem. The bag, which was designed by Cassidy's father, is actually fake at my behest, but Cassidy is a good secret-keeper and you'd never know that it didn't once swim green and free in the Nile.

Madison moves to give me the chair facing the reflective French windows while Phoebe sends a nearby non-Starlet – a civilian with hair so lank and unmemorable that we refer to her by number only – to fetch my morning mimosa.

'What have you been doing all this time, Siena?' asks Madison.

Libby looks up from the floor plan she's studying. 'Can't you guess? There's only one activity that messes up Siena's hair like that.'

'Horse riding?' blurts out Cassidy. She bites her lip immediately, because horse riding is considered to be such a reminder of Romy that Libby has banned the words as well as the activity. The other Starlets didn't argue, especially after her eye-opening presentation on the effects of dressage on the thighs, but then none of them is overly keen on animals anyway.

Libby narrows her eyes. 'Really, Cassidy. Isn't it obvious what Siena's been doing? Or should I say *whom*?'

Recently Libby has started to complain that she ranks second to her boyfriend Tristan's keen interest in synchronized swimming. While his aquatic social life is flourishing, she's increasingly intolerant of successful relationships.

Madison giggles. 'You and Jack are terrible, Siena. Didn't Mrs Denbigh just keep you after class to warn you about that behaviour?'

'Yes,' I say, pleased to be given this palatable excuse. 'But it's no wonder that she resents my romantic life when she's locked up here like a nun all year round.'

'We should set her up with someone.' Cassidy's eyes gleam. 'A toy boy, like the new synchronized swimming instructor, would be very on-trend. She's feisty, despite being so old. Perhaps she could even teach him a thing or two.'

Libby shakes her head before I can note that Mrs Denbigh is emphatically not Diego's type. 'We don't have the capacity to take on any more aid work right now. I could *perhaps* schedule it into September, if the charity safari doesn't come off.'

Libby is our social secretary, but in reality her role is even greater than that. Our lives are so high-octane, even without factoring in our academic commitments, that we'd never fulfil our charitable potential without her expert management.

'Are we ready for tonight?' I ask. 'Just tell me on a need-to-know basis, because I'm not interested in the details.'

'Are you sure, Siena?' asks Libby. 'Logistically this is a little complicated, and I'd hate for you to . . .'

'Really, Libby,' I interrupt, rolling my eyes. 'I'm sure I'll be able to follow what's going on.'

'Does it have to be fortune-telling?' Cassidy looks ashen. 'And does it have to be in the tower? It's going to be so . . . dark up there.'

'Fortune-telling was the *root* of Romy's crime, Cassidy,' Libby says patiently. 'The tower was the *scene* of Romy's crime. Hence the punishment.'

She hands her a box of candles. 'You can count these; it'll settle your nerves.'

'Cassidy's not supposed to think about the occult,' Madison says as Cassidy continues to tremble. 'We can't risk her being sectioned again, especially right before London Fashion Week. We won't get Frow tickets without her.'

Madison raises a good point, because Cassidy's father's high-end handbag line is responsible for most of our Frow access, and I'll need as much coverage as possible as I seek a wedding dress designer.

'Get on with it, Cassidy,' says Libby. 'We've a big night ahead of us.'

'Fortune-telling isn't real,' whispers Madison behind her hand. 'Romy was just good at faking it.'

'Excuse me?' says Libby alertly. 'You think there's another explanation for her accurate predictions, such as correctly foreseeing rain on the night of Winter Formal?'

'Romy watched the Weather Channel,' murmurs Madison. 'Rain was forecast.'

'She predicted that Cassidy would fail her Maths GCSE, and she did,' Libby says triumphantly. 'Would you care to explain that?'

'The prediction condemned Cassidy to failure,' Madison shrugs. 'She never stood a chance.'

'How about prophesying my balanced and fulfilling relationship with Tristan? I'd never have targeted him if it hadn't been for that.'

I wait for Madison to point out that this was merely a cruel joke on Romy's part, but thankfully she doesn't go that far. 'Fine,' she sighs. 'There's no other explanation.'

Libby loves psychic phenomena, and Romy's

excellent track record, along with my endorsement, has her convinced that she's the genuine article. It's ironic that the very talent that secured Romy admission to the Starlets aged twelve was the same that ejected her four years later.

I drum my hands restlessly on the chair arm and then stand up. 'Aren't you coming to watch swimming practice?' asks Phoebe. 'The boys' January diets haven't been enforced yet, so their Speedos will be really tight.'

'Not today,' I say regretfully. 'I'm having a manicure. I won't be back until this afternoon.'

'You could have told me,' huffs Libby. 'Now I have to rebook your midday detention, and you know I'm already working on a plea bargain with Mr Tavistock.'

'It's an emergency.' I hold out my hands as proof.

'It certainly is,' Madison says in horror. 'What on earth happened to you?'

Whipping out her phone, Libby photographs my artfully ragged cuticles at close range. 'Don't worry; I'll show him this. It should buy us a few days.'

Our Citizenship teacher Mr Tavistock is duty-bound to detain me every time I miss his lessons, and I'm currently in arrears. Judging by the hairiness of his own palms, I'm not sure that he'll empathize with a cuticle-based emergency.

I air-kiss each Starlet before heading for the door. Madison is holding a healing crystal to Cassidy's temple as, pale and shaking, she counts and re-counts candles, and Phoebe is patrolling to ward off unwanted civilian attention. At times like this we're a well-oiled quintet, and yet I can't surrender the feeling that we're a sextet rendered incomplete.

As I reach the end of the corridor I check that no one's around and then I double back, crossing the courtyard at a run.

Chapter Six

Romy

The stables are always deserted at this time of day, but, as I open the creaking door and enter the gloom, I still hold my breath as if doing so will render me undetectable. The smell is exactly the same as I remember; of wood and straw and January air, a hollowness that's always chilly whatever the weather. I wrap my arms around my chest for warmth as I run across the floor, my chin tucked firmly into my sheepskin collar.

My stall, complete with neatly stacked straw, is exactly as I left it a year ago. The door swings ajar to reveal an unnaturally bare floor, and the walls, stripped of tack, are depressingly grubby. In fact, no one appears to have been here since the day I left for France, when my father stormed in to remove my horse and everything associated with him.

I sit down inside, closing the stall door so that only strips of the room are visible through the slats. 'I'm sorry, Star,' I whisper as a band of despair tightens around me. 'I didn't choose this.'

That horse was supposed to teach you responsibility, my dad raged in handwriting that left deep grooves in his embossed paper. *You shouldn't be surprised to hear that I've had him sold.*

Now I realize the futility of my hope that he was bluffing in those desultory letters, and jealousy stabs me as I imagine Star living with a new owner: a child who loses interest in him as swiftly as she does her Christmas presents, or a teenager as selfish and entitled as some of the girls in this school.

I rest my head on my knees until the ache is replaced with an odd absence of feeling, and then I notice a glittering shape beside my foot. I pluck it and hold a tiny yet unmistakable gold star between my fingers, letting it flutter away as the main door swings open.

Siena's presence is always detectable, even when she can't be seen or heard, so I know she's there before her Ralph Lauren boots sound on the earthen floor and her golden hair flashes in the beam of sunlight that's impossibly followed her inside. She's been warned a million times about riding safety, and yet I'm not surprised when she leads her stallion Pip out of his stall without reins or a saddle. Unsupervised, she always rides bareback – barefoot if she can get away with it – and never wears a helmet unless Mrs Denbigh forces it onto her head.

What's the point of freedom if you're weighed down with precautions? she once said.

She's halfway across the paddock by the time I reach the doorway, but Pip is pure white, no doubt to attract maximum attention to their partnership, and her hair has come conspicuously loose from its fastenings. A haze of tiny gold leaves, of which she seems to have an endless supply, encircle her like a force field as her ribbon flutters away, and her hands are woven into the horse's mane as she leans into his ear to urge him onwards.

My memory of riding is so enmeshed with Siena that I've tried not to think about it, but now I remember the exact sensation; a thrill that's been buried beneath suspension and punishment and a father who shouts *What in God's name were you doing?* without once listening to the answer.

It's easy to imagine competing for the lead as I surrender to the lulling gallop. Siena is laughing, and so am I, even though she's beating me. She never laughs this way – excited and unselfconscious and loud – when we're with the other Starlets, and, as she and Pip vanish into the distance, I wonder if that laughter has been entirely suppressed by worshippers and boy dramas and ball gowns. It doesn't matter, because Siena does whatever she chooses and no one else bears any relevance to those choices. It's debatable whether she has any memory of these moments at all.

I force myself out of the stables before she returns, summoning the courage to walk back into school. The Sixth Form Common Room is the last place I want to enter, full as it always is with Starlets and Stripes, but, surrendering to the inevitable, I walk inside.

My face burns as the humming voices halt, and a hundred eyes swivel from me to Libby and back again.

'Disgraceful,' Libby proclaims in a clarion tone from the Starlets' seats that dominate the room like a club class lounge. 'Does this school have no regard for its students' safety?'

The voices strike up again, repeating my voice in waves. The Starlets crowd around Libby as if she needs a guard as I head at speed to the safer refuge of the Student Council's corner. Relegated to a group of hard chairs beside a draughty doorway, our Head Girl and Boy huddle over cups of hot chocolate, deep in conversation.

'Do you mind if I sit down?' I ask.

Ambrose responds by pushing his bag casually across an empty seat, while Avery hitches her chair forward to shrink their already cosy circle. Pretending not to notice, I push my way between them as they draw back in unison, looking affronted. They maintain that they aren't related, and perhaps that's true, but their identical freckles, long noses and skinny frames are more unnerving than ever now that they've entered into an official partnership.

'What's up?' I ask brightly. 'I'm looking forward to rejoining the Council this term.'

'Rejoining?' Ambrose says blankly. 'What do you mean?'

'I mean *joining again*,' I clarify. 'I've missed you.'

'You can't!' Ambrose's voice becomes a squeak and he clears his throat, ashamed of his outburst. 'What I mean to say is . . . what about the *incident*?'

I play dumb. 'Which incident?'

He sighs. 'You know I'm referring to your attack on Liberty Horsforth.'

'I've spent the last year being punished for that *incident*,' I say. 'You're President of the Human Rights Society! Don't you believe in rehabilitation and a clean slate?'

'The Starlets don't.' Avery pats her straw-like braid and looks towards Libby and Phoebe, who are hissing to each other like conspiratorial cockroaches. 'Libby doesn't want you back here at all. How can you sit on the Council as a student body representative when she's campaigning for your expulsion?'

'Libby isn't *the student body*,' I try. 'Libby is a single student. And you haven't replaced me, have you?'

Ambrose is studiedly casual. 'How do you know that?'

'Mrs Denbigh told me that my seat was still open.' I try not to let desperation creep into my voice. *What will I do if you won't have me back?* 'I wouldn't be here otherwise.'

'Your seat isn't vacant through choice,' says Ambrose. 'The fact is that no one will take it.'

'Why not?' I ask. The Council has never had a waiting list, but it seems odd that a replacement can't be found amongst the entirety of my year group. For all its lack of social prestige, it has benefits: responsibility for important decisions, advantages for university applications, and, I once believed, membership of a group that cares for its members.

'They're scared,' says Avery. 'The Starlets made it clear that they'd take a dim view of anyone following in your footsteps. No one will risk it.'

'That's crazy,' I say. 'My seat isn't jinxed!'

'Can you offer us an explanation for what you did to Libby?' Avery says timidly. 'You're such a pacifist – we couldn't believe you'd hurt someone so brutally.'

'The evidence is conclusive,' I shrug. 'I pushed her. Hard. Right down the ladder.'

'But why? *Starlets for all time*, and all that. Why would you hurt one of them? Such a high-profile member, at that?'

'I was on the Council for *four years*,' I remind them. 'I was loyal. I worked hard. I was even the Head Girl-elect. Does that count for nothing?'

'You have to understand our position,' Avery pleads. 'Council members endure enough spiritual tests without inviting an exile into our ranks. We'd never survive it.'

'Is there any way I can change your minds?' I ask. 'Would you have me back if I weren't an exile? If I were a Starlet again?'

'Life is certainly easier with Starlet endorsement,' concedes Ambrose. 'But let's face it, Romy. You have more chance of . . . of Jack choosing you over Siena than of the Starlets readmitting you.'

Before I can decide whether to tell them about the Starlets' note, Jack and some other Stripes enter the room with their usual fanfare. He's looking for Siena, of course, and I get up hurriedly before he notices me.

'Leave it with me,' I say. 'I've never let you down before, have I?'

'Romy . . .' says Avery. 'Maybe it's time for you to move on with dignity.'

I shake my head fiercely, ignoring her kind expression. I'm not sure if she means that I should move on from the Council or the Starlets or the school altogether, but none of the possibilities bears thinking about. I'm only halfway to the door when Jack notices me, and, although I'm almost running, he's caught my arm by the time I reach the corridor.

'Jack!' I back into an alcove and force an unconcerned smile. 'What can I do for you?'

He looks confused. 'What kind of question is that? You've been away for a year without any way for me to contact you. You deactivated your Facebook account . . . you changed your email . . . you didn't answer my letters . . . And I had to find out from *Phoebe* of all people that you were coming back today. I want to know how you are; what you've been doing; why we're having this conversation in an alcove . . .'

'Oh, *that*,' I say. 'I lost track of time, I suppose. Everyone knows that the internet barely works in France. Nor the postal service. And I didn't tell you I was coming back today because . . . I wanted to surprise you.'

41

'Well . . . okay.' He shakes his head. 'Thanks for explaining nothing.'

He's blocking my path, and he's too tall to push aside. Forced to look him in the eye, I contemplate sharing some details about my year away. It might be a relief, especially as we aren't in the habit of keeping secrets from each other. But then I notice that his shirt buttons are fastened wrongly; no doubt the result of recent activity with Siena.

'What do you want me to explain?' I sigh, defeated.

'How about *everything*? As if you'd push Libby off a ladder! Even if she deserved it, the idea is crazy. Why didn't you defend yourself and clear your name?'

'How could I?' I say. 'I pushed her. She fell. *Bang*. I got sent to France.'

'Why were you fighting with her?'

'Why do you think, Jack?' I say recklessly, hoping to embarrass him into letting me go. 'What do Libby and I ever fight about?'

'You fight about *everything*. How am I supposed to know . . .' He breaks off as the truth dawns on him. 'Not *again*?'

I nod. 'We don't fight over everything; we always fight over the same thing. But this time was different, because Libby *knew*. She knew the truth.'

He doesn't need me to explain, but, although his face is sympathetic, his words are not. 'I know you don't want this, but couldn't it be a good thing? A chance to come clean at last?'

I blink to hide pricking tears, but my voice sounds like a sob. 'I'm not ready to come clean, and I don't know if I ever will be.'

'I've missed you,' he says. 'I don't want to lose you again. Especially not over this.'

'Please don't make this harder,' I throw over my shoulder as I push past him. 'You and Siena made your choice years ago. The least you can do is live with it.'

'So that's it?' he asks. 'We can't be friends?'

'Think about what Siena wants from you, Jack,' I say. '*Really* think about it.'

He calls after me, but, as usual, he's too late.

Chapter Seven

Siena

We have to wear our black scholar's gowns for exams and meetings with the Headmistress, and the detestable Student Council members wear them every day – by choice, unless Madison's theory is correct that the gowns grow on them like fungus – but they spend most of their lifespans in our wardrobes gathering dust. So, even though they're very unflattering, with manmade fibres, batwing sleeves and billowing panels that swamp the most sculpted of figures – even *mine* – we all agreed with Libby that tonight would be an appropriately momentous outing for them.

The Starlets are neatly assembled when I arrive at our midnight meeting place in the courtyard. We're all wearing gowns over our nightdresses, and Cassidy smiles blearily, her tangled red hair and birdlike wrists emerging from oversized folds of fabric that render her more waifish than ever. She looks about eleven. Madison has added a skinny belt to her own gown and cut the hem asymmetrically to reveal several inches of bare thigh.

'I wish we could do this in summer,' says Phoebe grumpily. 'Whoever decided on January?'

She never tires of arguing. Sometimes she likes to

challenge Libby's position as second-in-command, and I usually let her, because it helps Libby stay at the top of her game.

'Would you prefer to leave Romy – a danger to herself as well as the whole student population – at large amongst us until the weather gets warmer?'

Libby tries to wave an arm for emphasis but is heavily weighed down. Her gown is the least flattering of all, customized as it is with inside pockets that hold her day planner, essential items of stationery, and her phone. She doesn't like to be reminded of her past as a Girl Guide – Patrol Leader, no less, and I have the pictures – yet their teachings seem more embedded in her psyche than anything she's learned since.

'Can we stop pretending to have the other students' interests at heart?' I suggest. 'We all know why we're here, and no one else can hear us.'

'How are we getting in?' asks Madison, who's been as uninterested in details as I have.

Libby loves the pay-off of successful planning, and so thrives on the resulting praise that she has trouble delegating all but the most menial tasks. She reaches inside her gown and produces an iron key.

'Mr Menzies keeps this in his shed, and it's really hard to get close to it,' she explains. 'Didn't you wonder why all the fire alarms went off this afternoon?'

'That was you?' Phoebe says in outrage. 'Don't you know that the alarms activate the sprinklers in the boys' changing rooms? My shirt got ruined, and it was vintage, so it's completely irreplaceable. Don't you ever *think*, Libby?'

'What were you doing in the boys' changing room?' asks Cassidy.

Madison smirks. 'Not *what* . . . Phoebe, why are you complaining about your shirt? I heard you weren't wearing anything except Chelsea boots anyway.'

'Oh, so *that's* why you were wearing a fireman's jacket afterwards, Phoebe,' says Libby. 'I assumed you were pioneering a literal interpretation of this spring's *workmanwear chic*.'

The clock tower that tops the main building has been the Sixth Formers' preferred hook-up venue for years. It's always been out of bounds, but security was heightened to Azkaban-like levels following last year's ill-fated incident which ended with Libby an unconscious heap and Romy on the first flight out of Heathrow. It would be beneficial if Libby's key theft were to restore the status quo, not least because I'm tired of getting splinters in my back from the floor of the woodshed.

Cassidy fumbles for my hand in my long sleeve as we creep up the spiral steps. Hoisting our gowns over our shoulders, we file up the ladder and through the trapdoor into the tiny tower room. As Shells we all fitted comfortably inside, but now it's cramped and the uneven floorboards are creaky. I often used to climb out of the window to sit under the clock face when I needed thinking time, but, as I open the window, the ledge looks more narrow and precarious than ever.

'Do you really think she's coming?' Madison asks as we light candles in every corner. Her face flickers in the intermittent glow.

'Of course she's coming,' Libby says. 'How could you doubt it?'

Madison shrugs as she searches behind sparse furniture and threadbare curtains.

'What are you looking for?' Phoebe giggles. 'If it's something that belongs to Siena, it's on the floor right behind that screen. You can see where the carpet's worn away.'

'I'd rather have lost it in here than in the swimming pool at Radley,' I tell her. 'During a *relay race*, of all things.'

Madison eventually liberates a bottle of vodka from a pile of dust sheets. I take double my share before handing it to Cassidy, who has the tolerance of a dormouse and thus relies on me to cover her ration without anyone noticing.

'You're very quiet.' Libby is watching her intently. 'Is something wrong?'

Cassidy jumps and takes a swig. 'Of course not!' she chokes. 'I was just thinking . . . what if we get caught? This could get *us* into trouble as well, couldn't it?'

Phoebe looks dismissive. 'Romy should have been expelled forever. If the school won't do the right thing,

47

it's up to us to wield the moral compass.'

A head rush of vodka makes Cassidy uncharacteristically – and unwisely – bold. 'We could ask Romy to explain herself. Maybe it was an accident, or . . .'

Libby looks appalled. 'Are you suggesting she could have a valid excuse for what she did to me?'

Phoebe nods. 'Romy's had more than enough chances to talk. There's no doubt that she hurt Libby on purpose, and she can't be allowed to get away with it. What would people say about us if we did nothing?'

Libby taps her bulky gown. 'Trust me, Cassidy. Tonight has been planned way beyond any margin of error. By tomorrow, order will be restored to Temperley High and none of us will have to see Romy again. *Ever.*'

She picks up a candle so that half her face is illuminated white, and Cassidy flinches. Ensuring that Libby can't see, I edge closer, intending to squeeze her arm in solidarity. Madison has got there first, though, and we both jump back as if, despite having been caught committing the same offence, one of us will break ranks and tell Libby.

Chapter Eight

Romy

The last evening I spent with the Starlets began a lot like this, in the tower room they love so inexplicably. Siena – of course – discovered it years ago when she and Jack were looking for *alone time*, and, despite the trouble it could have landed her in, it seemed as if she wanted to be caught up there. Anyone crossing the courtyard could have seen her on the window ledge, ivory in the moonlight, her small feet tucked under her and her hair fluttering in the breeze. She was lucky, or perhaps unlucky, that most people didn't glance up.

Tell Siena's fortune, Libby commanded me. We'd been playing drinking games and pretending to revise for exams, but Siena had injected a serious note into proceedings by wondering aloud when Jack would propose to her. She'd revisited this question intermittently over the years, but that night she spoke with palpable anxiety, as if she might soon be over the hill and no longer a viable match.

Do you really have a psychic gift? I'd once asked my mother. Her Tarot cards had been her constant companion for as long as I could remember, but I never knew where they came from, or why; only that, in the event of a house fire, she'd have rescued them before any of her family, and then consulted them for her next move. I wanted to sweep the whole pack into oblivion and force her to make her own decisions, even before she insisted that I learn to read them too.

Of course I have a gift, she told me as I inexpertly cut and dealt the cards during one of our lessons.

How will I know if I have a gift too? I asked in a moment of beat-them-join-them optimism. If I had to learn how to read these cards, I could at least develop a labour-saving method of doing so.

You'll just know, she said. *But if you pay attention to me, no one will know the difference.*

Do you mean I should fake it? I asked.

I mean that logic and guesswork are usually sufficient, she said carefully. *People are so predictable that a real gift is rarely necessary.*

I don't want to tell Siena's fortune, I told the Starlets in the tower room. The Tarot cards, which I'd by now inherited, were in my pocket, but predicting a date for Jack and Siena's engagement went way beyond my usual clairvoyant duties. The Starlets, who were gullible, were perfect subjects for cold readings, warm readings and anything else, and I was usually happy to prophesy about weather (based on television reports or looming dark clouds) or whether a particular boy was worth pursuing (because he inevitably wasn't); but Libby was in a markedly baleful mood that night, and Siena's marital future was not a prediction I wanted to undertake.

Nevertheless, having forsaken my free will when I'd first worn the Starlet earrings, I shuffled the cards. It should have been easy to conjure up mental images of Jack's romantic proposal and Siena's fake-surprised *yes*, and their ridiculously *Twilight* teenage wedding followed by a life of drudgery and resentful imprisonment. But, instead of seeing any of those things, my mind went blank, and stayed that way.

I don't see him proposing, I blurted out before I could stop myself, even as I should have been describing the crystal carriage whisking Siena to church, the Starlets' immensely flattering bridesmaids' dresses, and the Antiguan honeymoon.

The Starlets usually sulked and flounced when I gave an unpopular answer, but the enormity of this transgression was immediately clear. Madison looked bewildered, while Cassidy was close to tears, and Libby turned more rattlesnake than usual as she ordered me to retract my statement. Siena didn't speak, but she was pale as she followed the others down the ladder. I'd intended to follow them once I'd extinguished the candles, but unfortunately Libby stayed to help, initiating the events that preceded my year-long banishment.

The focal point of the tower room is a six-point star chalked on a candle-littered floor. The Starlets are cross-legged before their star points, gowns bunched in their laps.

'It's good to see you back, Romy.' Libby's arched eyebrows practically meet with the ferocity of her frown.

'Wow, thanks,' I say as sarcastically as I dare.

'*It's good to see you back*,' she repeats, 'as long as you promise not to try and kill any of us this time.'

I turn to Siena. 'I'm afraid I can't promise that. But I'm grateful for the opportunity to make amends, Siena.'

Glancing back at Libby, I see a flash of annoyance cross her face before a neutral expression reasserts itself. It's a petty victory, but still cheering to undermine Libby for an event she's masterminded.

Siena nods at the sound of her name, but she's not listening. She rarely does listen to anything going on around her, probably because it interferes with the constantly buzzing *Siena* feed inside her head. She's scrolling through photographs of herself on her phone as she chooses a new screensaver, and I can tell by her awkward posture that she's experimenting with a new Pilates movement.

'So what's the plan?' I ask.

'Isn't it obvious?' Madison waves at the circle.

'I don't tell fortunes any longer,' I say firmly. 'You know what happened last time, and you're crazy if you think I'll risk being expelled. In fact, if we're caught, we'll *all* be expelled.'

Libby looks angelic, as far as is possible for a regulation-clothed, sleek-haired Mussolini. 'We won't get caught. No one would expect us to come back up here after what you did to me.'

'I don't even have my cards anymore,' I say. 'I lost them that night.'

'Then you'll do it without them,' shrugs Libby. 'If you really have *the gift*, as you've always claimed, you won't need props.'

'Did you at least bring alcohol?' I ask. 'It's difficult to hold this conversation sober.'

Siena passes me a bottle of vodka. She stares at me as I take a swig – it's entirely possible that she's only just noticed I'm here at all – and we all jump as her phone rings. She makes a face as she answers, murmuring in response to an agitated voice.

'I'll call you back,' she says finally and hangs up.

'I could have taken that for you,' says Libby. 'Was it an overzealous fan?'

'It was Jack,' says Siena. 'Something about his mother miscalculating her lithium dosage. The usual.'

'Shouldn't you go and be with him?' I ask incredulously. 'Don't you care?'

'Spare me,' she snaps. 'It's your fault we have to be here at all.'

'*My* fault?' I raise my voice as latent anger – or alcoholic bravery – surges. 'You're blaming *me*, after I—'

'Calm down, girls,' says Phoebe smoothly. She attends an etiquette camp each summer where debutantes learn to exit a car without revealing their knickers to spying cameras, and, possibly, to conduct a

53

psychic reading untainted by incivility. 'Let's not ruin a lovely evening.'

'If I tell your fortune, can we go?' I turn towards Siena, but there's a gap in the circle where she was sitting.

'I didn't see Siena leave,' says Cassidy as everyone follows my stare.

Libby looks surprised, and then shrugs. 'You can't expect her to devote her whole night to this. She must have gone after Jack.'

I smile at the fact that Siena has followed my advice, and Libby scowls. 'She hasn't left because *you* told her to. She's left because she's extremely compassionate.'

The window slams, and Cassidy turns in panic. 'What happened? Is someone there?'

'Could I borrow your gown, Romy?' smiles Libby. 'I need to block up that draught. It's scaring Cassidy.'

'Why does it have to be my gown?' I ask. 'Use your own.'

'I don't want to use mine,' she explains. 'It'll get dirty. *Not* to mention that you owe me. *Not* that I hold grudges.'

I remove my gown, ignoring Madison's raised eyebrows at the oversized Metallica T-shirt that constitutes my winter pyjamas. My makeover, the result of a desperate visit to the Galeries Lafayette on my final day in Paris, was an attempt to convince my father that my sentence had changed me for the better. A personal shopper, horrified at my favourite leather jacket, chipped nail varnish and ripped jeans, devoted several hours to making me presentable and even forced me into the hair salon to remedy my half-grown-out streaks. Only when I'd left with an eye-watering array of new rainbow-hued outfits, my original ensemble shoved shamefully to the bottom of my now-obsolete backpack, did I realize that I'd forgotten to look for new nightwear.

'My Chanel is at the cleaners,' I say as Libby plugs a hole in the wall, but she's lost interest anyway.

'That's better,' she says as the candles stop flickering. 'Now I won't get pneumonia.'

'I'm quite cold, though,' I comment to a general lack of interest.

'Look into the flame, Romy, and tell us when Jack will propose to Siena,' says Madison tiredly. 'Otherwise we'll never get out of here.'

I try to visualize Siena's future logically, just as I can see Cassidy as a make-up artist and Madison a designer, Libby trapped in a deservedly unhappy marriage to a repressed synchronized swimmer, and Phoebe as a foil for a diamond heist gang; but once again I see nothing but swirling mist. *Siena*, I tell myself firmly, closing my eyes. *Siena and Jack*. Anger and jealousy vie for attention, filling my throat and choking me. Several long moments later, smelling smoke, I realize that I'm not being asphyxiated by emotion alone.

Opening my eyes, I see flames in place of my gown.

'Oh no, Romy!' Libby says in the voice she developed

for the line '*Out, damned spot!*' in last year's *Macbeth*. The *Temperley Tribune* called her an '*eerily competent villain*'. 'Your gown is on fire!'

The candles have gone out, and the room is now pitch black apart from the flames by the window. I should have been prepared for such a disaster, but I'm powerless as four shadows stampede towards the trapdoor. By the time I reach my gown, the fire has spread halfway up the curtain.

I'm shaking as I yank it onto the floor and stamp it out, thankful at least to be wearing my own boots and not the kind of Starlet-approved stilettoes that would have set my feet alight. Even so, my shirt is singed before the flames are extinguished. I lean on the wall, coughing and wheezing, in time to hear the trapdoor slam shut.

Chapter Nine

Siena

I've already told Jack that if his mother didn't change her meds so often, she'd be less likely to confuse her dosage. And it's not as if I can help. He'll only wait on a hard chair in the corridor as she's filled with charcoal and his father flies in from Singapore and promises to stay with them, and then they'll pretend it was a total accident and take her home. At which point she'll find a new hobby, like watercolours or patchwork quilting or even spending quality time with Jack's delinquent baby brother Edward, while her husband waits until he can reasonably return to his more enjoyable life overseas, reigniting the whole cycle.

I sit on the window ledge trying to explain this to him tactfully on the phone, ignoring my guilty resentment at Romy's comment. She of all people should know how committed I am to Jack, and that my reluctance to visit hospitals is no reflection on that.

'I wish you were with me.' His voice sounds miserable, but he's already en route to the hospital, so I'm safely off the hook.

'You'll be fine.' The ledge is so narrow that it's hard to balance, and I'm getting cramp. I flex my legs and wonder if they look thinner today, or if moonlight is flattering. 'You know it isn't my thing.'

He pauses, and when he speaks his voice sounds quieter than usual. 'I get that. But right now, *I* want to be your thing.'

'You know you're my thing.' My legs are definitely thinner. I've joined the swimming team and it's obviously working, but chlorine is so distressing for my hair that I'm in a quandary about whether to continue.

'You're totally my priority,' I add. I can pull off pretty much anything, but latex headwear is a step too far.

'I know exactly where I come on your priorities,' he says. 'Somewhere between your third-favourite pair of shoes and the number of calories you've just ingested.'

'That's not true.' As a conveyor belt of footwear runs through my mind, I relegate my YSL loafers to fourth place, behind my Lanvin flats. 'I'd be with you every step of the way if Libby weren't having a serious crisis right now.'

It's funny he should mention shoes, because tonight I'm wearing my lifelong favourites. They belonged to my mother, although she only wore them once. They shine variously white and crystal and silver in different lights, and sometimes – I like to think – in my different moods. They're embellished with sequins and embroidered flowers, but my favourite feature is their heels, which look like glass.

I'd never have worn them tonight if my alarm hadn't failed. I'd already laid out my Charlotte Olympia wedges, but, even though Libby woke me with a whisper that could cut through any degree of unconsciousness, I was rendered disorientated. As I've never worn the shoes outdoors, they're clean enough to sleep in, and sometimes (don't tell anyone I said this) I do. I didn't realize my mistake until we were in the circle, but now it occurs to me that I've always wanted to see what they'd look like up here in the moonlight.

I straighten my legs to admire the shoes, loosening one so it dangles from my toes. As I move, it's dislodged, and I jerk forward to save it, almost losing my balance.

'Damn,' I hiss, grabbing the ledge with my free hand. Tucking my phone under my chin, I wipe my sweating palm on my gown.

'I need you,' Jack says, as if it's an effort to tell me.

I consider the hospital and dismiss it as soon as I think of squeaky floors and heinous rubber shoes, and hot corridors and cupboards full of blankets used by contagious people, and clipboards and vending machines and wheelchairs and doctors who say *we just don't know*. It's natural to feel this way about hospitals, and until Chanel N° 5 can be pumped through the air vents and the invalids hermetically sealed, I have no intention of entering one.

'Libby needs me too,' I tell him. 'Really badly.'

I cover the receiver too late to muffle Libby's unmistakable screech from inside. 'You *bitch*, Romy.'

'I can hear that she does,' he says. 'I thought you were going to leave Romy alone?'

'What's she got to do with this?' I snap. It's disturbingly easy to visualize Romy beside Jack, unflinching at his mother's gaping hospital gown as she fetches slippers and keeps Edward out of jail and holds Jack's hand with an intensity borne primarily of support. 'Shall I ask her to join you? I'm sure she'd clear her schedule right away.'

'Goodbye, Siena.'

He hangs up, and I stare at the image of his face on the phone, trying to connect that smiling, happy-go-lucky boy with this conversation.

'Hospitals are a step too far,' I whisper. 'I never signed up for that.'

I'm restored to my precarious present by the sound of an unwelcomely familiar voice.

'What is it?' I ask without turning my head.

'You should come and see this.' Romy sounds a little hysterical, and my situation out here is beyond repair, so I lift myself carefully back inside.

'What happened?' I stare at the empty room and ebbing smoke clouds.

'Your friends happened. They started a fire – *with my gown* – and left. We can't get out.'

60

'Of course we can.' I run my hands around the trapdoor. 'Help me open it.'

She's frowning. 'It only opens from the outside. There's no handle in here.'

'I know that already.' I straighten up and reach for my phone.

'Don't you dare call Jack!' she tells me shrilly. 'He has enough to deal with right now.'

'I'm not calling Jack.' Cancelling the connection, I dial Libby instead. 'Where is everyone?'

'They couldn't get out of here soon enough, once they'd burned my gown as incriminating evidence,' Romy says. 'Don't play innocent.'

Libby isn't picking up, so I try Phoebe.

'No answer?' Romy is unbearably smug, despite the trouble she's in.

I ignore her, jabbing the screen for Madison and then Cassidy. Both calls ring out as Romy walks to the window. 'Come and look at this.'

I'd like to ignore her, but there's nothing else to do, so I limp unwillingly after her. 'Why are you wearing such ridiculous shoes?' she asks, pulling up my gown. 'Do you have a wedding to attend tonight?'

I lean out of the window to see the Starlets speeding across the courtyard, gowns billowing behind them. 'Why haven't they noticed I'm missing?' I mutter. 'Shouldn't Libby have done a headcount?'

They swarm in strict formation like a single entity. 'They all seem fine without you,' Romy muses as we watch figures who are so interchangeable that from this distance Libby could be Madison could be Cassidy could be Phoebe. I wonder if, amongst them, I might be interchangeable too. But this idea is absurd, because not one of them could be me.

'So what happens now?' Romy asks. 'Do they realize that this is going to get me kicked out once and for all? If not killed?'

'Of course they realize,' I say lightly as I pick up the vodka bottle. The burn in my throat is an effective antidote to my prickle of apprehension at being in line for a punishment.

She looks away. 'So this isn't a . . . twisted re-initiation or anything? You'd rather see me burn to death than come back?'

We survey the still-smoking gown detritus and the forlorn candle remains, and I wonder if I should have listened to Libby's insistence on details after all.

'Don't be stupid,' I say. 'The fire wasn't part of the plan. We'd never go that far!'

She raises an eyebrow and I blush, because, truthfully, Libby *would* go that far. It's not even the most extreme action she's taken against outside threats (not that this is the time for nostalgia).

'The other Starlets didn't know,' I say. 'I'm sure Libby was working alone.'

'I bet the prospect of a night with Jack's dying mother is quite attractive right now,' Romy says snidely. 'If only you weren't so selfish, you wouldn't be in this predicament. You'd have avoided trouble *and* his bad books.'

I throw my useless phone into my pocket and smooth my hair, because an unsightly mug shot is the very last thing I need. 'There's no predicament, because I'm not taking the blame. I'll say that . . .'

'I kidnapped you?' she suggests. 'Forced you up here at knifepoint?'

'*Yes*,' I say in relief. 'Knifepoint is perfect.'

'And I suppose I forced you to wear your gown, did I?' she continues. 'What a weird request for me to make. I must be even more sick and twisted than before.'

I consider removing my gown before remembering that my Victoria's Secret lingerie would curry even less favour with Mrs Denbigh than the misuse of official school robes. I could ask Romy for her pyjamas, but my mother would definitely consider expulsion preferable to me wearing that charred heavy metal T-shirt.

'Libby will get me out of this,' I shrug. 'And deservedly so, because this is entirely your fault.'

'You invited me here. You tricked me! Why couldn't you leave me alone?'

'You hurt Libby,' I say. 'How can we forgive you?'

She looks stubbornly away, even as I realize how desperately I want her to tell me that this isn't true; that there's been a terrible misunderstanding.

She doesn't, of course: she has the same mutinous

and stubborn expression as she did on the day she left. 'You hurt *me*. How can I forgive *you*?'

We're so caught up that we don't notice the banging trapdoor until it swings violently open, revealing Mrs Denbigh. She's wearing her housecoat over a nightdress, her hair untidier than ever. Her eyes widen as she takes in the candles, the gown and the vodka bottle.

'What's the meaning of this, Romy?' she bellows. 'I thought Liberty must be joking when she told me I'd find you in here up to no good.'

Mrs Denbigh hasn't rubbed in her neck cream properly and I wonder whether to tell her that it's congealed around her ears.

'Have you been . . .' She lifts her nose and sniffs incredulously. 'Have you been lighting *fires* up here?'

Romy gestures helplessly at me, and, in Libby's absence, I step forward. 'I'm glad you're here, Mrs Denbigh. I can't imagine what my mother would say if she knew that this dangerous tower wasn't cordoned off from students. I was about to report it to the governors when you appeared.'

Mrs Denbigh cuts me off. 'I'm waiting for an explanation. A *truthful* explanation.'

In the resulting silence, I count along with the ticking clock. At fifty, one hundred, two hundred seconds, she'll break.

Finally, at closer to five hundred, she gestures furiously at the ladder. 'Get to bed *now*. I want to see you in the morning, and, unless you're seriously reconsidering your future here, you'd better be ready to talk.'

I smile sympathetically at Romy, as it's the last time I'll ever see her, but Mrs Denbigh is still looking at me.

'*Both of you*,' she barks as she thumps her way back down to solid ground.

Romy and I see the discarded key at the same second. We both snatch at it, but I'm faster, and I smile as I hide it inside my gown.

'If you ever come back here, then you must have a death wish,' Romy mutters as I follow her down the ladder. 'You deserve whatever happens to you.'

I tread on her hand by way of reply.

Chapter Ten

Romy

Mrs Denbigh doesn't care about privacy, even for Sixth Formers. Siena gets off lightly, as she manages to close her bedroom door before Mrs Denbigh can block it, but when we reach my room, she grabs the door handle before I can do the same. I get into bed and pull my knees up under my chin, trying to control my shivering before she mistakes extreme cold for fear.

'What's this all about?' She walks inside and starts to fold the clothes I've thrown across the floor, repressing a grimace at a crumpled shirt. 'Do you *want* to be expelled?'

I open my mouth to tell her that expulsion would be a gross overreaction to creased clothing, but only a sob comes out. I hide my face in my bed sheets instead, emerging when my expression is under control. She's dropped the shirt on a towering, unironed pile, evidently at a loss as to what to say, or how to repair the various messes that constitute my life.

'Get some sleep,' she tells me as she leaves. Not until her footsteps have padded away do I wish I'd asked for reassurance that I wouldn't be expelled after all.

I edge my feet underneath the starched, freezing sheets until I'm lying flat. Last year I was in a dormitory, warmed by the bodies of five other girls whose regular breathing might not have cured my insomnia but at least allowed me to share it. Even if Sixth Formers didn't have their own rooms, though, it's not as if Siena would ever again push back our dividing curtain so we can spend the night whispering and trying not to laugh as Libby – for once unable to interfere – sleeps soundly across the room.

I clench my fists at the unfairness of everything: that I haven't slept properly in days, or months, or probably a year; that Siena, on the other side of our adjoining wall, might still be an ocean apart. In a wave of fury I sit up and hurl my shoes against the opposite wall, hoping that the sound, if not sufficiently loud to wake the corridor, will disturb her. But I'm railing against unmovable marble, and, if Siena hears, she makes no sound. More likely she's sitting before her looking glass as woodland creatures put on her nightgown and brush her hair and replace her glass-heeled shoes on their display cushion, while her conscience troubles her not one iota. Why should it, when she's so revered that she's never needed to suffer a moment's self-doubt?

Even as a Shell, Siena ruled the hallways with a sureness that cast no doubt on her future legacy. Older students avoided her gaze and shifted to let her walk catwalk-centre, and teachers were helpless to make her conform to the compulsory yellow-ribboned boater hat that made us as indistinguishable as ants.

My mother provided an explanatory note, she'd say

calmly when ordered to put on the hat, proffering a letter on thick cream paper that stopped all arguments. Defiant bareheadedness made Siena neatly distinct from her contemporaries, as well as exempting her from the most troublesome and prosaic affliction blighting the rest of us: an itchy head.

Burdened with boaters, Shells Phoebe and Cassidy used magnetic attraction and a couture wardrobe respectively to stamp their own identities on the school, while Libby, blessed with the kind of self-confidence of which tyrants only dream, turned potential embarrassment into a school-wide reputation as government cipher after Jennifer Zhou revealed that her much-fêted Mandarin business calls, conducted at echoing volume right across the campus, contained nothing more lucid than the phrase *Pass me the pigeons, favoured candle*.

When the rising bell drills through my ears, I have no idea if I've been asleep at all. Lacking time and inclination to excavate my bags for ridiculously tight and costly clothes, I throw on my oldest jeans. Tipping my head upside down in half-remembered Starlet advice to make my tangled hair look less like an accident, I long for the relative ease of school uniforms, when one's sartorial disasters at least remained within an agreed framework.

I drag my feet towards Mrs Denbigh's office, vaguely cheered to find Siena there before me. She's leaning her head against the back of her chair and her eyes are closed, giving her a deceptively childlike appearance. Her flaws are practically undetectable, but I'm gratified as I draw closer to see a tiny smear of eyeliner on her cheek; that her chignon is an inch out of line; and that the blue of her handbag doesn't quite match her nail varnish. I wonder fleetingly if she's been kept awake with worry, but this is unlikely.

It's very incongruous for her to be here at all: Libby should be dealing with this appointment, and, if she can't actually undertake it for her, should at least have provided a stand-in to endure the waiting room stage.

'Stop staring at me,' she commands in a whisper.

'Don't flatter yourself,' I tell her.

A smile plays across her lips as she opens her eyes to prove her point.

'There's nothing else to look at,' I mutter. 'Sue me.'

'You might glance at *yourself*,' she says scornfully as she takes in my outfit with a laser-beam gaze. 'What do you think you look like?'

'I look like me,' I say. 'What do I have to prove, to you or anyone else?'

'Nothing, I suppose,' she says after a pause. 'Nothing at all.'

She doesn't react as Mrs Denbigh bellows our names, not even to complain at being summoned in this way. I understand her passivity and obedience as she follows me into the office: it's classic Starlet behaviour to gauge a situation fully before reacting, and she's a master at it. Her white dress, draped modestly below her knees and buttoned neck-high like a pilgrim's, is a calculated, genius choice.

Usually Mrs Denbigh greets us from her array of mismatched and cheerful armchairs, handing us a biscuit tin that no Starlet would ever open, but today she gestures from behind her enormous oak desk for us to sit opposite her on plastic orange seats. Siena, wincing at this insult, mimics Mrs Denbigh's body language, crossing her legs and clasping her hands in her lap. I deliberately slouch and fold my arms.

Before Mrs Denbigh speaks, Siena holds out her phone. 'I presume you're happy to set up a conference call with my lawyer? Speed dial seven. He's expecting you.'

'That won't be necessary,' says Mrs Denbigh drily. 'I think we can handle this without legal representation.'

'In which case, I'd like an impartial student representative,' Siena tries. She must have read this clause in the School Rules, just as I did in my desperate final hours here before accepting that no one would be willing to represent me.

'Libby, you mean?' I ask. 'Yes, I'm sure she'd be very impartial.'

'That won't be necessary either,' says Mrs Denbigh. 'In fact, I think you'll be grateful to hear what I have to say without witnesses.'

Siena's expression is studiedly unconcerned but she drums her fingers against her glittery phone as if trying to hide the fact that they're shaking.

'This is very bad,' Mrs Denbigh says weightily. 'Very bad indeed.'

Siena stops drumming and looks meekly downward.

'I'm not going to ask what happened last night,' Mrs Denbigh continues. 'I don't see that assigning blame is going to get us anywhere.'

'I agree,' says Siena smoothly. 'That's a very helpful approach.'

'Of course you agree,' I mutter. 'The whole thing was your fault.'

'*No assigning blame*,' Siena reminds us both. 'We should focus instead on how best to move forward.'

Mrs Denbigh nods vigorously. 'You're right; we do need to move forward. I've been lying awake trying to decide how best to do that.'

There's no doubt that Mrs Denbigh loves us all as if we were her own children, but it's possible that she loves some of us more equally than others.

'What conclusion did you reach?' I ask. My pre-dawn hopelessness begins to recede as I consider the benefits of expulsion. It smarts a little that all these years of trying to fit in have come to nothing – not to mention the practical inconvenience of a nomadic existence – but ultimately there's something to be said for not perishing alone in a tower-room inferno.

Mrs Denbigh looks as tired as I feel. 'I've given out detention, lines, solitary confinement,' she lists. 'Extra homework. Laps of the football pitch. Letters home. Loss of privileges. *A year's suspension abroad.* Yet, at the age of seventeen, you're caught trespassing in a forbidden area at midnight, drinking alcohol and lighting fires. Can you give me any grounds for not expelling you on the spot?'

I pray that Siena will stay quiet, because I have a horrible suspicion that she wants to use her favourite defence: that she's too pretty to be punished.

'You need to understand each other's point of view,' Mrs Denbigh continues, breaking her own silence.

Siena smiles brightly. 'I'm a very empathetic person, so I already understand Romy's point of view. In fact, I took *Most Empathetic* in the last yearbook poll. It was unanimous.'

'Which award did I take?' I ask.

'*Most Lawless*,' she giggles. 'Amongst others.'

Mrs Denbigh ignores this. 'In order to do that, you're going to spend time together. Rather a lot of time, in fact.'

'What?' I say. 'You mean you *aren't* expelling me?'

'Of course not,' she says briskly. 'Where did you get such an idea?'

'From School Rule Number 43: *Unsupervised entry to the clock tower is punishable by expulsion*?' My Rules are well thumbed and I've committed most of them to memory. Last year I knew them better than my exam texts, for all the good it did me. 'Mainly that.'

'That Rule is exercised at my discretion,' she says. 'We've just got you back, Romy, and the last thing we want is to lose you again.'

'That's debatable,' says Siena. 'What if you expelled her for the good of everyone, like a mercy killing?'

'That's enough,' says Mrs Denbigh, but Siena is on a roll.

'How would this work? In case you haven't noticed, we move in *quite* different circles now.'

'I've noticed, Siena,' says Mrs Denbigh. 'That's why, this term, you'll be joining the Student Council alongside Romy.'

My mouth falls open in shock; Siena actually *shudders*. 'That won't be possible,' she explains when she's regained the power of speech. 'Although I'm passionate about politics and students' wellbeing, my existing extra-curricular commitments leave me little time . . .'

'Existing commitments?' I snap. 'Shooting tequila before breakfast, you mean? Designer-shoe shopping? Hooking up with Jack in every room in the school?'

'Romy, I know you're jealous of my life,' she says offendedly, 'but . . .'

Mrs Denbigh holds up her hand. '*Silence*. Siena, you will make time in your schedule for this. It's non-negotiable.'

I shake my head. 'This is more of a punishment for me than for her. The best thing about Student Council is that there's zero chance of meeting her coven there.'

'The Starlets aren't a coven,' she says. 'We're an enterprise.'

'Potato, tomato,' I mutter under my breath. 'Witches, bitches . . . Starlets, harlots . . .'

She ignores me. 'Mrs Denbigh, you must know that the Council won't dare take Romy back after what she did to Libby. Her only hope would be if we publicly forgave her; if we . . .'

She looks suspicious as she identifies the loophole.

'That's right.' Mrs Denbigh turns to me. 'Romy, you'll be rejoining Siena and her friends –' she stops short of saying *Starlets*, which I appreciate – 'at mealtimes and social occasions.'

'I'm afraid she won't,' Siena cuts in. 'As much as I'd like to cooperate with this *experiment*, Starlet membership is very exclusive, and there are comprehensive rules concerning . . .'

'Yes.' I agree with her for the first time in living memory. 'The Starlets are *very* exclusive.'

Mrs Denbigh nods. 'It'll be good for you to mix up your friendships; practise a little inclusivity. You should learn to appreciate each other.'

I wish I possessed Siena's talent for hiding human feelings behind a mask of bland magnificence. 'Please . . .' I whisper, and I sound as if I'm drowning. 'Anything but that . . .'

'There's no need to be so dramatic,' Siena says huffily. 'Most girls would die for this opportunity, and you must have been desperate for it yesterday to risk expulsion yet again.'

I hunch over and look at my shoes. 'I want to leave. I should never have come back.'

'We can call your father and talk this over with him,' Mrs Denbigh suggests as she takes the embers of my gown from her drawer and lays them across the desk. 'But I think he'll be displeased to see you in trouble again so soon.'

'If he even notices,' I mutter. 'And it's preferable to dealing with this.'

'It's not preferable to living out your days in your father's cellar, uneducated and unmarried,' smiles Siena. 'Which is what will happen once every school in Europe finds out about your criminal behaviour.'

'How will you make that happen?' I ask. 'Who listens to you outside this school?'

She continues to smile. 'Libby is somewhat prominent on Twitter. She's developed a rather excellent network of contacts across the public school system.'

'You wouldn't,' I say. 'That's a step too far, even for you.'

'Paris last year,' she continues blithely. 'Where next? It'll have to be so remote that no one has heard of you. Peru? Yemen? *Cumbria?*'

Siena's words soften Mrs Denbigh as if she's offering aid rather than single-handedly condemning me to a life of ruin. 'You two shared so much,' she pleads. 'Can't you remember your wonderful camaraderie?'

'Of course I can't remember it.' Siena's blue eyes darken when she's angry, and now they're almost navy.

'Because it *never happened*. Romy and I have never, *ever* been friends.'

Mrs Denbigh looks almost amused. 'I admire your ability to rewrite history, but there is much photographic proof suggesting otherwise.'

'That's what you think,' mutters Siena.

'I expect to see you beside Siena at all mealtimes, Romy,' Mrs Denbigh says as I snatch up my bag. 'Siena, the next Council meeting is this afternoon. Don't be late.'

We storm out side by side, reaching for the door at the same time and slamming it so hard that it almost falls off its hinges.

'It makes me so happy to see you working together,' floats Mrs Denbigh's disembodied voice.

Chapter Eleven

Siena

'This is entirely Syrena's fault,' I mutter.

Romy is keeping pace despite my attempts to shake her off. She's weirdly fond of my baby sister Syrena, and is smiling at the mere mention of her. 'What's she done now? Is it worse than pickaxing a hole in the attic floor and falling through your bedroom ceiling?'

'Yes,' I wince. 'Worse than breeding a badger colony in the summer house, *and* cooking my phone inside the Christmas turkey.'

'At least she gave you an excuse for not eating it,' she says. 'So what is it?'

'Surely you already know,' I say. 'She inextricably, hellishly, bound you and me together on our first day at this school, leaving us with the dismal consequences.'

Romy pulls an offended face, but I ignore her and take a sharp left down a narrow corridor. I momentarily escape her, but see in her place someone just as unwelcome.

Syrena, now six, was once a jaded two-year-old who stared contemptuously at the car keys my mother Seraphina rattled before her, as if she could be so easily distracted from the fish knife with which she was stripping paint from her nursery walls.

'Will you be taking Siena today?' asked our nanny Paula in surprise.

Seraphina gestured affrontedly at her travelling suit. 'To escort my eldest child to her first day at boarding school? Certainly.'

Paula nodded, because she was paid to be discreet and unquestioning.

'In fact,' Seraphina added spiritedly, 'I can do this alone. You stay here.'

'That's our mother,' my middle sister Stella, then seven, explained in a whisper as she strapped Syrena into her car seat. They had not been invited to accompany us, but blowing the whistle on Syrena would mean losing Stella's company too.

Paula hugged me tightly, tears streaming down her plump cheeks. She uttered a stream of orders in Spanish about the importance of good behaviour and kindness towards others before her words became unintelligible sobs. Paula had worked for us all my life, and sometimes, although it was disloyal, I preferred her advice to my mother's. I wondered if I might cry too, but then I noticed Seraphina watching as she pulled on her white gloves, and I wrinkled my nose until the sensation receded.

'I'll see you at the end of term,' I told Paula as I ducked out of her embrace. 'And of course I'll write to you. In Spanish, even.'

'Why is she so averse to me driving you to school?'

Seraphina muttered when we drove away. 'As if the idea were somehow unnatural.'

She looked, startled, into the rear-view mirror as Syrena made a noise from her baby seat. 'The others have joined us,' she noted.

Not until we were some miles away from Paula did I remember that my mother had begun her day with a Bloody Mary, eschewing the virgin option.

It was raining when we arrived at Temperley High, and we watched through windscreen wipers as students darted back and forth to boarding houses with their luggage. We'd wait all day rather than compromise our hair with damp humidity; not that clement conditions would entice my mother to carry bags and enter a communal living space.

Stella knelt on her seat and wrapped her arms around my neck, pressing her soft cheek against mine. 'I'll miss you,' she whispered.

I hadn't worried about leaving home until that moment, when I felt as if I were being literally uprooted. I held Stella's hands until a nod from Seraphina reminded me that, as the eldest, I was the setter of examples. I pushed her gently back into her place.

'Your gift, Siena.' Seraphina opened her handbag to reveal six jewellery boxes.

'Thank you.' I opened each box to reveal a pair of silver star-shaped earrings. 'But why do I need six? Syrena won't be there to eat them.'

'Only one is for you, Starlet,' she said, using the nickname my father had given me. 'You'll see that each box is marked with a number.'

The pair in the box marked with a 1 was bigger than the others, and inset with more diamonds. Seraphina put them into my ears and held up her mirror as she kissed me on the cheek. 'Never forget who you are.'

'Oh no,' said Syrena audibly as the back door swung open and Libby sprang inside.

Libby and I had been friends in a desultory sense through prep school, the reticence on my side. She'd occasionally visited us at home, and Syrena had taken an intense dislike to her that I secretly found funny. I'd gleaned that Libby had ended up on the rough end of her parents' recent divorce (in which her father had withdrawn all non-necessary expenses), so I was surprised to see her here. Temperley High, I was proudly aware, was the most expensive school in the county.

'Hello, Libby,' Stella said politely, motioning at Syrena to follow suit.

'Oh no,' Syrena repeated sadly.

'I thought you were going to a state school, Libby,' I said, trying to change the subject.

'Circumstances altered,' Libby primped, pushing up her sleeve to reveal a Tiffany charm bracelet. 'They altered considerably.'

To my surprise, Seraphina gave her an approving nod. 'Very nice, Liberty.'

Taking a closer look, I noticed that Libby had indeed improved over the summer. Her long hair was styled and blow-dried into professionally lacquered curls, and her eyebrows were neatly plucked. She'd been small for her age, ignored and drowned in a too-large school uniform, but she'd grown and was now pretty in a way that made sense, where everything fitted together as flawlessly as if she'd been constructed from a flat pack.

'Thank you, Miss Hamilton,' she said reverently.

My mother reached into her bag, and, handing me the box marked 2, gestured at me to pass it over.

'Really, Siena?' Libby gasped as she opened it with shaking hands. 'Does this mean I'm going to be your number two?'

'Yes?' I said dubiously, looking to Seraphina for clarification.

'*Yes*,' I repeated as she nodded.

Seraphina peered through the windscreen at the girls hurrying around us. '*Three*,' she pointed, tapping one of the remaining jewellery boxes.

Madison, already a knockout, was languidly following a posse of football-playing brothers who staggered under the weight of her fashion magazines, handbags, vanity cases and spindly-heeled sandals. Sample sizes hung as intended from her rangy frame, and her symmetrical face was pretty whether she wore make-up or stayed up all night giggling or played aggressive sports that made most people ugly.

She would later accept her earrings with nothing but a flick of her dishevelled straw-coloured hair.

'Nice bag, Libby,' I said, noticing the tote she was clutching. It was the new Primrose, one of a kind, handmade and obtainable only with the designer's personal recommendation. It was the bag I'd requested for my twelfth birthday; a request that had not been upheld.

'Thanks, Siena,' Libby said gratefully.

'*Four*,' Seraphina said measuredly as Cassidy slunk past like a stray kitten, compensating for what she lost in deportment with heavy auburn hair that glinted copper in sunshine. Cassidy was messily chic in a way that may have been accidental, with layers of impossibly beautiful clothes and handmade jewellery, and green eyes as bright and almond-shaped as a cat's.

'How did you get your bag, Libby?' I pressed.

'*Five*,' said Seraphina, as Phoebe, with a black velvet ribbon holding springy flaxen curls, patent shoes and snow-white knee socks, emerged from the back seat of a Rolls. Turning up her nose at the wet ground, she allowed her chauffeur to carry her over the gravel and deposit her at the front door.

Libby nodded, all the while making careful notes in her day planner. 'And number six, Miss Hamilton?'

Seraphina's gaze drifted towards a neat little girl called Emmeline, whose father was an earl and who, we'd later discover, had spelt her own name wrong on her entrance test. But, as Libby's pen hovered over the paper, Seraphina suddenly gasped in horror.

'Disgraceful,' she muttered.

It was unnecessary to ask to whom she referred.

I'd never seen a girl like Romy before, and, from the way Stella's eyes widened in shock, I knew she hadn't either. Unattended in the back seat, she'd been teaching something to Syrena. *Row-me,* she'd repeated patiently as Syrena tried to copy her; now they both fell silent.

Romy's tangled brown hair was sun-bleached into irregular highlights, and her face was tanned and freckled. She was inelegantly gangly, with a long scratch down one cheek as if she'd been crawling through hedges. Most shamefully, she hadn't adhered to the inventory, which was rare in an environment governed by efficient and experienced nannies. Without the regulation trunk, she heaved her belongings from a Daimler in a mixture of dented vanity cases and battered suitcases and decrepit holdalls. She appeared unconcerned even as the contents spilled onto the gravel, occasionally scooping up a sock or kicking a plimsoll along the ground in front of her.

'This can't be allowed,' Seraphina hissed. 'Should we call Security? Where is her keeper?'

'Romyromyromyromy,' said Syrena at speed.

'Well done, Syrena,' said Stella.

'What's she saying?' asked Libby. 'What does that mean?'

I sighed. 'She's a baby, Libby. She says lots of stuff that makes no sense.'

'Everything makes sense if you listen to her,' said Stella.

Romy twisted up her long hair with a fluffy-ended pencil and took a moment to refasten her blazer so that the buttons didn't match. I wondered how it would feel to wear my own hair loose and spilling down my back so that it became wet and curly in rainstorms and tangled in the wind. Involuntarily, I touched my head: as if sensing this silent rebellion, and just as Romy pulled a creamy, lop-eared rabbit from her pocket, Seraphina reached out a thin ivory hand and smoothed my ever-perfect chignon.

'She's not relevant to you.' My mother tried to turn my head gently away, just as she did when we passed homeless people on the street.

I might have let her, except that, as Romy vanished back into the depths of her car, her legs protruding indecorously before she emerged for a final time, she was joined by a dark-haired boy. He stroked her rabbit before slinging an arm around her shoulders, and her sulky face transformed, like storm clouds receding. She looked at the boy exactly as I imagined I'd look at him if he ever put his arm around me.

'How did that happen?' asked Libby, as if witnessing an injustice of epic proportions. '*Her*? With *him*?'

'Do you know him?' I adopted a casual tone.

'That's Jack Lawrence,' said Libby. 'Of the Goring Lawrences. They own half of Oxfordshire. I expect you've heard of them?'

I had, because the only book my mother had ever read to me was *Debrett's*. Stella and I had been a more captive audience than Syrena, who had recently shredded a section into a nest for her pet mouse.

The straps of a baby seat were no deterrent to a proficient escapologist – I knew this to my cost – and, during this conversation, Syrena had climbed into Stella's lap to peer out of the window.

'Rabbit,' she said.

'*No*,' Seraphina and I said in unison.

Romy was laughing now, as happy as she'd previously been angry, and Jack had joined in. I was still watching them when the car door slammed.

'Where are your sisters?' Libby abandoned her note-taking in confusion.

'Do I have to join you for breakfast?' Romy brings me back to the present, her voice as objectionable as Syrena's erstwhile chant of *Romyromyromyromy*.

'I suppose so,' I sigh as we approach the cafeteria. 'Although you should sign a confidentiality agreement first. I'll have Libby draw one up for you.'

'What?' She's staring in disbelief. 'Confidentiality about *you*?'

'Our table is the nerve centre of the entire school. Can you imagine the damage that could be done if you started carrying state secrets back to the general population? It would be like . . .' I search for an example, shaking my head as she starts talking about *water gates*. 'No, something really bad. Like the theft of Liz Hurley's holiday photographs.'

'I was a Starlet for five years,' she says. 'I know every single one of your secrets.'

You most certainly do not. 'You're an outsider now, and you'll be treated as such.'

'Why do you think you hold all the cards?' she asks. She's always been resilient – a trait I once *almost* admired. 'Wait until you try and spin this to your ladies-in-waiting. They might throw you out and force you to make your own way on Temperley High's mean streets with only me for company.'

'I don't know what you mean.'

'You do,' she presses. 'You loved *Lady and the Tramp*.'

Talking to Romy – just being near her – puts me in a state of irritation. 'How could they throw me out? I *am* the Starlets.'

'That's an interesting theory,' she considers. 'Yet they left you in mortal danger last night, trapped in a fire; every last one of them, even Cassidy, who's supposed to be the nice one, and Libby, who's allegedly your most loyal servant. And the worst thing is, they didn't even notice.'

'It was a simple error,' I clarify, 'with no bearing on my currency as a Starlet. Why are you picking a fight? Your life will be even harder if we're *all* against you.'

She laughs. 'You won't tell them the truth about this.'

'Of course I will! What else can I do? Announce that I've allowed you to rejoin us?'

'You'll lose face if you admit that you got caught when they all escaped. Facing a punishment, like a civilian, surely isn't the public image you want to project?'

I think this over.

'But then, perhaps you *do* have to come clean,' Romy muses. 'Because otherwise you have to pretend that you've joined the Student Council of your own volition. They'd drop you in a second. They'd probably have you burned at the stake.'

'What don't you understand?' I ask. 'I'm the heart and soul of the Starlets. Without me they would cease to exist. They'd *stop being alive.* I could do anything – *anything* – and they'd stand by me. Their support of me is as ingrained as their love of Chanel.'

'When will you learn that each of them has every bit the game plan you do?' she says. 'They're just cleverer about hiding it.'

We're now only feet away from the Starlet table, where Libby and Phoebe are audibly vying to be centre of attention.

'They seem to have no trouble existing without you,' smirks Romy. 'Have they noticed you're missing?'

'Shut up,' I mutter. 'Let me handle this, or I'll make it more painful for you.'

'They're palazzo pants all over again,' Phoebe is saying as she recalibrates her frittata. She takes pride in ordering the highest-calorie menu item, as if we don't notice that all she does is move it around her plate in circles before giving it a dignified burial under her napkin. 'They'll be out of style by the time they've even been delivered. Not to mention that they'll make your legs look stumpy.'

'You're wrong.' Libby jabs a manicured finger at a *Vanity Fair* spread on green slingbacks and tries to hide her hurt at this jibe. 'They're totally flattering, and this time next week you'll be eating your words. If not your breakfast.'

'It's not bad hair, exactly,' Cassidy concedes in a separate conversation with Madison. 'It's just a bit unexpected, because of the crimping. I can see where she was going with it.'

'Yes, so can I,' says Madison. '1998, at the latest.'

They all look up as I approach, smiling before they see who's behind me.

Chapter Twelve

Romy

Phoebe's mouth drops open. Cassidy looks scared. Libby flips through the day planner as though this is an appointment she's somehow overlooked. Madison adopts the aggressive position usually reserved for predatory Stripes. And Siena, who's moving her lips silently as if she's counting down from ten, slips into her seat before motioning me into my own. As composed as ever, she smiles measuredly at each of them in turn.

'What's going on?' she asks. 'And Libby, Phoebe's right. Those shoes are heinous.'

'As your breakfast companion appears to have crawled here from the underworld,' Libby says icily, 'I don't quite see why you're criticizing *my* appearance.'

I raise an eyebrow at Siena to provoke her into continuing. As much as she wants to tell the truth about her punishment, as much as she likes to believe that the Starlets love her unconditionally, she'd never disclose something as undignified as being left prisoner in the tower, like a child forgotten at nursery school. And as Madison whispers to Phoebe and they both laugh, and Cassidy makes some encouraging noises about Libby's horrible shoes while the latter continues to glare, I know Siena understands the only way to retain her power.

'Romy should be made answerable for what she did last year,' Siena announces. 'She'll be joining us for a trial period of rehabilitation, to prove she's truly sorry.'

'*Are* you truly sorry?' asks Cassidy.

'Truly,' I lie. *You can rejoin the Council*, I remind myself.

'You're not falling for this?' Phoebe asks the others in disbelief. 'I don't believe her for a second. She's up to something.'

'What could I possibly be up to?' I ask.

Phoebe frowns, unable to come up with anything plausible. 'Just . . . something.'

'You invited her back without a consultation?' Madison asks incredulously.

Siena once told me that she was taught as a child to hold a smile for up to six minutes without it wavering or looking fake. At the time I was baffled by her pride in this, but now I can see that it's an invaluable skill.

'Consider this your consultation,' she trills pleasantly through gritted teeth.

'This is unbelievable.' Libby shakes her head. 'Do you know that my scar still aches on cold days? My doctor said I could have died, or suffered a permanently reshaped hairline. I can't accept this decision, Siena. It's Romy or me.'

Madison, Phoebe and Cassidy look worriedly at Siena, while she darts a glance at me. I should have predicted this, and I can certainly predict Siena's reaction.

'The truth is . . .' she begins, right on cue. Losing Libby is unthinkable to her to the extent that she might as well be expelled anyway.

I interrupt before she gets any further. 'The truth is that you can't keep the sixth Starlet place open any longer.'

Siena glares, but the others are listening to me.

'I can see why you haven't replaced me,' I say. 'To make girls competitive and feel a futile sense of hope. Etcetera. But now it looks as if you can't fill the space. It looks as if no one wants to join you. It makes you look –' I pause for effect – '*undesirable.*'

'That's insane,' bristles Phoebe.

'It's true,' I say. 'I heard some Fifth Formers talking about it.'

Libby's head snaps up. 'Which Fifth Formers?' She narrows her eyes in a way that makes me fear for their safety.

'I'm not good with names,' I say. 'But that empty seat is damaging your reputation.'

'We can fill it with anyone we like,' blusters Phoebe. 'It doesn't have to be *you*.'

'Who else is there?' Siena rallies. 'The longer we wait, the more we risk lowering our standards. And wouldn't we all like to put our unfortunate history with Romy to bed?'

I nod. 'Readmitting me would make you look forgiving. You'd get to show your ultimate supremacy.

Not to mention that it might help me forget last night's fire.'

Libby is apparently wondering whether to admit that she knows the door only opens from the outside, and that she therefore deliberately imprisoned me in a burning tower. 'How did you get out?' she asks finally.

'I just did,' I say. 'Don't look so disappointed, all of you: anyone would think you actually wanted me to *die* in there. Don't you know that a murder conviction could seriously harm your university chances?'

Everyone stares at their plates, but I detect an unwilling admiration that could work in my favour.

'Romy has an interesting skill set,' Siena puts in. 'We could use her this term, if she puts it to good use.'

'You'll have to change,' says Madison. 'A new wardrobe isn't even a drop in the ocean. We have rules. Rules that *matter*.'

'I know you do,' I say irritably. 'I've heard them many times.'

'So . . . you aren't in any trouble for last night?' asks Libby tentatively.

'No, but I can predict that we'll *all* be in trouble if Mrs Denbigh finds out the truth. Don't you agree?'

Libby stares, and then the unthinkable happens. She pulls out the spare chair for me, and once again we're six.

'What really happened to your Tarot cards?' asks Madison. 'They can't have just disappeared.'

'I don't care, as long as they're far away from me,'

I say. 'I never want to experience another psychic reading again.'

I brought the cards with me to Temperley High in my first term as a small rebellion that my father would hate. I'd found them as I filled my arms with my mother's dresses and necklaces, books and magazine cuttings, and anything and everything else that I could carry.

Yet I bitterly regretted my decision when they spilled from my pocket as I slammed the car door on that first day. I scrabbled for them, muttering in embarrassment as I straightened up and almost knocked over two little girls, identical with their long fair hair, round blue eyes and perfectly serious expressions.

'Rabbit,' said the younger girl, pointing to the bundle in my arms.

'Do you want to stroke her?' I asked reluctantly.

'No,' said the elder girl, keeping tight hold of her sister. 'I mean – Syrena doesn't always understand how.'

'It's okay.' I felt a curious kinship towards Syrena, accustomed as I was to being told *no*. 'Do it like this.'

Syrena copied me, running her hand up and down the length of the rabbit's back.

'Stella,' came a voice from behind them, and I stood up as the elder girl turned. This third girl was probably my age, but otherwise looked exactly the same as her sisters.

Jack was waiting for me to catch him up. My heart

sank as he looked at the eldest girl, looked away, and looked again. Then he raised an eyebrow at me.

'Your boyfriend's waiting for you,' Stella told me. Her tone was pitying.

Jack watched Siena, and she watched him. Syrena stopped stroking the rabbit and turned between them.

I stepped deliberately forward, blocking Jack and Siena's view of each other under the guise of moving a suitcase. 'Yes, *my* boyfriend is waiting,' I reinforced. 'For *me*.'

Siena looked amused. 'Why do you have two names on your suitcase?' she asked.

Your name is Roma, Dad had told me as he'd painted my name on my case.

My name is not Roma, I'd argued, adding the word ROMY to the other side in black gloss, so large that it could be read from Italy, let alone across a crowded car park. Siena was looking at the ROMA side, so I turned it around.

'I prefer Romy,' I told her.

She smiled. 'That's a shame. I'm Siena, and I thought we had something in common.'

Stella started to smile at Siena, but I got the full force of it as she plucked a card from the pack in my hands and laughed.

'You're good at that,' she said, showing it to Siena before handing it back to me.

I looked at it only once they'd all gone: the Star card lit translucent in the emerging sun.

94

Chapter Thirteen

Siena

Romy is fidgeting and looking at her watch. 'Do you have somewhere to be?' I ask, trying to convey that, if she does, it had better be important.

'I'm sorry,' she says insincerely. 'I'd love to stay and hear more stories about bad hair . . .'

'It's not *bad* hair,' interrupts Madison, sounding annoyed. 'It's *unexpected*.'

'Where do you have to be?' asks Libby. 'You can't just flit in and out of debates without due regard.'

'I didn't realize that this was a debate,' Romy says. 'I'll have to reacclimatize.'

'You certainly will,' says Libby weightily. 'We haven't touched on half the topics up for discussion today.'

'So . . .' Romy prompts. 'What are they?'

There's a silence. 'You heard about Libby's shoes?' Cassidy says finally.

'Our thoughts on the re-emergence of feathered hair?' ventures Madison.

'We haven't even *considered* what to wear to tennis practice,' Phoebe adds.

'Wow,' says Romy. 'So your days are still action-packed. I wonder how I'll catch up on all I've missed.'

'Just go,' I sigh. 'We'll work on your attitude later.'

'Some warning would have been nice.' Libby turns on me the instant Romy leaves the table. 'You know I hate to be unprepared. My life coach says surprises are very bad for my mental balance.'

'Yesterday you complained that life had become predictable,' I remind her. 'Now we have a new toy.'

'But Romy?' she moans. 'Did it have to be Romy?'

'You know what they say about keeping one's enemies close.'

'I agree with that,' says Phoebe authoritatively. 'Romy learned from the very best, after all, and she could form a splinter group or something. She knows too much.'

I nod sagely. 'It's important not only to contain her, but to keep a close eye on all areas of the school until we're sure she's not going to start any trouble. That's why I've decided to take a *big hit* for the team.'

I take a deep breath before my second revelation. 'I've joined the Student Council.'

They all disintegrate into shock again, and I worry that Cassidy might faint. Madison fans her with a napkin without taking her eyes off me.

'I think I misheard you,' says Libby weakly. 'We've suffered so much turmoil that we're delirious.'

Phoebe giggles. 'Stop it, Siena. You're freaking me out. Have you been at Jack's mother's lithium again?'

'I've joined the Council,' I repeat forcefully. 'With Romy a Starlet *and* a Council member, I need to move

96

in parallel. With her at the helm, the Council could actually become influential.'

'This is so unselfish of you, Siena,' says Cassidy in admiration. 'Do you really think the Council is a threat to us?'

'This is a vulnerable and testing time,' I say. 'Next year is our last, and other students are already thinking about their legacies. We've been at the top since we were Shells, but we've never been threatened by opposition. We should be ready for a challenge.'

'But you shouldn't be fighting on the front line!' Libby protests. '*I'll* join the Council.'

'You're busy with my English coursework,' I say regretfully. 'And you have a severe head injury. It's only right that I shoulder some of the burden. This challenge will make us all better Starlets.'

Madison nods thoughtfully. 'We're so lucky to have you, Siena.'

Libby can't contest the seriousness of her injury, and gradually we drift into other conversations. I allow myself a secret smile as I wonder why I was so worried. It's typical of Romy to try and ruin my day like this. Now in one fell swoop she's back under control, and it seems crazy to think that it could have been otherwise.

'Aren't you going to answer that?' Phoebe waves my phone in front of me.

I hadn't noticed that it was ringing, and now I stare without enthusiasm at the image of Jack's face on the display. I haven't thought about our last conversation yet this morning, but now I see a stream of messages. *Do you even care about this?* says one.

Before I can cancel the call, Libby has swiped the phone. 'She's right here,' she tells Jack briskly. 'Yes, I'm feeling much better, thank you.'

She raises an eyebrow at me as I remember using her as an excuse last night, and I shrug helplessly as she hands over the phone.

'Siena?' he says. 'Where are you?'

'I'm at breakfast,' I tell him. 'Where are *you*? I've been looking for you everywhere.'

'I'm still at the hospital,' he says flatly, and my heart sinks. The longer he stays there, the greater the chance of me being expected to visit. 'Are you going to make it here? You've got two free periods.'

'I'm tied up all day,' I say contritely. 'You know I'd make it if I could.'

He hangs up abruptly and I register relief that he's accepted the decision so easily. I'm about to rejoin the debate, which is now tackling the pros and cons of drop pearl earrings, when Libby's phone clangs with its annoying bell tone.

She reaches for it like a reflex, answering within the first ring. 'She's always hectic,' she says distractedly. 'But I can move a few things around if it's really an emergency. I could have her with you by eleven, with a clear forty-minute window. Forty-five, if I ask Henry to step on it.'

I'm only half listening until she puts down the phone. 'You should have said you needed to be at the hospital with Jack. I know I can be a taskmaster but I'll almost always grant leave on compassionate grounds.'

'That was *Jack*?' I say. 'You told him I could visit the hospital today?'

She's beaming, completely oblivious to the subtext. 'Of course! He sounds so lost without you that I was glad to help, and we can reschedule your *Three Sisters* audition. It's frankly an insult that you have to audition at all, even if it is just a formality.'

I stare at her, feeling my face burn with annoyance.

'You don't seem pleased,' she says, sounding less confident. 'Did I do something wrong? Don't you want to support Jack in hospital?'

'Of course I do,' I say, pulling myself together and smiling as sincerely as I can. 'More than anything. Thank you, Libby, for rectifying the matter so efficiently.'

'You're welcome,' she says in relief. 'That's what I'm here for. What else would I do all day?'

I'm quietly furious as I storm through the courtyard at the appointed time. Libby has her own on-call chauffeur, Henry, and I nod as he opens the car door for me.

'Hospital?' he says as we wind down the long driveway. I force a smile in case he reports on my mood to Libby.

'Has the world changed much since you left it?' he asks after a few minutes.

I laugh despite myself, because Henry always professes to find it strange that we love school so much. He can't understand why we always cry on the last day of term, but never the first; why deep gloom descends as he drives each of us towards an enforced, extended separation; why our panic and alienation at leaving school don't lift until we return.

'It looks the same, I suppose,' I concede, although I never notice my surroundings much. I check the mirror for visible signs of stress, and, the next time I look out of the window, we're at the hospital.

Henry takes out his newspaper as I pinch my cheeks to restore colour to them. 'I won't be long,' I say, more to reassure myself than him. 'It's a flying visit.'

'You take all the time you need,' he says. 'I'll be waiting.'

His unswervingly good nature annoys me. I step out of the car, approaching the entrance with unnatural sloth.

I hope that Security, or confidentiality, or *something*, will stop me advancing beyond reception, but I can't catch a break, and as soon as I say Jack's name I'm waved through. I trudge up three flights of stairs, partly to delay the inevitable and partly to burn off the apple I ate earlier.

Jack is sitting at the far end of a dimly lit hall, beneath a strip light that flickers and buzzes so loudly that I can't understand why it's not driving him crazy. I decelerate further, still hopeful of finding an escape, but he turns at the sound of my shoes.

It's too late to turn back, but I wish I could, because the flickering light is bright enough to show tears streaked on his pale cheeks. He turns away to wipe them with his sleeve as I sit beside him. I know I'm blushing, and that neither of us wants to acknowledge what's happening, and so I examine my manicure, focusing on a tiny chip as I reach for my nail file.

He watches as if he's interested in what I'm doing. Then, as I consider the best place to start, he snatches the file and tosses it right down the corridor. I watch, stupefied, as it skitters to a halt.

'What was that for?' I ask. 'I'm here, aren't I?'

'You think I wanted to book an appointment through Libby?' he asks. 'You think I wanted to force you here kicking and screaming?'

'I'm *here*,' I repeat. 'That's what you wanted.'

Unexpectedly, he takes my hand. 'Can't you see that, if this were happening to you, I'd be by your side in a heartbeat? I'd do everything possible to make it easier on you. I'd never make you go through it alone.'

'Where's your dad?' I ask, looking around. 'I thought he'd be here by now.'

He laughs. 'He's in the middle of a deal. He says he came last time, and the time before. Like he's in credit for hospital visits or something.'

'So how is she?' I ask stiffly. Even this question feels unnatural.

He clears his throat. 'It's too early to tell. You

know she's done this before?'

I nod, because *everyone* knows that she does this at least three times a year. His dad's regular donations to the ward ensure her a premier service, but even so, her insides must be hewn from titanium.

'They think she might have permanent damage,' he says. 'They won't know until she wakes up.'

He ducks his head and I hear him sob properly. We've been together for over four years, but I feel like a stranger as I gingerly rub his back.

A nurse comes out of the door beside us. 'Are you ready?' she asks, sounding far gentler than I ever do. But then, Nursing College probably offers a module on Sympathetic Voices, while Mrs Denbigh's Manners classes have never yet touched on bedside technique in any medical sense.

I scowl as she squeezes Jack's shoulder, even though I should be pleased to have someone do my job for me.

'You can go in too, sweetie,' she tells me.

I look up quickly. 'Isn't it family only? I'm not . . .'

She looks at our entwined hands. 'I didn't think you two were related. It's fine.'

Jack is looking at me hopefully. 'Please, Siena. Please come in with me.'

I don't tell him that sitting in this antiseptic corridor, underneath a buzzing, flickering light that makes me want to scream, is already more than I can cope with.

We'll never come back, will we? I asked on the day

I left a hospital just like this one.

Paula was wheeling my mother's chair slowly and cautiously to avoid upsetting both her and the sleeping bundle on her lap, but my mother leaned forward, urging her to speed up.

Blinking into the light, she gulped raw spring air before taking my hand in her cold fingers.

We'll never come back, she promised.

I close my eyes and try to imagine that I'm not here at all, but riding Pip through a field at sunset. I concentrate on his thundering hooves, and his coarse mane twisted through my hands as I lean so far into him that my head is almost buried. And for a second I'm able to think of nothing else.

'Don't let us keep you.'

My eyes snap open to see the nurse, much altered from the recent moment in which she called me *sweetie*, looking annoyed. I shouldn't be surprised that she's taking Jack's side over mine, but I ignore her anyway as I stand briskly and smooth my skirt.

'Come on,' Jack says, already on his feet.

'Let's get this over with,' I mutter as I follow him.

The buzzing of the light is replaced immediately by the buzzing of whatever machine it is that his mother is rigged up to. He's beside me as we enter the room but he stops short at the sight of her.

'Haven't you been in here yet?' I whisper.

He shakes his head. 'They wouldn't let me in last night. And today . . .'

The nurse cuts in, still sounding irritated. 'He was waiting for you. It's a shame you were so . . . detained.'

She looks about forty and is wearing a wedding ring. I'd put money on her having teenage sons herself and hoarding pent-up resentment from watching them wait for girls to respond to their calls or texts or inadequate conversational overtures.

This makes me picture Jack alone in the corridor underneath a malfunctioning light, going to increasingly desperate lengths to make me arrive; risking never seeing his mother again unless I'm by his side.

'You shouldn't have waited,' I mutter. 'What if she'd . . . before I got here?'

'I couldn't do it alone,' he says. His teeth are clenched, but his whole body is shaking.

I start to back away. He looks at me in disbelief and I avoid his eyes; for some reason, it's not him who changes my mind, but the nurse. Her expression, disbelieving and knowing and contemptuous all at once, makes me snatch up his hand and hold it tighter than I ever have before.

'I'm sorry I wasn't here for you,' I tell him, allowing myself a second to glare at her. 'I promise I won't leave you again.'

We sit on opposite sides of the bed, the beeping of the monitor even more distracting than the flickering light, and I pray that I can make it to the end of visiting time without running out of here as fast as I can.

Chapter Fourteen

Romy

Student Council meetings take place in a damp room underneath a staircase, the main benefit of which is that no one can find and vandalize it. It's remarkable that the Starlets ever allowed me to be a member during my previous incarnation, and I can only think it was to allow them a clear hour each week in which to discuss my wrongdoings behind my back. There would never have been a conversation shortage.

I wait at the door for Siena, who's predictably late. Only as I'm about to go inside without her do I hear her familiar Louboutins clacking on the polished floor.

'Where have you been?' I ask curiously, because she's flustered, her hair untidy and her collar creased. She looks upset, although this quickly mutates into annoyance.

'I'm here now, aren't I?' she glares as she fastens her hair.

I shrug. 'It's no skin off my nose whether you turn up or not.'

'I think you'll find we both have to keep our end of the bargain. Good job at breakfast, by the way. I don't think the Starlets suspected anything.'

'Where's your gown?' I ask. 'We're supposed to wear them to meetings.'

'Where's *yours*?' she snipes, turning up her nose at my outfit for the second time today.

Having made an effort for my return, I've lost interest in clothes. As opening my wardrobe requires energy I don't possess, I'm already in direct defiance of the Starlet Statute that requires *all members to change ensembles a minimum of twice a day; thrice on Saturdays.* I've thrown on a rust-coloured jumper I found abandoned in my old locker, and it's only now that I notice a hole in the sleeve and a piece of hay woven into the cuff.

'Was that heinous knitwear too stylish to cover up, or have you lost yet another gown?'

'*My* gown,' I remind her, 'is now a pile of ashes on the tower room floor.'

She unsnaps her handbag and produces her own gown. I know it hasn't occurred to her to lend me one, even though it's her fault that I'm without *and* she has a shelf full of spares, pristinely ironed and subtly customized. I pull an oversized black cardigan around my shoulders and hope that no one will notice the difference.

She blanches as I open the door. 'Is there nowhere else you could meet? Like Soho House?'

I remind myself that she's exceeded expectations just by turning up. It seems petty to feel annoyed that she's made me late for the very first meeting of term.

The Council are assembled, but conversation grinds to a halt as we sit in the remaining empty spaces. One of the youngest girls, who's been doodling crowns and hearts and wedding rings on her notepad, drops her pen and stares at us in unabashed amazement, while another starts to shake visibly.

'This is Siena Hamilton,' I announce. 'She'd like to join me on the Council this term. That is, if you'll have me back.'

I say this with sarcasm, because bringing Siena onto the Council is so far beyond the dreams of any of its members that I could throw Libby headfirst down a ladder a million times over before they'd kick me out again. But no one's even listening, because Siena has adopted the smile she always exhibits when forced to meet and greet the general public. Introducing her is as absurd as introducing Kate Middleton; as though everyone in the room doesn't already know every single fact and unverified rumour about her life in as much detail as their own. But Siena probably doesn't have the faintest idea who any of these students are, even though she's lived with them for four years, and shared classes and swimming pools and even dormitories with them.

The Council has about twenty members, and frankly that's a tremendous achievement. Most year groups are better represented than ours, which today comprises just me and Siena, and that's possibly because they're unhindered by the disapproving – and by that I mean *downright threatening* – existence of the Starlets. Their hatred of the Council might be borne simply as a reaction against a rival power-seeking group, but my involvement certainly intensified it.

'Why would you do this?' asked Libby when I first requested to join. 'I know you don't fit in *here*, but surely you can see that joining the Council would be completely off-brand?'

'Why would you do this?' the Council members asked with equal bemusement. 'You don't fit in *here*.'

'I know that,' I told both sides. 'But even if I don't fit anywhere, I have to be *somewhere*.'

Finally I persuaded the Starlets that I could enter the Council as a double agent, keeping a foot squarely in both camps and ensuring that their priorities were adequately heeded. Given that the Council handles the budget for all social events as well as academic affairs, there were advantages to giving me my way.

Siena holds out her hand. 'Pleased to meet you,' she greets each member as she makes her way around the table. The shock of being in such proximity to her apparently prevents them being offended that she follows each handshake with a pump of sanitizer. Despite a changeover of Head Girl and Boy, and the appearance of a few nervous-looking Shells, the Council is much the same as I left it. This is possibly because it attracts a very clear type: everyone is pale and earnest with a pathological loyalty to the school crest and a world-weary duty to impart rules upon individuals

Welcome to Tile Hill Community Library

Customer ID: *********5959

Items that you have checked out

Title: Siena
ID: 38002022038899
Due: 27 November 2018

Total items: 1
Account balance: £0.00
30 October 2018
Checked out: 1
Overdue: 0
Hold requests: 0
Ready for collection: 0

Thank you for using this unit - tilself01
Tel: 024-7678-6785
www.coventry.gov.uk/libraries
email.tilehill.library@coventry.gov.uk
Opening Hours
Mon - Tues 9am - 7pm
Wed - Closed
Thurs - Fri 9am - 7pm
Sat - 9am - 4pm

who will never be grateful to learn them. One might as well wear a bullseye as a Council badge, and so the only volunteers are students who care about library provision and prep and helping Shells make friends more than they care about keeping their hair free of spitballs and not being tripped up or flushed down a toilet every time they venture out in public.

'Eric's missing,' I frown.

'Eric left the Council,' says Ambrose tremulously, pushing his glasses up his nose.

'*Again?*' Eric is in the Lower Sixth like me, and, despite being a loyal and helpful member, is periodically forced into hiding amid safety fears. 'Shall I go and fetch him?'

'It won't be any use,' sighs Avery. 'He's really left this time.'

'Why did he leave?' I ask, looking suspiciously at Siena.

Ambrose and Avery exchange glances. 'There was an incident,' begins Avery carefully. 'More of a misunderstanding, really. I'm sure the Starlets would *never . . .*'

I groan, but Siena isn't listening to me; rather, she's taking a Smythson notebook from her bag and unscrewing the lid of her silver fountain pen. *Siena's Student Council*, she writes on the first page, underlining the words twice and admiring them. Her handwriting is elaborately curvy and covetable; like all the girls in our class, I've exerted considerable effort over the years to subvert my own spider-like scrawls into some semblance of it.

'What did you do to Eric?' I ask her.

'Who's Eric?' she asks without looking up.

'He's quite short,' explains Avery. 'Quite freckly. Quite pale. He often carries a bag of rocks and a Tupperware box of frogs.'

'I don't believe I've had the *pleasure*,' Siena says delicately.

'You know perfectly well who Eric is,' I snap at her. 'You've known him for four years. Tell me what you did to him.'

She clicks her pen lid thoughtfully. 'If we're thinking of the same person, it's possible that Phoebe recently enlisted him to help with her photosynthesis experiment.'

'She buried him,' whispers Avery. 'In the shrubbery.'

Around me is a simultaneous group shiver; a Mexican wave of girls and boys fearing for their lives.

'She did nothing of the sort.' Siena is righteously indignant. 'She *planted* him. Like the specimen he is.'

'Underneath some of his rocks,' Ambrose adds. 'He wasn't discovered for a while.'

'He's not there anymore,' Siena reassures me. 'I'm sure I've seen him since. If anything, the experience has improved him. He's flatter now, and the exposure has ameliorated his complexion.'

'Where is he today?' I ask.

'He felt that Council membership was making him

a sitting target,' says Ambrose. 'He took up Samurai training this term instead.'

'But we need him!' I say. 'We require a male Lower Sixth Council member as Head Boy-elect. Should I talk to him?'

'You could try,' Avery says. 'But it's best to keep a six-foot distance. He carries an electric cattle prod, and he can be quite *jumpy*.'

'So who's going to be Head Boy next year?' I ask. 'We need a new Council member.'

'In the circumstances, we have permission to look outside the Council for a candidate,' says Ambrose. 'I'm sure we'll find someone just as charismatic as Eric.'

'You might consider dragging the Headmistress's pond,' suggests Siena. 'You'll find plenty of life just as charismatic as Eric, if you go deep enough.'

I look furiously at her, but she only taps her pen. 'What important issues are on the agenda today?' she asks.

There's a terrified silence, which I break with a sigh. 'Could you give a summary of what you've done while I've been away?'

'We campaigned for a new floor in the Woodlands girls' bathroom,' Avery ventures finally. 'The lino is cracked.'

'That's good,' I say encouragingly. 'I haven't seen it yet – what's it like?'

'We didn't get it,' she admits. 'There were . . . other priorities. It was decided to have a new home strip designed for the Stripes instead. It's tighter than their other kits, and the shorts are smaller. The Starlets campaigned for it.'

I ignore Siena's approving nod. 'What else?'

'We devised an orientation programme for the Shells, to help them make friends quickly,' Ambrose offers.

'What a great idea!' I say.

'Hardly,' says Siena. 'No offence, but why would any of them look to you for ideas about being popular?'

'No one said your notion of popularity had anything in common with making friends,' I tell her. 'I'm sure it was a success. I'd love to hear about it.'

'No one signed up,' admits Ambrose sheepishly. 'We had to cancel it.'

Siena laughs. 'So the point of the Student Council is ...'

I refrain from reminding her that the Starlets' main priority this week appears to be choosing Phoebe a new eyeshadow following the discontinuation of her favourite cerulean.

'Let's focus on the future,' I say instead. 'We all went through a lot of changes last year, I'm sure. What's first on today's agenda?'

'We're discussing the library catalogue.' Avery turns to Siena. 'The Council is given a budget to choose books and journals.'

'Books and journals?' Siena asks alertly. 'That's very interesting.'

112

'Is it?' says Avery in surprise.

I can read Siena as if she were a book herself. She's planning to order coffee table souvenirs about the Olsen twins and the history of Chanel, to force us to transfer our *Economist* subscription to *Vanity Fair*, and to educate the Shells to revere Grace Kelly instead of Hillary Clinton.

'Academic books and journals,' I clarify. 'Not fashion and celebrity magazines.'

'*Anyway*,' cuts in Ambrose after a quick conferral with Avery. 'Your return does give us an important discussion point, Romy. As the longest-serving Council member, you've become the Head Girl-elect.'

'Really?' I say doubtfully. 'Yesterday you said . . .'

'Never mind that,' Avery says with a hasty glance at Siena. She couldn't be more misguided if she thinks Siena would ever take my side, but there's no need to tell her that.

'Romy was thrown out of school for anti-social behaviour,' Siena argues. 'What's going on here?'

Avery crumbles instantly. 'Mrs Denbigh believes this responsibility will be good for Romy,' she whispers.

Siena rolls her eyes, and I almost join her, because the image of Mrs Denbigh plying the Council with Garibaldis and guilt-tripping sentiments of Christian forgiveness is embarrassingly easy to visualize.

'You don't have to do everything Mrs Denbigh says,' claims Siena, as if she isn't here as a punishment imposed by the very same. 'She has no real power.'

'Mrs Denbigh also reminded us that Romy is the only remaining Lower Sixth Council member,' adds Ambrose. 'Until you arrived, Siena, of course.'

He frowns as we take a moment to remember the fallen: the procession of bookish, idealistic girls driven out of the Council as fast as their Mary-Janes would carry them by name-calling and ridiculing, and, in some cases, with apples embedded in their heads.

'But you're so . . . anti-establishment,' Siena complains. 'Like that Russian punk band. Or Jessica Simpson. Isn't this a little conformist for you?'

'The only way to change a system is to be in it,' I tell her.

'What do you get for being Head Girl?' Siena looks Avery up and down. 'Nothing, I presume? Not even a shoe allowance?'

'There's a special presentation assembly.' Fifth Former Nicole speaks up for the first time. She and her best friend Bethany harbour a particular fascination for the Starlets, sitting exams for them, taking their places during wintry PE lessons, and acting as Siena's official stand-ins and seat-fillers at formal events. Her voice trembles slightly and she addresses her words directly to the table. 'It's called Elevation.'

'Why have I never heard of that?' Siena asks.

'Because, I believe,' I remind her, 'you miss every assembly in order to spend *quality time* with Jack.'

She barely conceals a smirk.

'Jack is so gorgeous,' sighs Bethany, as Nicole nods. 'You're so lucky, Siena.'

Siena looks at them imperiously. Both are deeply earnest in their spotless uniforms, faces innocently scrubbed make-up free. 'Luck has nothing to do with it.'

'No, it's more about trampling on everyone to get what you want,' I agree.

'What else does one get?' Siena turns away from me. 'I'm not sure that a special assembly is sufficiently enticing.'

'The Head Girl's fees are paid by the school,' says Nicole timidly. 'That's a big financial incentive.'

I can almost see the cogs in Siena's head whirring as she processes this. Her school fees are probably paid, like most students', by an absent and guilty father, so the financial saving would no doubt benefit her directly. I'm sure she's currently choosing the handbag on which she could blow the whole lump sum.

'And the Head Girl always goes to Oxford,' adds Bethany.

'That's not a rule,' I point out. 'It just seems to end up that way.'

'You want to go to Oxford?' Siena asks me.

'Why do you care?' I begin before breaking off. 'Oh, I know why you care. You don't want me to go to the same university as Jack.'

She looks astonished. 'Jack's job in the Firm –' spoken as if the Lawrences are on a par with the Windsors – 'is already guaranteed. What does he need university for?'

'A degree?' I suggest. 'Life experience? Self-improvement?'

'To get the best job possible, so he can take care of you.' Nicole speaks in the saccharine tone of someone who wants for nothing but a smile from Siena.

'You could consider going to university yourself,' I suggest. 'Imagine being educated by a source other than *Vogue*.'

She's horrified. 'Lecture theatres with plastic communal seating? Halls of residence? Public transport? *Students?*'

'So what are you going to do with yourself for three years while Jack's away having the time of his life?' I ask. 'What if he goes somewhere you can't follow, and doesn't want to come back? What if he likes independence and self-discovery and freedom more than the prospect of eternity with you?'

'Jack doesn't need to go to university, because he already has everything he needs,' she snaps. 'Right here.'

I know she's planned her wedding and her married life, which will comprise lunching on rocket leaves and Moët and going to the gym with other newly wedded Starlets before fobbing off babies onto a nanny and a pre-prep school, perpetuating the whole dismal cycle.

'Well, if you're sure,' I say. 'You know him better than I do, of course. Now, shall we discuss something cheerful? Like the football championship?'

I'd expected this to lighten the mood, but yet another

awkward silence forms, and Siena scowls more blackly than ever.

'Isn't it next week?' I ask. 'Aren't we going to rally the school in support?'

'The Stripes aren't having the best season,' whispers Nicole. From Siena's expression, I guess this is an understatement.

'Surely that's all the more reason to support them?' I say. 'We never missed a single game while I was here, and they always appreciated it.'

Ambrose looks ashamed. 'I suppose the support has dwindled, as none of us can be considered *soccer fans*, and their performances have diminished in the interim. Let's put on a big push for them this week. Well suggested, Romy.'

'That's settled, then,' says Siena, looking at her watch. 'We'll support them. Are we finished?'

'No!' I say. 'We haven't discussed the details. What support are we intending to offer? What's our budget? How will we keep up morale if they lose?'

'I'm not interested in details,' she says automatically.

'It was that attitude that got you here,' I tell her. 'We're supporting your boyfriend!'

'Jack knows he can count on my support in all his endeavours,' she says loftily. 'I don't need to carry pompoms to prove it.'

I don't know what makes me continue, except that she's annoyed me more than I can take. 'Then you might want to ask him why he was reading the Oxford prospectus in the library today. And why he's signed up for an open day.'

She looks furious. 'You're very lucky to be back in this school at all. If you want to stay, you should remember that.'

'We should wrap up,' says Ambrose hurriedly. 'I think we've covered everything.'

'*Fine*,' says Siena. 'If I have to spend another minute with any of you, I *swear* I'll throw myself headfirst out of the window.'

She picks up her bag and storms out, slamming the door behind her.

'Whoa,' says Bethany, shaking her head.

'I know,' I murmur. 'She's a nightmare straight from the pits of hell.'

Nicole stares at the door as if Siena is still there. 'Thank you for bringing her to us,' she whispers. 'I'll never, ever forget it.'

Chapter Fifteen

Siena

'What's up with Jack?' Cassidy asks, nodding across the cafeteria where he's staring into a cup of coffee. 'I didn't even notice him come in.'

My hospital trip was only yesterday, but, thanks to the hideous diversion of the Council meeting, I'd managed to forget my promise to go with him again today. Now it washes over me and I glare at Libby before I can stop myself.

'Did something bad happen at the hospital?' she squeaks. 'Did I . . . did I do wrong in scheduling the visit?'

'Of course not,' I say magnanimously. 'It was *so* helpful of you to set my priorities in order and enable me to be with Jack in his time of need.'

I have to grit my teeth to say this, but I can't put up with Libby's wounded expression any longer. It could throw her off her game, and none of the other Starlets is capable of managing my schedule. Besides which, I want to borrow a pair of her shoes.

'I've been so worried that our friendship would change with Romy back,' she admits. 'She was always such a bad influence on you. Sometimes, when you two were together, it was as if the rest of us didn't even matter.'

I look around the table in case this view is widely held.

'No one blames you, Siena,' says Phoebe quickly. 'We all know how manipulative Romy is. We know you didn't *really* prefer her to us.'

I try to listen to Phoebe, but, as much as I fight it, I can't shake Romy's voice, or her luminous green eyes, out of my head.

Admit that they're boring, she challenged me in a conversation I thought I'd forgotten. It was two years ago, and we were avoiding a debate about acceptable heel height for the Henley Regatta. *Admit that you don't like talking about kitten heels and blusher any more than I do.*

I'm not admitting anything. Of course the Starlets aren't boring.

Then why do you escape and hide from them at every opportunity? she asked. *Usually it's not even my idea.*

I'm not hiding. I shrank into the apple leaves at the sound of voices on the ground. *This tree just happens to be a comfortable place to sit.*

I shifted awkwardly, because a branch was digging into my back.

Why don't I invite them along? She reached into her pocket for her phone.

No, I said quickly. *Let's just stay here for a while. On our own.*

She shrugged. *We can stay as long as you like.*

Cassidy smiles at me now. 'It's all in the past, safely buried. Romy's departure freed you to become the wonderful person you were always destined to be.'

To ensure that Romy's reappearance hasn't damaged my standing, I hold out my hand across the table. '*Nothing* is going to change,' I stress.

'For all time?' Libby asks tentatively, putting her hand on mine.

I nod as the others pile their hands on top of ours. 'For all time,' we repeat.

'Are you seriously still doing that?' says Romy as she throws down her tray. 'Do you know how childish you look?'

'I'd forgotten you'd be joining us,' I say coldly. 'It allowed me a brief moment of happiness.'

She shrugs and takes a bite of toast. This is the kind of complex carbohydrate that hasn't passed a Starlet's lips for the last ten years.

'Are you going to digest that?' asks Phoebe with genuine curiosity. 'Like, fully?'

'I thought I might,' she says. 'I usually do try to digest my food after swallowing it. I realize this concept is alien to you.'

'Interesting,' murmurs Phoebe. She has a plate of toast too, but so far her progress involves only cutting it into star shapes and covering it with jam.

'I'm surprised you didn't go and sit with Jack,' I tell

her. 'You don't often miss an opportunity to poison him against me.'

Romy puts down her toast, her appetite apparently gone.

'*You* should go and talk to him, Siena,' says Libby. 'You've got . . . almost fifteen minutes before registration. You last did your hair ten minutes ago, so you can leave that for another forty-five. You should give him the opportunity to thank you for all your support. He's so lucky to have you at his side.'

'And maybe you could cheer him up,' suggests Cassidy. 'I mean, he has a lot on his mind. *Of course*. But don't the Stripes have that big game soon? We don't want to get the blame if it goes badly.'

'Are you for real?' Romy asks. 'You're going to talk to Jack about football? *Today?*'

Libby nods. 'The Stripes' ongoing uselessness is becoming a reputational problem for us. People think we have a direct effect on their performance.'

'Everyone was so mean to us when Phoebe turned off Harry's alarm clock and he missed the bus to the Winchester play-offs,' Cassidy complains. 'And there was a very hostile atmosphere the day they lost to Bedales, which was a total misunderstanding. How was Mads supposed to know that she and Sam were dating exclusively, or that he and Taylor would discuss such *intimate* details about their—'

'Enough, Cassidy,' I say, getting up. 'I was going anyway.'

'Don't,' Romy blurts out. She blushes as everyone stares at her. 'Just . . . leave Jack alone.'

'I'll do what I like,' I tell her, leaning closer. 'My relationship with Jack is one area of my life in which you'll remain uninvolved.'

'You're planning to distract him with sex,' she says. 'Which is inappropriate, even for you.'

'I think I know better than you what Jack needs,' I snap. 'So watch and learn.'

Jack seems not to notice as I sit beside him. I move his cup away, because I'm wearing fawn and his hands look unsteady. He still doesn't look up, but, despite the awful smirk that Romy gives me, I'm not deterred. This is the kind of challenge that makes me the best at what I do: the tendency of boys to fall to pieces whenever I give them so much as a smile isn't exactly scintillating, and the last thing I want is for indiscriminate male attention to make me complacent.

Normally a first move wouldn't be required of me, but I'm on limited time, so I run my thumbs gently up and down his stomach, watching as he jumps and inhales.

'Siena,' he says. Instead of replying, I kiss him in a circular pattern starting right under his earlobe. His eyes are closed and his breath comes raggedly. I substitute my thumbs for my fingernails, running them along the waistband of his jeans. He half opens his eyes, so I circle lower. I kiss along his jawline to his

123

mouth and circle the tip of his tongue with my own. For a second I feel him go slack.

'*Siena.*' His voice is hoarse but determined and he pushes my hands away.

'What?' I try not to sound irritated. We still have almost ten minutes before the bell, which would be plenty if he'd stop talking.

There was a moment yesterday at the hospital when he ducked his head and stayed motionless for so long that I wondered if he was praying. His hands were clasped white-knuckle tight, his face set in quiet desperation, and, as my mind raced through the ways in which I wanted to help him, I believed there was nothing I wouldn't do. When he flexed his hands and exhaled, I saw a tear on his eyelashes, and it sent a shockwave through me.

But that moment, with no spectators to sense weakness in me, or to threaten to separate us, was poles apart from this. Stealing another glance at Romy's triumphant expression, I shrug my dress strap off my shoulder. Without missing a beat he picks it up and replaces it.

'What?' My pout makes me hate myself, even if I don't understand why. 'What else are we supposed to do in the cafeteria to prove to Ro— to everyone that we're a couple?'

'Not now,' he says.

'You said you needed me. I want to make you feel better.'

'But *that* won't make me feel better. Can't you see that hooking up isn't always the answer to our problems?'

'What else is there?'

'There's love,' he says. 'Isn't there?'

'That's the same.'

'Not always.' I've never known him to be so stubborn. 'Sometimes love means conversation. Empathy. Support. You were so nice yesterday: what's changed?'

He looks at the Starlets, who have opened magazine spreads across the table, and gives a short laugh as Romy averts her gaze from us and pretends to study them too.

'No need to explain,' he says. 'I see this isn't about me at all. You're just proving a point to Romy.'

'I'm not,' I say. 'I've been generous enough to let her sit with us. Doesn't that show what kind of person I am?'

'You're making this about you again. You don't even care enough to ask how she is!'

I wonder who *she* is before remembering his mother, but he hasn't stopped talking for long enough to notice. 'Just because you don't care about your family doesn't mean that I shouldn't care about mine.'

I'm stung by this. 'I don't care about my family?'

'You don't give any indication of it. You never take any notice of your sisters, for one thing. Do you even know when their birthdays are?'

I don't answer this, because my family and birthdays are not a happy combination. My mother flatly refuses to get older, and none of us likes to mention the unhappiness that descended when Syrena fell to earth. 'I care about my family,' I tell him, and then I mimic him. '*Let's not make this about me.*'

'You make everything about you.'

'I was joking,' I tell him.

'Whereas I was taking our relationship seriously,' he shoots back. 'Was there something else you wanted?'

I've had enough, football championship or none. I'm pretty sure I can start a rumour about Phoebe that will cause enough of a fight with her boyfriend – Jack's vice-captain – to take the heat off me. As for Romy, she might look happy right now but I'm sure even she's smart enough to realize that she won't get away with this.

He calls me back as I stand up, and I wait for him to apologize. 'My mum's going to be okay,' he says. 'In case you were wondering.'

'Of course I was wondering,' I tell him untruthfully, but he's already turned away.

Chapter Sixteen

Romy

'Why were you allowed to come back halfway through the year?' Siena asks as we walk to the Common Room. Mrs Denbigh has taken to tailgating us at every opportunity, herding us not only into each other's company, but into ostensibly civil conversation. Right now she's wedged, beady-eyed, behind a pot plant. 'Why is your French no better than it was when you left?'

'*Va-t'en*,' I mutter under my breath.

'What was that?' she asks.

I smile. 'My French is still better than yours, apparently.'

Siena veers out of Mrs Denbigh's vision down a dark corridor leading to the Art block. 'Do go away!' she snaps as I follow her. 'She can't see us now, can she?'

'I'm not risking it,' I say. 'She could reappear at any time.'

'She's not supernatural,' she says exasperatedly. 'You could give me ten minutes alone. Or are you hoping I'll lead you to Jack? Because I should tell you that, whatever problems you *falsely* perceive us to be having, nothing will ever send him back to you.'

'I'm glad you remember that I knew him first,' I say.

'He never talks about his time with you,' she says. 'One would almost think your relationship never took place.'

'He never talks about his mother with you anymore either,' I remind her. 'Perhaps he steers clear of meaningful subjects.'

We're too busy arguing to notice the approach of our Art teacher Mr Kidd until it's too late.

'*Merde*,' we say at the same time.

'We can't both turn around,' she mutters. 'It's too obvious.'

'Then let me go,' I say. Mr Kidd, one of the few teachers who didn't disown me last year, sent me a monstrous amount of work to hand in on my return. It occurs to me now that missing the deadline isn't the best way to show my gratitude. 'Why do you need to avoid him? You're everyone's favourite, no matter how bad your work is.'

Mr Kidd's rolling gait is deceptively fast, and neither of us succeeds in escaping before he's in front of us. 'I'm glad I stumbled across you two,' he says mildly. 'Although I could have just followed the noise. You missed my lesson yesterday, as I expect you already know.'

Siena opens her mouth to begin an elaborate excuse, but he shakes his head. 'Save it for next time. You need details of this term's project. As everyone else now has a partner, it looks as though you two will be working

128

together. I understand from Mrs Denbigh that you will be delighted to do so.'

'What's the brief?' Siena's voice is tight.

'*Inspiration*.' He sounds pleased with himself. 'But there's a twist or two. Firstly, Siena, you must exhibit Romy's inspiration, and vice versa.'

'What's the other twist?' she asks miserably.

'You must use Romy's medium, and she yours. So Romy will work with oil paints, and you, photography.'

'I always partner Tristan,' she protests. 'We share the same light aesthetic, as well as a keen interest in minor Swedish royals. Our project is already planned.'

'Not this time,' he says. 'I was moved to wonder if your intended depiction of the Royal Wedding with you as the bride would be treason. Not that it wouldn't have been compelling to see Mrs Denbigh as the Duchess of Cornwall.'

'It's not treason,' I tell Siena reassuringly, because Mr Kidd is the only teacher she has any respect for, and she looks stricken at this. 'It's sociopathic, but that won't land you in the Tower. Probably.'

Mr Kidd smiles benignly. 'I'm expecting something spectacular from you both,' he says as he departs.

'You're taking this very well,' I comment when he's gone. 'I expected you to complain far more loudly.'

'It's a fake project,' she says dismissively. She starts walking at speed, navigating a convoluted route back to the Common Room. 'Mrs Denbigh put him up to it.'

'Doesn't matter, if we still have to do it.'

'What we *don't* have to do is talk about it,' she says. 'Especially not now,' she adds hurriedly as we enter the Common Room to the sight of an overexcited Libby. She's shaking, her cheeks flushed, and she giggles as she grabs Siena by the wrist and pulls her to the Starlet sofa. Waiting for silence, she casts around a triumphant glance until she has everyone's full attention.

'Remember when Jack told you that this would be your most exciting term ever?' she asks. 'And you thought—'

'What of it?' asks Siena impatiently.

'He's got the rock.' Libby manages to hiss and squeak at the same time.

Siena is at once fully alert. 'Where is it? How do you know? Are you sure?'

Libby nods. 'He brought it to football practice by mistake, and Tristan got a good look at it before he left to put it away. He confirms that the diamond is a good size, though smaller than Princess Charlene's, and of excellent clarity.'

'How long do you think he's been carrying it around?' Siena asks. 'I'm always diligent about checking his pockets and I've never found anything terribly interesting.'

'It must be a recent thing,' says Libby, lighting a candle. 'But why are we speculating when Romy can verify the details for us? She still owes us a fortune-telling session.'

'I don't . . . I can't . . .' No one's listening. 'I'm not doing this!'

'*Focus*,' says Libby. 'Just for once, can't you do a nice deed for someone deserving?'

I've never pitted Jack as the type to propose to Siena before their school careers were over, but the evidence seems pretty indefatigable, and who knows how much his mother's mishap has upset him. He must want comfort and security at a time like this, and he loves Siena enough to make this eminently possible, if not eminently stupid.

Let them get married, if that's what they want, I tell myself. *Divorce might teach them a valuable lesson.*

'What do you see?' whispers Cassidy.

As my psychic gift is yet to show itself, I close my eyes and hope for the best. My head fills with blankness instead of Siena, and I play for time by flipping through the other girls instead, fleetingly glimpsing an injection of cash for Libby, a nervous collapse for Cassidy and an academic warning for Phoebe. Conflict is slamming towards Madison, but Libby is talking again before I see more.

'Hurry up, or I'll have to tell Mrs Denbigh how uncooperative you're being. I imagine she's very close by – we can't seem to shake her off this term.'

'I see the tower room,' I say hurriedly, throwing all semblance of honesty to the winds. 'I see candles and . . . roses.'

'What else?' breathes Cassidy.

'I see the school hall,' I say. 'It's a dance.'

'That's interesting,' says Libby. 'Especially since the Council put a complete embargo on social occasions when you left. Even if they were persuaded to change their minds, I doubt any budget remains following their lunatic library refurbishment.'

'I'm completely sure.' I wasn't aware of this Council policy, but it doesn't matter. It might actually be best to predict an event so implausible that even Libby won't try to make it happen. 'I see a very *expensive* dance with chandeliers, and glass slippers, and crystals, and roses, and gold crockery, and dancing animals, and . . .'

I open my eyes to see Tristan hovering nearby with his phone. 'Why is he filming me?'

'How else do you expect us to document this?' asks Libby. 'Shorthand?'

'What am I wearing at the dance?' asks Siena dreamily.

'A dress?' I say, running out of steam. 'Definitely a dress.'

'Don't start that nonsense again,' says Libby. 'What colour dress? What length?'

'This is silly,' says Madison. 'It's no fun if Romy tells us everything beforehand. Some things have to evolve.'

I smile gratefully. 'Mads made Siena's dress,' I say as she smiles back. 'And it's beautiful. I know that much.'

'This discussion is a waste of time,' says Phoebe. 'We've never had a dance like that, and we're not likely to have. I'm not even sure which animals know how to dance properly.'

'We'll see,' says Siena. 'You've forgotten that I'm on the Council now, and I decide on our events. *All* our events.'

'You're the Council's newest, least important member,' I remind her. 'What makes you think you can push this through?'

She looks me right in the eye. 'No one gets the better of me. Not you, not Mrs Denbigh, and not the Council. By the end of term, no one will *ever* doubt that again.'

Chapter Seventeen

Siena

I'm so happy about the emergence of the ring that I make a special effort to support Jack's big game. There's no sense in enduring the match itself, because it will outlast my attention span and there's a risk of being hit by a ball, but I pass the playing field on my return from the hairdresser just before it's due to end. It goes without saying that the Starlets are absent, but a huge crowd is in attendance nonetheless.

Students are supposed to attend all home matches, but support has been desultory since the Stripes began their losing streak. Today almost the entire school is here, with the Council a stalwart presence. They're wearing team colours, and some have even dyed their hair into red stripes. They're waving banners predicting an unlikely victory, with Romy's messy handwriting evident on each as if she's marking territory.

'Siena!' calls Avery enthusiastically. 'Come here!'

I give her a wave and a regretful shake of the head as I hurry onwards, because protecting my hair from drizzle so that I look my best in the post-match photographs is far more supportive, long-term, than being near the pitch. However, by now the entire

Council is shouting at me, and making so much noise that I have no choice but to turn back towards them.

'It's a draw so far!' says Avery happily. 'It's their best match in ages. All this support must have boosted morale.'

'Drawing doesn't sound very good,' I say. 'Isn't that the same as losing?'

Ambrose starts to explain something about points, and why drawing and losing are two different concepts. I worry this will take a long time, but, just as I start to edge away again, the whistle blows.

'It's a corner kick!' says Nicole breathlessly. She and Bethany have painted matching stripes across their cheeks and look even more wretched than usual. 'Jack's taking it!'

'Would you like to borrow my scarf, Siena?' asks Avery. 'You seem cold.'

Her striped scarf is unappealing, and I'm glad I've had a few shots of vodka, which has the same warming effect as unflatteringly bulky outerwear. But just then Jack looks up and sees me. His expression, of incredulity turning to happiness, is so unexpected that I take the scarf Avery proffers and drape it around my neck. The manmade fibres feel very unpleasant, but I try to put that aside as he takes the kick, and not to imagine that acrylic is tightening around my windpipe like a serpent. There's a lot of jostling, and so I miss the exact movements of both Jack and the ball, but judging by the frenzied reaction I guess it

135

ends up where it's supposed to be, and then the game appears to be over.

'It's amazing to have you with us!' Avery says. 'We've never seen you here before.'

'How funny,' I say. 'I suppose I'm not usually in the cheap seats.'

'Do you like football?' she asks.

'I love it,' I say, preparing to leave. 'All that mud, and men falling everywhere and congratulating each other . . . What's not to enjoy?'

As the Stripes finish their victory huddle and head towards us, I prise Avery's *Go Stripes Go* banner from her hand, intending to shield myself from their muddy clothes.

'You came!' Jack says. 'I can't believe it.'

'Of course I came,' I say. 'Someone had to coordinate the Council into some kind of order. You should have seen the state they were in before I took over.'

'You mean . . .' He looks in amazement at the Council's painted faces, banners and scarves. 'Do you mean *you* put this support together?'

'That depends,' I say cautiously. 'Do you like it?'

'Do I . . .' He shakes his head in disbelief. 'Siena, this support won us the match!'

I smile modestly. 'Then yes, I was responsible for this . . . circus. When I joined the Student Council I was determined to make a difference, and restoring morale to our talented but troubled football team seemed the perfect place to start.'

'I feel as if . . . as if this is a twilight zone,' he says, sounding dazed. 'I thought you said you'd joined the Student Council.'

'I'm extremely passionate about student politics,' I explain, showing him the Council badge I hide under a lapel for obvious reasons. 'I can't believe you didn't know that.'

'To think . . .' He sounds ashamed. 'I didn't even expect you to turn up today! I'm so sorry for underestimating you.'

Romy is furious, and some of the Council look a bit concerned, as if she should be getting some credit, but luckily the other Stripes descend on us at this point.

'Siena rallied the whole school in support!' Jack tells them. 'She won us the game!'

'I suppose I did,' I acknowledge as they all break into applause. Romy must have worked hard to persuade so many people to come along in such cold weather, but I was solely responsible for the winning goal, so everything he's saying is true. Not to mention that my help is more newsworthy than Romy's, who has nothing better to do with her time.

'So why have you joined the Council?' he asks, slinging an arm around me as we head back to school.

'I've been somewhat selfish,' I say, because he deserves to think he's right for once. 'Neglecting those less fortunate. This helps me give back to my community and work towards a common goal; enjoy my favourite sport and the great outdoors.'

137

'You hate football,' Romy hisses as she appears at my right ear.

'*Au contraire*,' I say. 'The football field is where Jack and I first became acquainted, so it holds special memories.'

'In that case, why did no one see you before the final moments of the match? Where were you for the first eighty-nine minutes?'

'There was much to coordinate,' I explain. 'I was in the wings, working tirelessly backstage for the stars up front. After all, today wasn't about me.'

'So you didn't get to see most of the game?' Jack says. 'I can't believe I called you selfish. You even joined the Council so you could support me! Can you forgive me?'

'Let's never speak of it,' I say as I lead him away from Romy.

'My mum's doing a lot—'

'Let's never speak of it,' I say more forcefully. 'Let's concentrate on the living.'

He looks a bit upset, so I try again. 'I mean, the able-bodied. Let's concentrate on us.'

The Common Room is packed by the time we arrive. The Starlets are always present at this part of proceedings, and I wrench off my scarf too late.

'What on *earth* is that?' says Libby in revulsion. 'It looks like some kind of noose.'

I kick it blithely along the floor. 'It pays to keep your man happy.'

'It certainly does,' Phoebe says as Jack arrives with a bottle of Cristal. 'Siena, why is everyone saying you won the football championship?'

'I'm not sure.' I shrug. 'Perhaps in the way I win every game, just by existing.'

They nod in understanding, and then we roll our eyes as Romy storms up. 'You're taking all the credit! You're stealing my hard work, and making it all about you. This has to be the most selfish thing you've ever done, and there's some stiff competition.'

'How about when—' begins Phoebe.

'No need for examples, Phoebe,' says Libby. 'As long as Siena's behaviour is always classed as superlative, that's all we need to know.'

'I did win the game, Romy,' I say as I steer her out of earshot. 'I didn't notice the Stripes winning before I arrived. I won *our* game too, and don't forget it. Jack is *my* boyfriend, and it's staying that way.'

'You have no redeeming qualities at all, do you know that?'

I sigh. I was hoping to delay pulling this particular rabbit from my hat, but she's so angry that I can't guarantee she won't open her mouth and blow my reasons for joining the Council as well as my primarily supervisory role in today's game. 'Actually, I've been doing something entirely selfless for you for a whole year.'

'You had me exiled for the good of my health?'

'More *everyone else's* health. But something besides

that. You should collect it from my room before I have it made into stew. Now go away and let people congratulate me.'

She doesn't move, but the Starlets edge her backwards until she's out of sight and sound, banishing her far enough that I can enjoy my party without further conflict. Unfortunately she ends up beside Jack, where they share a deep conversation before he leaves her to join me.

'What were you talking to Romy about?' I ask.

He shrugs. 'Nothing that would interest you.'

'It might,' I say, annoyed. 'Don't assume I'm never interested in the things she is.'

'I'd have invited you to offer your opinion on the French election if I'd known you cared so much,' he says.

I stop listening in relief. I should have known that Romy would be incapable of anything approaching flirting.

'She also had some great words of support about my mum,' he adds. 'Do you know she sent flowers?'

'You'll always find a supportive ear here,' I say. 'Oh, they're playing our song!'

I drag him to the centre of the makeshift dance floor as my request, *The Bad Touch*, begins its opening beats.

'Our song is *Flying Without Wings*,' he corrects me. 'You always get that wrong.'

I relax as he wraps his arms around my waist, relieved that we're back on track.

'I know things have been strange between us,' he

says. 'But I have the perfect way to make it up to you.'

'What is it?' I remind myself that begging for presents is rude, not to mention Syrena-ish, but it takes all my willpower not to extend my left hand.

He kisses me on the nose. 'Be patient. I can't tell you until the end of term.'

My heart is beating faster. 'You have to give me a clue!'

He thinks to himself. 'Okay . . . I was beginning to wonder if I'd made the right decision, but everything that's happened today has made up my mind.'

'Another clue?' I suggest.

'It's about a very big event that's going to take place in the summer,' he says.

'Does it involve celebrations and dresses?'

He kisses me again. 'Everything in your world involves celebrations and dresses. I'm sure this will be no different. Now stop asking questions, or you'll ruin the surprise.'

'I won't say another word,' I promise.

'I'll believe that when I see it. Although I can think of one way to keep you quiet. Do you think anyone will miss you for half an hour?'

He takes my hand and I look around for Libby as we leave the room. 'It's really happening!' I mouth to her. 'He's going to propose before Easter!'

Showing, as always, that the truest friends can be happy for others even with nothing to gain themselves, Libby looks almost as joyful as I feel.

Chapter Eighteen

Romy

I sit moodily with the Starlets as Jack and Siena dance in the centre of the room, so miserable about the afternoon's outcome that I ignore their horrified expressions and work through a bowl of crisps and half a discarded bottle of champagne.

Phoebe's silk scarf slips as she reaches for her wine glass, and Madison pulls it down to reveal a mark on her neck. 'Is that a hickey?'

'Nice,' I say, pushing away the crisps. 'Very classy.'

Libby looks disapproving. 'Have you forgotten the Statute, Phoebe? Hickeys are unacceptable for anyone over the age of fourteen.'

'You're disgusting,' I tell them. 'You act as if you're so refined, but your minds are in the gutter.'

Phoebe pats my hand sympathetically. 'Still a terminal virgin?'

'You'll feel differently when you find someone special, Romy,' Cassidy says.

Phoebe cuts in. 'Speaking of which . . . Romy, you're amongst friends, so you can tell the truth. Has your jealousy over Jack and Siena stopped you finding anyone else for yourself?'

'Something like that.' I fix my eyes on the table.

'We could find you a new man!' Cassidy exclaims.

Libby shakes her head. 'How many times, Cassidy? We aren't taking on any more aid work. Our plates are full, and we haven't even thought about the poor souls in the north of England.'

'But we all have boyfriends right now, even Libby,' says Phoebe. 'Kind of. It looks weird that Romy doesn't. We're out of sync.'

'I'd hate you to be out of sync,' I say.

'Didn't you find anyone special in Paris?' asks Cassidy. 'It's *four years* since you and Jack broke up.'

I think back to the many evenings I spent in the bathroom on the uppermost corridor of my French boarding house. The window overlooked Notre Dame, but it was a view I rarely saw, obscured as it invariably was by the soaking wet towels we'd be smoking into. Lying on the floor, our legs vaguely entangled as we stretched them up against the wall, Max and I had discussed everything and nothing. 'There was someone called Max who was . . . special.'

'What's love like?' Cassidy sways slightly as Phoebe removes a champagne flute from her hand.

'It's like being lit up from the inside,' I say. 'Warmth and light.'

They stare in disbelief, and I immediately regret drinking so much champagne.

'Like Ready Brek?' Phoebe giggles.

'What do you know about love?' asks Libby.

Trying to avoid their eyes, my gaze falls on Siena and

Jack, who are still dancing. Siena kisses him slowly and deliberately, and his blindness to everyone else in the room makes it obvious that it doesn't matter what she does, or how much she hurts, or abandons, or betrays him; that he'll love her until the day he dies as if no other girl exists but her. He's a reassuring anchor to her willowy, ribboning form; he tips her back and I stare at the glitter dusting her shoulders and her jutting collarbone, finally meeting her azure eyes. She's at the heart of the dance floor but she seems to fill the room, and the Starlets watch as if they draw their life force from her.

Siena has strict rules about the right time to leave parties, although I've never found out why. Irrespective of how much fun she appears to be having, or how much alcohol remains, she always disappears before the clock tower strikes twelve. I endure the party until then, and head back to her room in Woodlands, climbing the stairs in time with the chimes.

She appears unwillingly at my third knock, wearing a very expensive-looking nightdress. She's brushing her hair, which, untethered from its usual comb, falls heavily over her shoulder.

'What?' she asks. 'It's late.'

'You told me you had something of mine,' I remind her. 'I want it back.'

'Oh, yes,' she says. Her memory is astonishingly, if selectively, bad. 'Come back tomorrow. I'm extremely busy with this fishtail braid.'

I'm too tired to argue, but, as I turn away, one of the nearby bedroom doors opens. Before anyone emerges, she grabs my hand and pulls me inside with such force that I nearly fall over. She slams the door as soon as I'm through it.

'No one should see you outside my room,' she explains, as casually as if her behaviour is reasonable. 'Can you imagine the uproar?'

She has the corner room, which is the biggest on the corridor. She's managed to transplant last year's dormitory cubicle (the largest, and the only one with its own window) here on a more fabulous scale. The Starlets' cubicles, like everything else in their lives, were practically identical; explosions of popularity manifested in one-off designer pieces, shoes they couldn't stand in, supposedly spiritual items picked up on the rare occasions they left six-star holiday resorts to patronize local residents, and walls obscured by photographs of them intent on showing the world exactly how magnificent their lives were.

I remember Sports Days, prize-givings, gymkhanas and Halloweens; full moon parties, pool parties, hunting balls and Sweet Sixteens. These were the days when my Starlet membership was genuine, and seem so long ago that I search for myself in the images in order to connect that girl to whatever I am today.

Except that I can't find myself in a single one. My memory has been expunged, my presence cut with clinical precision from each photograph.

'I was in that picture,' I say, staring hard at the Starlets at Hogmanay. 'I was in the middle, between you and Mads.'

'You can't have been, because you aren't there now.'

'I was there,' I say exasperatedly. 'And in this one . . . we were standing next to each other in half of these.'

'Libby decorates my room,' she says, and I can't tell if she knows the truth. 'She's the gallery curator.'

'Then Libby should know that doctoring photographs to change history is a bit . . .'

'A bit what?' Siena's tone is cautionary but I don't care.

'*Sinister*. What else does she have planned? Will I be eradicated altogether?'

She raises an eyebrow. 'Suggesting that you're the one in danger from Libby is a bit rich, isn't it? You can't blame her for wanting to erase troubling memories.'

I give up. 'Tell me what this is about so I can leave you to your important work. What's next? Painting over the school signposts in the hope that I'll wander off a footpath and perish in a ditch?'

'Look.' She sits on her bed and points over the far edge. I hold back, in case Libby is lying in wait with a mace, but she reaches down and grabs a bundle of fluff.

'What the hell is that?' I ask as she places the bundle in my arms. Staring in confusion, I make out floppy ears, a twitching nose and a rapid heartbeat.

'It's your pet rabbit, of course. I've been looking after

her, and it's time you took her back. I'm not running an animal hospital.'

'This isn't my rabbit. This isn't *any* kind of rabbit. It's pink!'

'My sister dyed her,' she says impatiently. 'You're always saying that appearances are only skin deep, so I didn't think you'd mind. She's definitely yours – look at her collar.'

I twist the collar around, while the pink rabbit burrows into me as if she's ashamed to be seen in public. *Elisabeth*, reads the familiar tag. Beneath her lurid cerise rinse, I make out white roots. 'What if she licks it off and gets poisoned?' I ask in horror.

'She won't. It's perfectly safe.'

'How do you know that?'

She sighs. 'Because, after dying her, Syrena drank the remainder of the bottle to make herself match.'

'Did it work?'

'Not noticeably,' she says. 'But she's in excellent health, so it's unlikely that the rabbit will be adversely affected. We keep only vegetable dye at home since Syrena made over her friend Octavia with bathroom bleach.'

'What happened to Octavia?'

'Her hair grew back,' she says. 'After a year or so. I'm sure the experience was character-shaping. Anyway, this will wear off if you wash her enough times.'

'That's reassuring,' I mutter. 'Rabbits just love being washed.'

147

She nods at a photograph of a fair-haired toddler clutching a stuffed toy with the ears and teeth of a rabbit, but a giraffe's neck, and demonically red eyes.

'You owed Syrena the chance to see what an anatomically correct rabbit looks like,' she says. 'As opposed to that stuffed *monstrosity*. I didn't want her growing up with strange ideas.'

I laugh. 'You gave her that thing? I thought you were going to burn it!'

'Of course I didn't give it to her! She found it and screamed whenever it was taken away from her. She still sleeps with it now, for all I know.'

'It served you right for stealing my Textiles pattern,' I remind her. 'You were going to take credit for my work, as usual.'

'Stealing your pattern was supposed to save me valuable time that could have been better spent,' she says. 'I trusted you not to trick me by replacing your real template with that deformity.'

'You still won,' I note. 'You got an A for originality, and *Creatures from the Great Beyond* is now the official brief. And I got a B-minus for my anatomically perfect rabbit.'

'You don't seem very grateful about this,' she says. 'Pets aren't allowed in rooms, so I've taken extreme risks to keep this animal safe for you. Not to mention the amount of shoe space I've sacrificed to house it. *Or* the time she chewed through the lead of Mads' hair straighteners. I had a very difficult time blaming that on Phoebe.'

I remain silent, and she scowls at me. 'I wish I hadn't bothered. You haven't even mentioned the rabbit since you got back. I thought you cared about her?'

'I do care,' I say. 'But my dad threw out so many of my belongings, I didn't want to think about what he might have done with her. I'd added her to my list of collateral damage, right below Star.'

She looks stricken. 'Have you tried to find Star?'

I blink away tears. 'What's the point? My dad won't let me have him back.'

Awkwardly searching for a new subject, I notice a wooden cage under the bed. 'So why did you take care of Elisabeth for me? And where did you get this cage?'

'The Stripes made it in Woodwork,' she says. 'As for *why*, because your dad looked so angry when he came for your stuff that I thought he might cook her. Never let it be said that I don't put others before myself. Especially defenceless animals.'

'You own a crocodile-skin bag,' I observe, seeing the pink tote hanging on her door. 'Or don't you consider crocodiles defenceless?'

'My bag is fake,' she hisses furtively. 'It's fake, okay? Don't push me.'

She returns her attention to her hair. 'You can go. I'll have a Stripe bring the cage to your room later. And next time I do something to help you, remind me that it's a bad idea.'

149

I snatch up Elisabeth and leave, slamming the door behind me. 'I went in the wrong room,' I say wearily to a bulge in the curtain directly opposite. 'I got lost on my way to bed.'

Libby emerges from folds of ruched satin like a bridesmaid from someone's nightmares. 'I know you think you can weasel your way back into Siena's life, but you're wrong. Your days here are numbered.'

'How are you going to swing it this time?' I ask. 'Same trick as last year?'

'Stay away from Siena, do you hear me?'

'Siena can make her own decisions,' I say. 'You'd be surprised – she's a lot more independent than you give her credit for.'

'*Independent*?' she says indignantly. 'I don't think so.'

'You might not see it, but she's changed since I left.' It's very easy to scare Libby. 'For all we know, she might want to become a career woman instead of marrying Jack.'

She's desperate to know if I can see a corporate path forming in Siena's future, but can't bear to ask me for help. 'We're on the home straight as far as that engagement is concerned,' she says. 'Don't do anything to sabotage it.'

'Who knows?' I hold my own door ready to slam behind me. 'She might do that all by herself.'

Chapter Nineteen

Siena

By the middle of term I've officially lost interest in Council meetings. Today's gathering is so longwinded and pointless that I concentrate on a problem cuticle to block out Romy's heated earnestness and Bethany's nasal whine.

'They're bad for the environment,' Romy is saying. 'What's wrong with tap water?'

'There isn't a sink near the library,' Bethany argues. 'Without a water cooler, students have to walk two flights of stairs to a tap. They're missing valuable study time.'

Oh please. 'You've been talking about water coolers for ten minutes, do you know that?' I slam down my nail file. 'How is that even *possible*?'

'Stay out of this, Siena,' warns Romy. 'I'm sure the environment isn't high on your list of priorities, but we're not all as self-obsessed as you.'

'The environment is a very high priority for me,' I correct her. 'That's why I'm so concerned by all your talking and lack of positive action. Do you know how many trees in Madagascar have been felled since your argument began?'

Ambrose and Avery look impressed, but I have a

feeling that Romy is going to ask me *how many?* so I move quickly on, scanning the agenda for something – *anything* – more diverting. I fail.

'We need to decide how to spend our excess budget,' says Avery. 'Should we go for the vegetable allotment or the student scholarship?'

'That's a difficult one,' frowns Ambrose. 'We know that fresh, organic food has a beneficial effect on learning. It improves concentration and morale, and generates an all-round good atmosphere.'

'That's so true,' nods Avery. I notice that her freckles are extra-bright when she's feeling inspired. 'On the other hand we must consider the benefits of opening our doors to those less fortunate. We can't grow as a community unless we offer opportunities to all students deserving of a good education. Perhaps we should put the allotment on hold in favour of an extra scholarship.'

Everyone around the table furrows their brows. 'Should we take a vote?' asks Ambrose quietly. 'Show of hands for the allotment?'

I don't bother to count how many hands are raised, but it's more than one might expect when the subject matter is radishes.

'The scholarship?' Avery asks. 'I don't mind saying that I, for one, would never have benefited from this wonderful education were it not for the existing support.'

'I have another suggestion,' I say.

Ambrose jumps in surprise. 'Please, Siena. We'd love to hear it.'

'We should have a ball,' I announce. 'That would be the very best use of our money.'

'Hmmm.' Ambrose nods heavily. 'You make a good point, but . . .'

'We need this,' I say forcefully. 'It's been a hard winter. We've suffered. And when you think about it, allotments don't boost morale. Dances do.'

'Siena, if you want a ball, be honest about your motivations,' Romy says. 'Don't pretend it's for the good of all of us.'

'Romy, the whole concept was your idea.' I turn to the rest of the Council with a smile. 'Romy is a total inspiration.'

'Really?' Avery is dubious. 'I can't imagine Romy having an opinion about this . . .'

I flick through my phone until I find the pertinent video. *Chandeliers, and glass slippers, and crystals, and roses . . .* Romy is saying in a dreamy voice. Her eyes are closed, conveying extra passion.

'That's not what it looks like,' Romy says in exasperation.

I appeal to the table. 'Who's with me and Romy that a ball is the most powerful thing we could spend our money on?'

'The allotment and scholarship are laudable projects,' says Ambrose tentatively.

'So is a ball,' I say. 'Dances bring us together as a

community. They promote inclusivity, which is an issue very close to my heart.'

'This would blow our entire budget,' Romy says. 'How can we justify spending all our money on one evening?'

'That's a very blinkered attitude,' I say. 'Memories last a lifetime, and you can't put a price on that. Especially for people like you – it'll be like having friends for a whole night.'

Bethany and Nicole shoot up their hands in support, along with some deplorable specimens I don't usually look at directly.

I contemplate Ambrose. 'It would also be the perfect opportunity for ineffectual, unpopular monarchs to leave a misleadingly significant legacy.'

He coughs self-consciously. 'What do you mean by *legacy*?'

Behind me are a number of portraits from a different period of the school's history, when being on the Council must have been desirable. 'You'll get portraits,' I say. 'And history rewritten. And a big party.'

Romy laughs derisively. 'You can't *buy* Ambrose and Avery, Siena. They have more integrity than anyone else I know.'

Ambrose and Avery confer for a moment and then nod sheepishly.

'Everyone wants to be remembered, Romy,' Ambrose says. 'This is nothing more than we deserve.

If the Starlets can help make the Council relevant again, we can pass a legacy to future generations. This isn't a selfish endeavour.'

Everyone but Romy raises their hands. 'So that's settled,' I say, drowning out her protestations. 'We'll throw the best dance the school has ever seen.'

'Who's going to be responsible for organization?' asks Romy. 'Theme? Décor?'

'The Starlets will do all the crucial work,' I establish. 'Obviously we'll take on help for low-level admin.'

'What's the *crucial work*?' she asks. 'Spiking the punch? Flashing your underwear? Tombstoning from the library window into Dr Tringle's ornamental pond?'

'Phoebe's actions don't always reflect the beliefs of the group,' I say smoothly. 'And I'm pretty sure it was a swan dive. Phoebe *is* captain of the diving team.'

'And your theme?' Bethany asks eagerly.

I try to ignore Romy, because she's smirking as if I don't have a single thought in my head that hasn't been put there by Libby.

'Cinderella,' I announce. 'The theme is Cinderella.'

Chapter Twenty

Romy

'Cinderella?' I ask in the awed silence that follows Siena's announcement. 'Is that how you get Jack in the mood?'

She scowls. 'I suppose you have a better idea? Water coolers or something?'

'Don't you listen to anything I say?' I snap. 'I'm *against* water coolers.'

'Cinderella,' Bethany sighs. 'What a wonderful concept.'

'Thank you,' Siena tells her graciously. 'I already have so many ideas.'

Nicole's fountain pen scratches eagerly across her page. 'I'll record them for you.'

Siena stares at her poised pen as she attempts to make her brain cells connect. For a second I think she'll achieve it; then she shakes her head in defeat and reaches for her phone. 'Let's invite Libby. She'll really take this to the next level.'

Gloom settles as Libby arrives almost before Siena's SOS has been delivered, as if she's been hiding in the broom cupboard at the end of the corridor.

'What do you need, Siena?' she asks anxiously as she fans her with a spare agenda. 'Is the greyness infecting you? Do we need to stage an intervention?'

'I'm hosting a Cinderella ball at the end of term,' Siena announces. No one asks her when this became *her* ball. 'We need your expertise, Libby.'

'A Cinderella theme has so much scope.' Avery has by this time completely abandoned her pretence of caring about scholarships. 'All the girls in white . . .'

'*All* the girls?' Libby says haughtily. 'I think you mean *one girl*.'

Of course. At a Cinderella ball, there's only one princess.

'Does that mean only one girl gets glass slippers?' I ask. 'Only one girl kisses a prince?'

'We're in a recession,' Libby reminds me. 'It's a time of austerity and self-sacrifice.'

'Of course,' I say. 'But how do we choose the lucky girl? Obviously the selection process should be equitable and transparent.'

Libby taps her pen on the table. I know she's wishing, more vehemently than usual, that we were still separated by the English Channel. 'Of course it should. I think the fairest method will be to choose the girl who's most likely to marry a prince.'

Before I can tell her that, although many Temperley High girls must have a good shot of marrying aristocracy, this method is non-quantifiable, she hunts in her bag and emerges triumphant with the centrefold of the last yearbook. *Most Likely to Marry a Prince*, reads an insipid swirly headline above a large photograph of Siena. The very existence of the category is beyond depressing.

'You see?' she says. 'Siena will be Cinderella, and Jack will be Prince Charming. It'll be just as you saw it in your vision.'

'You know you can't stop people from wearing what they want?' I say. 'It might breach their human rights.'

'We'd never *dream* of telling people what to wear,' Libby assures me.

'There are plenty of other characters for students to depict,' Siena puts in. 'Like mice, and rats, and . . . toads, probably. There's so much choice.'

'And students are welcome to come as a *pre-ball* Cinderella,' Libby agrees, glancing over my outfit. 'That look would come very naturally to *some people*. But I doubt anyone would dream of contesting Siena's right to be the princess. It's instinctive for students to stand back and watch her shine.'

I flick through the yearbook at speed. Past images of Siena under *Best Hair, Best Figure, Most Likely to Become a Supermodel* and the no-brainer that she wins every single year, *Most Beautiful*; past me with felt tip bars and *Most Likely to Need a 4 a.m. Attorney* scribbled over my face; and then there's Jack. *Most Whipped*. The accompanying picture shows him carrying Siena's pink Birkin and a matching candyfloss bundle that I now know to be my rabbit, as Siena, weighed down only by Prada sunglasses, follows him towards Libby's chauffeured car. Not only is he whipped, but he's completely aware of the fact and completely accepting of his fate.

'I hope you're proud of yourself,' I tell her. 'You've successfully emasculated him.'

She smiles indulgently at the photograph. 'I'm very proud.'

'Shall we go?' Libby asks Siena. 'I think we've covered the main points, and we're missing valuable outfit-planning time.'

Siena nods in relief and follows Libby from the room, blowing a perfunctory kiss to Avery and Ambrose as the door closes.

'How could you agree to spend all our money on a party?' I ask the room at large as soon as they've gone. 'And how could you agree to collaborate with Libby?'

They still look scared. The effect of Libby on a room is notable; it's as if we're all recovering from a state visit from Maleficent.

'A party is a good idea,' Avery says. 'It's a long time since we've had one.'

'We could have spent the money on something worthwhile,' I argue.

'The time is right,' says Ambrose, as if we might not have noticed his legacy plans. 'And with the Starlets in attendance it's a guaranteed success. Think about it, Romy – we can actually *make* money.'

'Think again,' I say, remembering my predictions for crystals, chandeliers and gold crockery. 'You'll find that this party is the most expensive the school has ever thrown.'

'Well, we have Libby as events planner,' says Avery. 'I can't imagine safer hands.'

'It must be wonderful to have such a loyal friend,' Nicole says earnestly. 'Libby would do anything for Siena.'

'It's creepy,' I tell her. 'And unhealthy.'

'I have an idea that will cheer you up.' Avery confers with Ambrose, who nods effusively. 'We'll use the ball as an official kick-off for the coronation of the new Head Girl and Boy. We'll announce your name alongside his during the evening.'

'You haven't even told me who the new Head Boy is going to be,' I point out. 'What if you've chosen someone awful?'

They smile broadly. 'We're still finalizing the details, but he's going to be *such* a hit,' gushes Avery. 'This will be an unforgettable night, and now the Starlets want to be a part of it, we can all embrace an inclusive Temperley High. What a wonderful start to your Head Girl tenure!'

'If you think the Starlets want to work alongside you, you're completely wrong,' I say. 'They don't work with anyone except themselves, and half the time they can't even manage that.'

Chapter Twenty-one

Siena

'I feel bad that you had to handle that meeting yourself,' Libby is saying as we hurry to her room. 'You should have called me immediately.'

'It was fine. It's not as if they were going to argue with me.'

'So Romy's prediction came true,' she says. 'How annoying that she should be right, even if it is our ideal outcome.'

I wonder dimly if causing a prediction to come true is enough to validate it, but Libby has already opened her wardrobe to run her hand along a row of dresses. Her expression is beatific as she pulls out a shimmering gold dress and holds it against herself.

'You can't wear that,' I tell her. 'Gold is shiny and eye-catching.'

'So? Nothing stands out more than white. And no one stands out more than you.'

'I know that,' I frown. 'But you do want the Fairy Godmother position, don't you?'

Panic crosses her face. 'Who else is in the running?'

'Well, I'd never dress my Fairy Godmother in gold, any more than I'd dress my maid of honour in gold at my real wedding,' I explain. 'That would be madness.'

'This isn't your real wedding,' she whispers. 'The colours don't have to match.'

'It's a rehearsal,' I say. 'It should replicate a wedding.'

'So what colour *do* you have in mind for your Fairy Godmother?' she asks.

'Green.'

'I'm a Spring!' she pleads in horror. 'Green will make me look jaundiced. Or worse.'

'I have a second choice,' I tell her consolingly, because she does look peculiarly washed-out in green. 'You're very welcome to wear burnt orange.'

'Green it is,' she says manfully. 'Maybe my skin tone will change before the ball. If not, I'll just have a chemical peel.'

'Whichever you prefer. How are the other arrangements coming along?'

'I've only been working on this event for ten minutes,' she says. 'But everything's well under control.'

'This *has* to be flawless. Otherwise how will Jack understand the joy of weddings?'

'Is something wrong between you and Jack?' she asks. 'Surely you aren't worried about this?'

'Everything's great between us. Especially since the football game. But there's no harm in ensuring that his decision is firm and non-retractable. We've had a few challenging moments recently.'

'Why?' she breathes. 'Is it Romy?'

'Of course not,' I say. 'Maybe. She hasn't helped. Should I have to *make* this proposal happen? Is that how relationships are supposed to be?'

'Of course it is,' she says. 'How else would men know what they want?'

'It's tiring to have to manipulate everything into happening,' I admit. 'I wonder if it's sustainable.' I search for a simile. 'It's like trying to keep a rose garden in order when the roses keep changing course and colour and growing in ways they aren't supposed to.'

Libby is asking me what I'm talking about, and if I've gone mad, but I don't reply because my head is full of a rose garden instead. A garden, originally comprising red roses only, that was a wedding present from my father to my mother. He added to it with pink roses when I was born, and, after Stella's arrival five years later, with white.

'Grace and joy,' he told me one day as we stood, hand in hand, before our abundantly swirling petals. 'That's what pink roses mean, and why I chose them for you.'

'White roses are innocence and secrecy,' he told Stella, who was five. 'And silence,' he added when she failed to reply.

The garden was complete and self-contained, but that day we watched the gardener dig over a new patch of soil, creating a portentous space beside Stella's roses. Our mother had woven Stella's hair into plaits, making her eyes bigger than ever in her small face. I didn't like them on her, and I shook them out so that her hair fell in curls to her waist.

'You're wise,' our father agreed. 'That hairstyle could get an awful lot of boys into an awful lot of trouble. How do you think I ended up here?'

Stella let go of my hand and stood over the soil patch, staring intently. 'What colour roses will the new baby have?' she asked.

He was apparently too startled to reply, and, looking from him to Stella and back again, I saw that she'd beaten him to the chase. He'd brought us here to explain that we were to have a new sibling, but, for unexplainable reasons (certainly not weight gain on our mother's part, or anticipation on our father's), Stella had already known.

We don't need a new baby. I dared not speak out loud, because I had a dim sense that, once I voiced this opinion, it could never be unsaid. But, as I met my father's eyes, I understood instinctively that he felt the same.

'What colour roses for the baby?' Stella prompted him.

'Black,' he said drily.

I tried to draw Stella back towards me, but her eyes were trained on the soil patch as if at any second a baby might begin to grow before our eyes; a changeling whose roots would kick and push themselves between me and Stella until it belonged so undeniably that no one would remember a time when it hadn't lived amongst us.

Our mother appeared and snaked her arm into our father's, her hand flat against her still-small waist; her pale cheeks flusher than usual. She leaned into him, but he remained rigid, staring at her red roses instead of greeting her.

'What do red roses mean?' I prompted him. 'Do they mean love?'

'One meaning of red roses,' he said as our mother waited eagerly, 'is *job well done.*'

'What about beauty?' Stella asked as she dragged her eyes back towards us.

Seraphina nodded, but our father's expression was hard to define as he stepped away. 'Surely that goes without saying,' he said. 'For all of you, beauty is one thing that will never be in short supply.'

'How does he make the greatest compliments sound insulting?' our mother muttered as we watched him leave.

My heart pounds as I begin to identify with my mother's frustration. She must have wondered on that day, as I wonder now, what would happen to her if my father changed his mind: how she'd face life if it came to pass that beauty were insufficient, and manipulation ineffectual.

Libby pats my shoulder. 'We'll leave nothing to chance. We'll follow Romy's predictions to the letter.

The décor will be exquisite, and Mads can make the dresses. It'll be the most perfect evening you've ever had, and I guarantee that, by the last dance, your hand will be so weighed down by the Lawrence rock that you'll never play tennis again.'

'Do you really think so?' I ask.

'I know so,' she says. 'Otherwise I wouldn't be a very good Fairy Godmother.'

'You're the best Fairy Godmother in the world,' I reassure her.

'I'm the *greenest*,' she mutters as she contemplates her reflection.

Chapter Twenty-two

Romy

Siena's room is the largest in Woodlands, so, although she dislikes clutter, she generously opens her doors to guests before the Cinderella ball.

I haven't been privy to any dress discussions, but it's been made clear that the Starlets will have final approval over my wardrobe. I queried this as a human rights issue with Mrs Denbigh, but she was too enchanted by the concept of a united Cinderella cast to offer useful support, so I arrive as instructed in my dressing gown, ready to accept whatever horror of a gown is thrust upon me.

Cassidy, Madison and Phoebe are insipid in matching bridesmaid pink, while Libby sulks in bile green. 'What are you supposed to be?' I ask. 'Should I make a guess?'

'No stupid jokes.' Phoebe adjusts her headpiece of pink roses. 'We're Cinderella's attendants. Siena briefed Mads on the designs to ensure that we look exactly right beside her.'

'I'm sure she did,' I agree, taking a closer glance at the pouffy pink layers that render the Starlets' figures lumpy and anaemic. As a saboteur of rival beauty, Siena is the maven.

'How are you controlling what the other guests

wear?' I ask. 'I expect it would be terribly embarrassing if everyone looked like blancmange.'

'All civilian outfits are Libby-approved,' explains Cassidy. 'Ugly Sisters and Stepmothers are permissible, but, other than that, girls can only come as rodents or pumpkins.'

There's no need to ask why no one has contested this decree. With a stranglehold that defies belief, the Starlet juggernaut not only gets its own way, but convinces students that its decisions are for the greater good.

'We must be community-minded,' nods Phoebe. 'It's so important that all students feel part of this event.'

'A community means having wider purpose, doesn't it?' I ask. 'Working for others?'

'That's exactly right,' says Phoebe. 'Speaking of which, what are you planning to contribute, now you're back? You can't keep freeloading from us.'

'I'm sorry,' I say. 'I wasn't aware that I was using up your resources.'

'If your return is going to be prolonged,' Libby says as one forced to utter these words, 'we need to assign you a role. The build-up to the wedding will be frantic, and our posts are already formalized.'

'What's your role?' I ask.

'Mine's obvious.' She shakes her hair like a proud horse. 'I protect the talent.'

'The *talent*? Whose talent?'

'Siena is the talent,' Libby says slowly, as if I'm an idiot.

'*What* is Siena's talent?' I ask at the same speed.

She sighs in exasperation. 'Talent is what she *is*, not what she *has*!'

I give up and turn to Cassidy. 'What are you?'

'Hair and make-up,' she says. 'Want to see?'

Taking my shrug as a *yes*, she opens a vanity case to reveal an extensive cosmetics empire. I jump in shock as she thrusts a hairdresser's dummy, complete with long blonde locks, towards me.

'And you?' I ask Madison.

'Stylist.' She hands me her big black book and I flip through hundreds of designs, mood boards and scraps of fabric; abstract sketches and quotations.

'Mads, this is beautiful,' I say in surprise. 'You're really talented!'

'We shall see,' sings Libby like an operatic narrator who knows that tragedy is forecast. 'Siena hasn't seen her dress yet. I hope she'll like it, Mads, for your sake.'

'Otherwise I'll have to set fire to it,' Madison mutters, biting her nails. 'And then set fire to myself.'

'And you, Phoebs?' I ask hurriedly. 'Are you her bouncer or something?'

'I'm her attitude coach,' Phoebe says. '*Swagger coach*, we sometimes call it.'

'Do we?' I ask. 'With a straight face?'

Libby thrusts me her iPad. *How many calories is too many? . . . Slingbacks or wedges? . . . Is acrylic ever acceptable? . . .*

'This is the *Ask Siena* Twitter feed,' she explains.

'Each week we give the Shells a chance to tweet Siena their questions, and she gives them the honour of responding to a very small selection. Or, rather, we do it for her, because she's extremely busy.'

I scroll through the questions. 'The Shells are stupid enough to do this?'

'They're *dedicated*. None of them wants to miss the prize draw.'

'It's always an object of sentimental value,' Cassidy says. 'Last week we gave away a piece of Siena's vintage French homework. For an especially good question we might donate disused nail varnish, or even a hairpin.'

'That's disgusting,' I say. 'You give away used hairpins?'

'*Genuines*,' Libby clarifies. 'We had an incident last term where some Fourth Formers were caught selling fakes. Now all prizes come with a certificate of authenticity signed by Siena herself. Or, rather, I sign them for her because she's extremely busy.'

Cassidy quivers as a bell sounds from the room next door. 'That means Siena's ready for hair and make-up,' she explains. 'Did we tell you that Libby's bedroom has been part-converted into Siena's dressing room? She was very cramped with all her belongings in here.'

I take a happy moment to imagine Libby, pushed out of her own living space to sleep on a bale of straw in a corner, but she interrupts me by snatching her iPad out of my hands.

'You were about to answer a question!' she accuses. 'Without training!'

'The questions aren't about physics,' I say. 'I'm unsure what training is required.'

She jabs the screen. 'See here, where a Stripe has infiltrated the feed to ask a question about Siena's lingerie? This should have been blocked. We *never* speak about Siena's lingerie!'

'Siena's clothes are tight enough to show off the washing instructions,' I say. 'Last night you ran laps of the courtyard in bikinis. One can't call her lingerie a secret, exactly.'

'The courtyard run was part of a controlled photographic display,' Libby explains. 'It was for a potential modelling contract.'

'You hired someone to spy on you and take pictures?' I ask.

'*Controlled photographic display,*' she repeats. 'Don't make it sound tacky.'

Phoebe and Madison stand like courtiers as Cassidy returns to announce Siena's imminent arrival, while Libby runs around in circles hiding discarded tights down the back of the radiator. I can almost hear the strains of *The Arrival of the Queen of Sheba* as Siena sweeps in, hair and make-up flawless, wearing a pink silk dressing gown.

'I'm ready to see my dress,' she commands.

Madison is visibly nervous as she fumbles with a mannequin. The room hushes as she pushes it into the centre of the room, while Siena inspects it from all sides.

Madison has interpreted the *before* part of the Cinderella story, and Siena's dress evokes the initial rags. But it's completely beautiful. The yellow gossamer shimmers with butterflies and floats gauzily in tissued layers. It's unstructured, and it rises and falls like wings. It's the polar opposite of every dress I've seen Siena wear, and yet it takes no imagination to see her in it. This is the Siena I thought no one but me ever saw: it's not the neatly chignoned, crossed-ankled Siena, but the Siena who lets down her hair and rides bareback across open countryside and laughs at the top of her voice.

I feel a rush of relief for Madison, but this only lasts until Siena breaks her silence. 'What is this?' she asks, her words like dripping ice.

'I – I went for something a little different to the traditional ball gown,' Madison stammers. 'Because tonight signifies a new chapter for you and Jack, I wanted it to represent sunrise, and a new beginning, rather than the wedding dress which is the end result.'

'I knew it was a mistake to give you free rein.' Siena's words grow colder with each syllable. 'If only I hadn't read that piece in *Harper's* about giving struggling designers a chance . . . I swear, my compassion will be my downfall. Are you trying to ruin me? Or *kill* me?'

'I worked so hard!' Madison is close to tears. 'It took

me weeks and weeks, and the least you could do is show a bit of gratitude.'

'*Gratitude*,' Siena mutters as Phoebe and Cassidy wince.

'What's so wrong with it?' Madison asks plaintively. 'Tell me why you don't like it.'

Siena takes three steps towards her. '*I. Hate. Yellow*,' she says as if she's spitting venom.

'Libby didn't tell me you hated yellow.' Madison sounds as if she's drowning. 'Libby, please . . .'

'I deny that!' Libby shrills, her cheeks puce against green satin, even though Siena has done nothing more than raise an eyebrow. 'You knew all eyes would be on Siena tonight and so you plotted to get yourself attention as a designer. I had no reason to believe that you weren't working on the white dress previously discussed.'

Siena storms out onto her tiny balcony while Phoebe scoops up everyone's phones and scuttles after her. We watch through the window as she makes multiple calls.

'You sold me out, Libby,' says Madison furiously. 'I made these pink *things* for us, and green for you, exactly to the specifications. How could I have known there was a problem with yellow? Siena's never mentioned it. Isn't it your job to know these details?'

Cassidy is trembling in a corner, Cristal spilling from her glass as she tries to take a sip. I can't see any medication lying around, so I grab the remaining pink dress from its hanger to distract her before she becomes catatonic. 'Do I really have to wear this?'

'If we can find enough tissue to stuff it with,' says Libby, not too deeply embroiled in a crisis to insult me. 'Your *ironing board* excuse of a cleavage will never keep it up.'

'*Fine.*' I grab a discarded tuxedo that one of the Stripes must have left behind, putting it on and tying the cummerbund tightly enough that it can't be easily removed. 'Will this make you happy? It'll make going to the bathroom a lot easier, and anything is preferable to the toilet roll holders you're wearing.'

'You're not attending like that!' says Libby. 'Consider your next move *very* carefully.'

Siena enters stage left and jabs a mobile phone to terminate a heated call before tossing it into a full glass of red wine.

'That was my phone,' whispers Madison.

Cassidy spills Cristal onto the bedspread and yelps in terror as Siena bestows her most frightening stare on us. 'You'll all be fired in a minute if someone doesn't fix this,' she says. 'Phoebe faces immediate demotion for her lack of assistance.'

'It's such short notice,' Phoebe says plaintively. 'Valentino isn't picking up.'

Siena thrusts another phone at her. 'Then get me Donatella.'

'She's on the red-eye,' Phoebe says in despair. 'I've tried to cut across the flight path but I can't make contact without serious risk to other planes.'

'You already own a million dresses,' I point out. 'No one will know if you repeat.'

'*Repeat* . . .' Phoebe mutters as if I'm a rambling lunatic. 'The scrutiny she's under . . .'

'Why won't you give my dress a chance?' Madison begs. 'I know it's not what you expected, but I swear, it will look great on you . . .'

'Romy, will you put that on!' Libby hurls the pink monstrosity through the air, almost knocking me off my feet. 'Or stay behind!'

I've been through a lot for the Starlets, but this is one humiliation too far, and I decide to head it off at the pass. 'I've just had a vision about Siena's ball dress,' I lie.

Libby and Siena regard each other uncertainly. 'I thought you couldn't see what Siena's supposed to wear?' says Libby. 'You said the stars wouldn't align.'

'The fog has cleared,' I say. 'It's a psychic miracle. Siena is definitely supposed to wear this pink dress.'

'But then I'll be the same as all of you,' says Siena. 'Surely that can't be right?'

'You'll never be the same as us,' says Phoebe sincerely. 'You'll always stand out, whatever you wear.'

'You do like our dresses, don't you?' Cassidy is sweet and trusting, in frills that clash hideously with her red hair. 'You picked them because they suit us all?'

I'm surprised at the ease of this plan. 'Yes, *obviously* you love the design, or you wouldn't have chosen it for your very best friends. And pink is your signature colour. It all makes sense.'

Unable to admit that she chose her very best friends the least flattering gowns she could dream up, Siena focuses on me. 'Who are you supposed to be?'

'I'm Buttons.' I twirl around so that my jacket flies out wide. 'What do you think?'

'I think that I'm not surprised,' she says. 'Is this another feat of epic incompetence on Mads' part?'

Madison is crying openly, but no one moves to defend her. This is exactly the way I remember the Starlets, bickering with a hierarchy so firmly embedded that their roles are immovable, no matter where justice lies.

Libby and Phoebe grab the dress as if it's an exotic bird, and wrestle Siena into it. When her face emerges from the voluminous frills, she looks like a sulky little girl too old for her dressing-up box. The cut is unflattering across her thin collarbone, and the pink silk makes her pale and translucent. If she's the most beautiful girl at the ball, it will only be by default.

'Is this definitely what I'm supposed to wear on my engagement night?' Siena asks me.

Something about her intense expression makes her hard to lie to. I almost come clean when I see a light go on in Libby's eyes. 'If it's not the right dress, Siena will have to wear this,' she says generously as she reaches for the zip of her green mutation. 'I can find something else. *Anything* else.'

176

I use the interruption to consider the magnitude of Siena's aims. If she has to resemble a retro dessert for Jack to see that they're not ready for marriage, then so be it. Not to mention that I haven't forgiven her for duping the Council into running this ball.

'No doubt,' I say, fingers crossed in my suit sleeves. 'And Libby has to stay in green. That message is coming to me very strongly.'

'You both look wonderful,' Cassidy says staunchly. 'What a night this is going to be.'

'Romy should take the official photograph,' Libby says. 'It makes sense for her to remain behind the lens. After all, she can't attend the ball without a dress.'

Siena looks impatient. 'No pictures,' she says. 'I'm going outside.'

'You can't ban Romy from the ball,' Madison bursts out as soon as Siena has gone. None of the Starlets has ever taken my side before, and I can only assume that the evening's distressing events have caused her to lose her mind. 'She organized it!'

A portentous silence descends. '*Romy* organized it?' asks Libby.

Madison collapses onto the bed, her courage reserves empty, as the other Starlets put on their shoes and pick up their bags.

'What about Mads?' Cassidy whispers as they reach the door.

'She and Romy can *both* stay here,' Libby throws over her shoulder.

'You can't stop us coming,' I say. 'I'm a Council member. I have to be there!'

Libby looks me meaningfully up and down, her gaze lingering on my tuxedo. 'I can't stop you coming to the ball?'

I lapse into silence as she continues. 'Why don't you and Mads both atone for your mistakes by cleaning Siena's room? I'm sure she doesn't want to come back to this mess.'

'Don't be ridiculous,' I say, but I don't make it to the door before she slams it shut. A key turns in the lock, and then her footsteps fade. I rattle the handle uselessly as Madison exhales in a desperate sob. Then we start to pick up piles of clothes from the floor.

Chapter Twenty-three

Siena

'Where's Romy?' I ask Libby as we cross the courtyard behind Cassidy and Phoebe.

'She's reassessing her priorities,' says Libby. 'It's for the best. What if she'd orchestrated a sabotage to stop Jack proposing?'

'You're right,' I concede. 'She might have been planning anything, for all we know. So what do you think of my dress?'

'It's fine,' she says. 'Don't give it another thought.'

I'm walking as fast as I can, but the dress is heavy and hot. 'I haven't made a mistake?'

'You have not made a mistake,' she repeats. 'Mistakes are an alien concept to you. The dress represents you perfectly. It's a princess gown that will be perfectly accessorized in –' she checks her watch – 'three hours' time with a flawless Princess cut diamond.'

'Yes.' I look down at my pink dress; the dress I've never imagined myself wearing on this, or any other occasion. 'I chose perfectly.'

'Ready?' says Phoebe as she and Cassidy pause outside the hall.

'Of course.' I stand on my marker, exactly centre, and they swing open the doors.

'Are you having a wonderful time?' Libby asks each time she and Tristan swing past me in the throes of a complicated ballroom move.

'*Wonderful*,' I tell her with increasing conviction, in the hope that she won't ask again. '*Spectacular*.'

Jack might not be quite as good a dancer as Tristan, but he's holding his own, and as always he's by far the best-looking boy in the room.

'This is quite an event,' he says as he glances nervously upwards, as if a chandelier might plummet and annihilate him.

'Do you like it?' I ask. 'We did it for you.'

He laughs slightly and shakes his head. 'I'd have been happy going to the cinema,' he says, but I'm pretty sure he's joking.

He must be, because I'm telling the truth when I use the word *spectacular*. I've never seen a dance like this. The room is glass-slipper themed, with chandeliers and sharp-edged crystals that hang over us like giant diamonds. Libby was dissuaded from installing a glass floor by the prospect of expensive law suits brought by girls in short skirts, but the marble has been polished and I imagine I'd be able to see my face in it as clearly as I can in the surrounding rainbow prisms. Libby has eschewed a food budget in favour of alcohol, and the long tables are festooned with buckets of pink Cristal – my mother's favourite champagne.

And for once the students have been brought into

line on dress code. Not one of them competes with me as Cinderella: they are mice, ladies-in-waiting and possibly unintentionally Ugly Sisters, but I am, as intended, the unequivocal star of the night. The other Starlets might be wearing pink, but my dress is surely the pinkest; the biggest; the best. And it's matched by the pink roses which decorate every corner of the room.

'Where did you get these?' I ask Libby as she brings us a handful. She presses one into Jack's hand and ignores his wince of pain.

'We should stop dancing,' he suggests, glaring at her.

I almost ask him why, but then accept that this is a good idea. My corset is cutting into me and my feet hurt.

We sit at opposite sides of a glass table, slightly too far away to hear each other over the pounding beat. I nod politely when he says something indecipherable; he does the same for me. Our reflection ripples in prisms, and I see us as if we're strangers. In our rainbow likeness, we're a couple that sits in airports, restaurants, ornate drawing rooms, watching the gap between us stretch until it's too cavernous to mend.

Although this couple is nothing like me and Jack (aside from anything else, engagement duties and wedding preparations will give us no excuse for a moment's silence), I'm almost relieved to be joined by Avery and Ambrose. Ambrose looks faintly horrified as he inspects a gold goblet; for a moment I wonder if he's going to bite it.

'I'm not sure we'll recoup our money,' worries Avery. 'This seems very expensive.'

'Memories are priceless,' I remind her, although I wonder if they'll like to be reminded of a dance for which they apparently dressed up as frog footmen, and at which no one noticed them for the whole night. The thought actually makes me a little sad.

Ambrose is speaking, and I shrug to notify him that I have no interest in his words.

'I said, *Where's Romy?*' he shouts, standing up to get closer to me.

'She couldn't come,' I say regretfully. 'She sends apologies.'

Avery turns crimson. 'You can't be serious? She advocates spending our entire remaining budget on this and doesn't even attend?'

Libby swoops in before I can respond. 'It's not the attitude one would expect from a Head Girl-elect,' she says elatedly. 'I've been left entirely in charge, and it's not as if I don't have enough to do. My dance card is so full that I can't divide the songs small enough.'

Ambrose nods reluctantly. 'I expected more commitment from Romy than this. We should liaise with her about the budget too. This décor is very decadent, and I want to check that we didn't overshoot.'

'I'm afraid Romy definitely overshot.' Libby casts a rueful glance at the decorations she ordered without Romy's knowledge. 'Let's hope nothing she hired gets broken.'

She trails her handbag over the table as she leaves, sending crystal goblets shattering to the floor.

Jack rolls his eyes. 'I'm not surprised Romy's given it a miss. I can't imagine her getting sucked into this kind of rubbish.'

'What do you mean by that?' I ask.

'Matching pink dresses and roses and champagne?' he says. 'I'm getting toothache just sitting near you.'

I wonder if I've heard him wrong. 'Don't you like my dress?' I ask, because even if I don't, strictly speaking, like my dress, it can't be the case that he doesn't.

'I love it,' he says hurriedly. 'It's so . . . pink. And big.'

Feeling subdued, I search for someone to blame my mood on. 'Can we stop talking about Romy? Does it matter if she's here or not?'

'Actually, it matters a lot,' says Ambrose heavily. 'You know we'd planned tonight as the kick-off for next term's Head Girl and Boy handover.'

'You can go ahead without Romy,' I say. 'No one will even notice.'

'I suppose we'll have to.' As Ambrose gets up to leave, he gives Jack what's obviously supposed to be a man-to-man backslap, and the result is painful to watch. 'We'll start soon, Jack. Then the floor is all yours.'

'What does he mean?' I ask Jack, who looks nervous.

'You'll see in a minute – I don't want to ruin the surprise.'

Of course. I reach for his hand in relief. *He's going to propose on stage.*

The song cuts out as Avery and Ambrose take to the microphone.

'This is my cue,' says Jack. He kisses me and then makes his way to the front, while I push in the opposite direction towards Libby. The Starlets, like flamingos, pull me into the middle of their flock. Avery and Ambrose drone on and we all hold hands during our last moment before my life – and by extension their lives – changes forever.

'Did you anticipate an onstage proposal?' Cassidy asks.

'I suppose I expected something a little more intimate,' I admit. 'But this will be perfect.'

Jack is his usual confident self by the time he takes the microphone. The students cheer and I bask in vicarious enthusiasm, even though half of them are dressed as vermin.

'It's an honour for me to stand here,' he says. 'This is a relatively new ambition of mine, but I know that on some level it's what I've always wanted.'

'You should get closer to the stage,' says Libby. 'He'll call you up there any minute.'

I follow as she forges a path through the crowd. I've lost the train of Jack's speech somewhat, because he's talking about leadership and the life-changing effects of navigating the Stripes to their recent victory. Then he smiles directly at me. 'Siena, I told you I had something big to announce. This is for you.'

Libby is almost hyperventilating. 'Get on with it, Lawrence,' she mutters. '*Ask her*.'

He flashes a huge smile. 'Classmates, I'm proud to tell you that I'll be your next Head Boy.'

I'm aware of cheering around me but I can't gather my thoughts. Everyone's jostling and for a second I'm actually grateful for the suffocating layers of fabric that cocoon me from the worst of this moment.

'What the hell happened?' I ask Libby, trying to maintain a smile. 'That was his big announcement? Is he *kidding* me?'

'He must be,' she says, looking as shocked as I feel. 'There's no way . . .'

'What happened?' asks Cassidy. 'When's the proposal?'

'Later,' Libby reassures her, snatching Tristan's pina colada. 'Don't worry, everything's fine.'

'Tell me what to do!' I say urgently as Jack leaves the stage. 'Tell me how to fix this.'

Libby looks up at the clock. 'It's not midnight yet. You still have time to make this right. Get to the tower room.'

'Why?' I say. 'How will he know where I've gone?'

'He'll follow you anywhere,' she says. 'This is recoverable, as long as you act fast.'

I push through the crowds, running out of the room and across the courtyard, not stopping for breath as the clock strikes half past eleven.

Chapter Twenty-four

Romy

'Why didn't you follow the rules and make her a white meringue?' I ask Madison as we sit on the floor, slotting rings back into their display boxes. We spent an hour in hopeless silence as she sobbed and tried to make calls on a phone filled with Chianti, but finally she's calm enough – following the discovery of Cassidy's lost Valium – to help me tidy up.

She speaks in a rush. 'I started with a meringue, but Jack laughed at the pattern, even though he didn't know what it was. He said . . . actually, he said the same as you.'

'Toilet roll holder?' I try not to smile.

She nods. 'Exactly. So I tried something different. Libby never told me that Siena hated yellow. She really didn't.'

'I believe you.' I take the dress off the mannequin and hold it up against myself. 'Siena should have given this a chance.'

'Try it on,' Madison suggests. 'At least one person should wear it.'

She helps me into it, twisting up my hair so I can see it properly, and I turn from side to side. Even on me it's a masterpiece. 'This would have suited her,' I say. 'It's so original; no one would have been dressed like her.'

'As it is . . .' Madison grimaces at her pink-clad reflection. 'I should never have made this freak show. I've lost my integrity, and they turned on me anyway.'

I rip off her voluminous puffed sleeves and some heavy layers of skirt, which is a big improvement. She hunts the room for remaining alcohol, lining up bottles and drinking from each in turn. In the absence of any better ideas, I copy.

'Siena always listens to Libby over everyone else,' she says. 'And she always gets what she wants. That's just the way it is.'

I wonder if she'll say something less favourable, but a bottle of wine is insufficient for her to break ranks. 'Siena deserves to get what she wants, because she and Jack are meant to be together. Even though it was a shame for you.'

'A shame?' I take a mouthful of white wine and then red, even though I don't like either. 'That's one way of putting it.'

'You're so cryptic,' she says impatiently. 'If you're still angry about what she did, then say so. You never give a straight answer about how you feel.'

'You never ask the right questions,' I say.

'Would you like Siena and Jack to break up?' she asks. 'There's a question.'

I remain silent.

'You can't deny it, can you?'

'No,' I whisper. 'They aren't right for each other.'

'Okay,' she says. 'Tell me what really happened between you and Libby. I mean, none of us believed that you could . . . but when you left without trying to explain . . .'

To avoid answering, I open the window and climb onto the balcony. 'We should get out of here, don't you think?'

'How?' she says moodily. 'We're going to be shut in for ages yet. Siena won't even come back tonight if things go well.'

'Siena doesn't always use the door. You weren't planning to stay until someone remembered to let us out?'

'You know another way?' she asks. 'We've been in here for hours! Why didn't you say something before we missed the entire ball?'

'I forgot,' I say. 'Or perhaps I didn't think you'd be too upset about missing it, all things considered.'

She looks irritated, but then shrugs. 'You're right. An evening dressed like a begonia, drinking from gold goblets and hiding from Libby, probably isn't that much fun.'

'It's much less fun than spending the evening with you,' I tell her.

'I agree,' she says, sounding surprised. Then she looks over the balcony edge and shudders. 'It's high. I can't imagine Siena doing anything like this.'

'Then you have a lot to learn about Siena.' I grab the trellis and haul myself over the edge.

She lays her hand on mine before I start to climb down. 'Does it still hurt?' she asks. 'That Jack and Siena . . .'

I think of the day four years ago when I missed football practice because of a twisted ankle, to watch Siena take my place as the only girl in the Shells' First Eleven. *You campaigned so hard for girls to be allowed on the team*, she told me as she borrowed my kit and kissed me on the cheek. *I'll bridge the gap so no one forgets you*.

Having expressed nothing but disgust at the concept of co-ed sports and mud and shorts and kneepads, Siena played with ruthless efficiency, weaving and shooting and scoring in my centre forward place as she deceived both teams into giving her everything she wanted.

Watch the ball, not the girl, screamed the coach, turning purple as he blew a whistle that didn't even penetrate the boys' ears. Smiling, Siena lifted her shirt to wipe imaginary sweat from her forehead, exposing her midriff as Harry scored an own goal. The boys were devoted to their game, but that day no one even remembered the score.

At twelve, Jack was more interested in football than girls, except for girls like me who wore black and carried *The Catcher in the Rye* in a battered backpack and made sarcastic comments about the Starlets, despite being one of their number. But that day, as I watched Jack and Siena leave the pitch together without a backward glance, her hip touching his and their hands twisted like vines, I learned that all boys follow the same rules. He didn't contest her as she steered and tagged him lightly; he only laughed as they ran until he was out of sight and out of range and beyond reason and blind to everything but the glow of the autumn sun on her golden hair.

'Does it *hurt*?' I ask Madison in disbelief. Shaking off her hand, I climb down the trellis, speaking my answer to branches instead of her. 'It hurts every single day.'

Chapter Twenty-five

Siena

As soon as I push through the trapdoor, I understand why Libby has sent me here. The tower room has never looked like this, transformed from its usual mess into something like a fairy tale. Candles cover every surface, flames dancing in the breeze that blows through the open window and casts unearthly shadows against the silky drapes. And besides candles, there are flowers. Pink roses – the roses my father named for me – scatter the creaking floorboards, while loose petals are a coral drift around my feet. *Thank you for doing this*, I text Libby.

A back-up location is crucial, she texts back. *So is a second chance.*

Jack arrives as I put away my phone, staring me up and down in a way I don't understand. Crossing the room, he picks up a fallen long-stemmed rose to save it from being crushed underfoot and hands it to me.

'I have something else to tell you,' he says.

I wait, decorously holding my rose, just as my mother told me. *Let it unfold*, she always said regarding the protocol of this moment. *Let him unfold.*

'I'm not going to work for my dad next year,' he announces.

I'm thrown off-course; too much to respond.

'I'm going to apply to university instead.'

'But . . . why?' I say stupidly.

He begins an enthusiastic explanation of his Economics syllabus, which is an overshare too far and includes something called Game Theory, which sounds as if it should be interesting but definitely isn't. I've no choice but to engage with this unexpected subject matter before it descends any further into farce.

'University is for people who need an education to become marriageable,' I tell him. 'The poor. The uncomely. Not people like *you*. You already have a job and good looks. There's nothing for you there.'

'It's for people who want opportunities, and to offer something to the world,' he says emphatically.

I laugh. 'Your dad owns a global company. In a few years it'll be yours. How many opportunities do you want?'

'I don't want to follow my dad.' He sounds stubborn. 'I want to make my own way.'

'Won't that be harder?'

'Of course it'll be harder,' he says. 'That's what will make it worth having.'

I try to process this change in our fortunes; a relationship with Jack based not on company profits and bonuses and corporate events, but student loans and microwaved carbohydrates and diluted beer in plastic glasses.

'Maybe you should think about university too,' he suggests. 'You'd be clever if you ever paid attention in lessons.'

'Of course I would. That's not the point. We're supposed to be *together*.'

'We've still got one more year here,' he says as if this is the most natural thing in the world. 'And after that we can see each other during the holidays.'

'What will become of us?' I ask.

'No one knows the future,' he says. 'Ours or anyone else's. You don't know what might happen, or what we might achieve.'

'You already have me! Why isn't that enough?'

'You don't listen to me, Siena,' he says. 'You don't hear my point of view.'

'I hear *our* point of view,' I say. 'Everything I do is for us.'

I have a dim memory of hearing these lines on one of Cassidy's soap operas – the one set in a burns unit in Buenos Aires – but that doesn't make them less sincere. 'I'm working towards our future. A future that was supposed to start tonight.'

Involuntarily I clench my left hand, manicured and cleared of rings for this purpose. Jack looks at it before staring around bemusedly.

'That's why the room is decorated like this.' He closes his eyes in disbelief. 'That's what the ball was for. You thought I was going to *propose*.'

His inflection suggests that the concept is absurd.

'You said this term would be *the most important of our lives*,' I remind him. 'You said this term would change everything. I thought . . .'

'We're seventeen!'

'Almost eighteen,' I persist. 'Our parents were both married by that age.'

'Look at the mess they made!' he says. 'Their marriages were – are, in my parents' case – cataclysmic. Why would I make the same disaster of my own life? And yours?'

The Starlets – minus Romy, who would probably have set fire to it – have worked for hours to make this room perfect; this room that should mean something to him. But looking around, I see it through his eyes, and it becomes ridiculous. Some of the candles have burned out and others spatter wax onto the floorboards. Drapes of silk and lace hung to conceal cobwebs and dust (the Starlets have drawn the line at actual cleaning) are not gauzy and romantic, but portentous and haunting.

And, at the centre of this tableau, Jack and I are as spectral as our surroundings, inhabiting a space relevant only to times past.

He takes a deep breath. 'Siena, I don't want to be engaged to you or anyone else. I don't even want to think about marriage yet.'

'You had an engagement ring. Libby told me that Tristan told her that—'

'My dad gave me the ring when my mum was in

hospital. He wanted me to have it in case . . .' His expression flits between confusion and pain. 'It's a reminder of the way our lives could turn out if we don't guard against it. My dad told me not to repeat his mistakes.'

'This is a chance to *rectify* their mistakes. If we get married, we'll succeed where they failed.'

'No,' he says. 'We'll walk into the same trap.'

Something tightens in my chest like a corkscrew. 'You think I'm a trap?'

He evades the question. 'I still feel the same about you.'

'You don't.' I back away from him. 'Unless you never cared about me.'

'Of course I cared,' he says impatiently, his past tense – perhaps unconscious, perhaps not – more painful than any of his other words.

'*Care*,' he corrects himself meaninglessly. 'I care about you. But there isn't going to be a wedding, and there never was. This is something you and Libby have concocted and given a life of its own.'

I wonder how emptiness can be so overwhelming; how a void can be so tangible; how a chasm of my entire belief system can take me over with the slamming force of a riptide. I force myself to stand still, even though I can hardly bear to be in my own body, until the clock strike cuts through me as if it's slicing me in half.

It's a quarter to twelve.

'Why are you so obsessed with weddings?' he says. 'It's not normal. Sometimes I wonder if it's even about me at all.'

He's still talking as I try to control the pain in my stomach, but it only ripples outward, weakening my arms and legs and throat as my future, such as it is, realigns itself inside me like a river forced to change course. I'm enduring an endless summer without the diversion of an engagement party; I'm watching my contemporaries flit into finishing school and university and PR jobs and marriage. Jack is part of that exodus, leaving me to stand petrified, without ambition, achievements or human connections, until my future stagnates in replication of my mother's, who took to bed on the day my father left and has never really risen since.

'What am I supposed to do now?' I whisper.

He laughs as if my question is absurd. 'How can you ask that? You're seventeen, you're healthy, and you're *alive*. You can do anything you want. *Be* anything. *Go* anywhere. Don't trap yourself in a place like this; in a past that doesn't even belong to you.'

Only as he reaches for my hand do I realize I'm gripping the rose so tightly that its thorns are embedded in my palm.

The clock is ticking like a heartbeat, growing stronger and louder as if it rather than my heart is responsible for pumping blood around my body. I hear nothing but the clock as it ticks closer to midnight, towards a point of no return and no future and no salvation. And because this is my last chance I reach out for him, unsure which of these words are my own, and which are memories from which only his proposal can liberate me.

'Why are you doing this?' I ask.

'I'm trying to show you that this is the best thing for us.'

My hand stings and I hold it away from him. 'How can the *best thing* hurt like this?'

I tug at the rose, shaking drops of blood across the bodice of my dress.

'Don't do that,' he says as I pull out the last jagged thorn as violently as I can; as if it will offset other pain. I stare at my hand as red spreads like poppies.

'We should get out of here,' he says uneasily. 'It's creepy.'

'*Don't leave me,*' is all I can say, but the sounds are indistinct, choked and tremulous as if I'm crying. Putting my hand to my cheek, I feel to my amazement that this is true. I hardly ever cry.

'I don't want to leave you here,' he says as he stands over the trapdoor.

'I don't want you to go,' I tell him, but he's too logical for these endless circles. He shakes his head and starts down the ladder.

'Please consider this,' he says before he disappears. 'Do you want to marry me because you love me?'

The last thing I see before he disappears is his watch.

It's hideous, but he insists on wearing it because it was a gift from Edward. Amongst its numerous dreadful features is a glow-in-the-dark facility, which he never remembers to deactivate. I'm mesmerized by its light until he and the watch are gone.

Chapter Twenty-six

Romy

Libby has orchestrated a farcical – even by her standards – charade, forcing all students to congregate beneath the clock tower, each holding a pink rose to throw at the happy betrothed when they dismount the stairs. She'd originally envisioned a kiss at the open window, but had fretted about Siena's hair getting windblown.

Everyone is in position by the time Madison and I stumble down the line, seeking sanctuary before we're uncovered and publicly hanged with piano wire.

'What are you doing here?' Cassidy hisses as she grabs each of us by an elbow.

'How long were we supposed to stay up there?' whines Madison. 'The room's tidy . . . the ball's over . . .'

'Yes, but . . .' Cassidy glances fearfully around. '*She* didn't say you could leave.'

Libby is in full throttle, marshalling students into miserable submission as she empties a sack of roses and loose petals onto the stone slabs.

'Where did she get all those?' I ask.

'Siena's mother sent them.' Cassidy reaches reverently for a flower. 'Do you know that Siena's father had these roses named for her? They represent her so perfectly.'

The roses are pale pink with a rippling swirl. I don't tell Cassidy that I agree with her, but it's true that the pale colour is that of Siena's cheeks when she's happy; the brighter swirl when she's riding.

'We should all be so lucky to have a father like that,' I say instead.

Cassidy blushes. 'She doesn't see him very often,' she says carefully. 'But whose father wouldn't do anything for them?'

Libby zooms back into view before I can answer, patrolling like a sergeant major lumbered with a particularly dim-witted troop.

'Stop trying to create symbolism,' she hisses to an unfortunate Shell who drops a moulting rose in sheer terror. 'Pick off one more petal and you're out.'

I look up to see flickering lights gradually extinguished. In darkness, the tower merges into the moonless sky, and I squint as I think I see a figure at the window. But it's too high, and too dark, and the clock has begun to strike.

'Ready, everyone?' Libby raises her voice and there's silence as everyone gives her their full attention. 'She'll be out at any second.'

The clock strikes as if it's splitting in two, and I feel every one of the vibrations in my bare feet.

Chapter Twenty-seven

Siena

I'm aware of my movements as I approach the window, but still I climb out onto the ledge. Gripping the clock is only instinct and habit. Falling is easier than clinging on, and falling is my only remaining course of action. I've never learned another way out.

My breath clouds before me and I suck in April air so cold that it hurts my teeth. My dress flutters in the wind, giving the illusion of a swelling shape beneath the fabric. I'm thin enough that my hip bones protrude, and yet I put my hand to my stomach as if it's swollen. I see my father's car on the ground below as clearly as if this is real; as if I'm not on the edge of the clock tower but back at home, on the balcony outside my parents' bedroom window, exactly seven years ago.

And just as my parents' clock begins to strike, so does the clock in the tower.

One.

'Come back!' my mother screams as my father's rear lights fade into darkness. Staggering to the balcony rail, she grasps at freezing air with one hand and her stomach with the other.

Two.

'Don't leave me,' she's saying over and over again, her voice breaking and smashing until the words are unintelligible.

I've listened, hidden in the curtains, as she begged my father not to leave; as he packed his bags as calmly as if he were leaving for just another conference, placing a dispassionate hand on her stomach while telling her to *look after this one* before removing it hurriedly, as if he'd received a kick. She continued to beg as he disappeared down the stairs, reappeared outside and got into his car; even as the engine revved and the car moved down the drive, out of sight and sound.

Three.

Gripping the balcony, she climbs onto the edge and reaches out as if she can still touch him.

'No!' I scream as I fight my way out of the curtains.

Four.

My appearance is at best too late or too slow; at worst, the cause of everything. She turns to me for an instant and I see many things in her face. I see despair, and resignation, and a strange kind of triumph as she surrenders to gravity and to my father, propelling herself towards the place he's just vacated. Before I've moved a single step, she's gone.

Five.

My legs shake uncontrollably as I force myself to look over the ledge. She fell silently and I have a dumb, childish hope that by some miracle she's landed, Persian cat-style, on her feet. Or even that she's defied gravity altogether and soared upwards, somewhere far from me but safe.

'Mum.' I try to speak her name out loud but manage only a whisper, and she never answers to that word anyway. 'Mother . . .'

Six.

Fighting my way back through the curtains, I run downstairs. The house is full of half-burned candles, my mother having prepared for quite a different evening, and I snap on the light switch as I wrench open the front door.

Seven.

She hasn't disappeared or landed like a cat. She's motionless on the stone floor right underneath the point she fell, one hand still outstretched.

But there is blood. Her lace and chiffon dress, pure white only moments ago, is now red with poppies that blossom across its skirts.

Eight.

I take her hand; I test her pulse; I beg her, uselessly, to wake up; I don't prevent Stella from sitting beside me, even though I know she shouldn't see this.

'She's coming,' Stella tells me.

Nine.

'She can't be coming!' I can think only of the due date seared across our collective consciousness, more than six weeks away.

Stella takes my hand and I feel the baby kicking

and kicking and kicking, as if she's striking out at the parent who's left her.

'Stay there, baby,' Stella says, leaning further until her hands and white nightdress are wet and sticky with blood. 'We aren't ready to meet you yet.'

Ten.

As people converge on us, Stella holds her hands where the baby's ears might be.

'Is the father here?' someone asks.

'We don't have a father.' I look up wildly as I realize that the low voices surrounding us are wondering which of the casualties to save first.

'Mother,' I whisper as fiercely as I can through tears that stream down my cheeks. 'Mother, *of course.*'

Eleven.

Beside me Stella is perfectly silent and still, and yet I hear her words reverberate through the very core of our beings; as rhythmical as the clock that fails to drown her out.

I'm no longer in Hampstead. I'm on a narrow ledge in the clock tower, and I'm losing my balance. I feel for the open window behind me and fall backwards through the gap, knocking against the electric light switch and landing painfully on wooden floorboards.

The glow of the candles is replaced by the yellow glare of a bare bulb, vulgar in its garishness. Stripped of enchantments, the room is debris and litter and hopelessness. Something tugs me from the window

205

and down the ladder; down the stairs; out of the school.

Sister, Stella said that night over the peal of the clock, in a voice that existed only inside her, inside me, and inside a cord that flowed between us like a lifeline.

Just as there's only one voice I can hear, there's only one place I can go. Stella's voice chimes as penetratingly as the clock's final strike.

Save my sister.

Chapter Twenty-eight

Romy

I count the doleful peals, craning my neck as the door opens and a ripple runs through the crowd. Everyone's been prepped – on pain of death – to throw their rose at the correct moment, but they lower their arms instead, looking around in confusion.

I step out of line far enough to see Libby accost Jack as he approaches alone, and then I duck out of my place to join them.

'Go away, Romy,' Libby says frostily, apparently too preoccupied to ask how I've escaped. 'This doesn't concern you.'

'Stop speaking to people that way,' snaps Jack with uncharacteristic venom.

She looks outraged and he gives me a slight smile. 'I'm not under her jurisdiction anymore,' he explains. 'You should try it; it feels great.'

'This is just cold feet,' says Libby agitatedly. 'Get back up there and apologize. Here, take her some roses.'

Jack recoils as she thrusts a handful at him. 'I've seen enough roses to last me a lifetime. I'm not going back up there. I'm going home.'

'What about the proposal?' Libby blocks his way. 'Don't tell me you've been leading her on all this time.

Don't tell me we organized that ball for nothing.'

Jack is staring at her in disgust. 'You know what? If there's one good thing about what's happened tonight, it's never having to tolerate you again.'

Predictably, she ignores this insult and homes in on what she considers most important. 'What do you mean? What *has* happened tonight?'

Jack turns to me. 'You know what, Romy? There's something I should have done a year ago. Out of misplaced respect, I didn't.'

He takes my hand and shakes it firmly. 'That's for giving Libby what she deserved. Next time, push her harder, and off something higher.'

And then he's gone.

Libby stares after him, her mouth opening and closing, and then she gets to work, dismissing students line by line. 'Siena and Jack appreciate your good wishes but value their privacy,' she repeats. 'They ask you to join them in celebration at a later date.'

The students disperse, Madison concealing herself amongst them, until only Cassidy and Phoebe linger. 'You too,' Libby says ruthlessly. 'Time for bed.'

'What's wrong, Libby?' asks Cassidy. 'What happened up there?'

'Absolutely nothing,' Libby says. 'Everything went entirely according to plan. But you know Siena and Jack are a very private couple. Siena would prefer to see only me tonight.'

Like the lobotomized victims they are, they leave the

scene, while Libby turns on me. 'I didn't say you could leave Siena's room. Get back up there and keep tidying!'

'*Pick the clothes up, Cinderella,*' I say. '*Make the dinner, Cinderella*. I don't think so, Libby.'

'You're not Cinderella,' she says. 'Don't forget it.'

We turn as Siena's silhouette appears. She seems smaller, even though that's impossible, and her dress more cage-like. She pauses in the doorway, leaning one hand against the frame and holding the other to her waist as if she's short of air.

'I need you, Henry,' Libby is now barking down the phone. 'It's an emergency. I know I always say that . . . but it always is.'

Up close, Siena's face is tear-streaked and her hair untidy, but the most shocking aspect of her appearance is how dazed she seems.

'Siena?' I extend my hand as I'd approach an unbroken horse, and, when she doesn't spook, I hold it to her cheek. She's crying silently and almost indiscernibly.

'What are you wearing?' she asks.

I'm almost surprised to see that I'm still in Madison's dress. 'You said you didn't want it.'

She reaches for the fabric, combing her fingers through its shimmering yellow drapes. 'It's beautiful,' she says. 'Perfect.'

She looks from me to Libby as if she's seeing something she hasn't before. *Listen to your instincts*, I will her. *Listen to me*.

She says nothing else before she walks away. She

209

moves as slowly and painfully as if the dress is made of thorns; she's almost doubled up by the time she reaches the car.

'This would never have happened if you hadn't come back,' says Libby. 'Either we rectify this, or I'll make sure every person in this school knows the truth about you.'

Then she's gone, and I'm alone.

Chapter Twenty-nine

Siena

Neither Henry nor I speak as I fall into the back seat of the car, and he drives away from the gloom of Temperley High into a new kind of darkness.

Some time later he pulls up before my house, but, when I make no effort to move, he drives around the back and opens the windows as if he's trying to help me reacclimatize. The headlights sweep the garden, illuminating austerely mowed lawns, symmetrical beech trees, and, finally, the rose garden that forms the centrepiece. I hold my breath as a phantom scent fills my nose and throat.

'Is anyone home?' he asks.

'Of course.' I sound more confident than I feel.

'Good,' he says dubiously. 'Then . . . enjoy your holiday.'

I'm hardly at the door before Stella appears. She's a candle of golden hair and white nightdress, her face lit with happiness. 'You're home?' she says in wonderment, bouncing up and down. 'You're really home? With us?'

When I pick her up and whirl her around, she wraps her arms so tightly around me that I can hardly

211

breathe; so tightly that I hardly mind; so tightly that I can believe I'm still her centre and her core and her beginning and her end and the only sister whose roots are intrinsically entwined with her own.

I try to put her down but she won't let go, so I walk with her bare feet on top of mine, as our father used to dance with us. She's twelve now, but so small that it doesn't hurt to do this.

'You remembered Syrena's birthday!' she says when she finally moves away. 'We weren't expecting you.'

She gestures at the little shadow behind her that had escaped my notice. I should have known that Syrena would be up past midnight to see in her seventh birthday, but it was easier for those first few seconds with Stella to imagine that, not only are we still two, but that Stella is content for us to be that way.

I take Syrena in now, a little Russian doll replica. She's growing tall, and it strikes me as curious that she takes after me in stature rather than Stella, when we have nothing in common and they have everything. They're almost the same height, with identical features, but to me they could hardly be more distinct.

'Hello, Syrena,' I say politely.

She says *hello* back, her voice cautious. Stella whispers that she's set off fireworks in the summer house, destroying the ceiling. This doesn't fully explain her reticence, but, although I don't like to have her look at me so, I can't bring myself to extend my arms to her. To her credit, she doesn't appear to expect it.

'Where's Seraphina?' I ask.

Stella nods up the stairs. 'In her room. She said we weren't to expect her.'

Our mother has spent each of Syrena's birthdays in her own bedroom, feigning a spectrum of ailments from a headache to the onset of a tropical disease.

'I should go to her,' I say reluctantly.

They follow me upstairs, circling me like little birds, but shrink away as I open our mother's bedroom door. This is unnecessary because she can't see them anyway; she's never seen anything more than the shadows they've made themselves. She sees only me.

She's in bed, facing away from the door, but she watches the mirror as I cross the room to sit beside her. I compare our reflections, even though one section of the glass is obscured by her wedding dress, hung as though she's expecting a reprieve.

Our features grow more identical with each passing year, and today there are further characteristics to link us: corpse-pale faces, prominent cheekbones and eyes darkening from cornflower to violet. Our expressions, too, are indistinguishable. It's strange to think that tonight's intention was to eradicate forever her expression of frenzied disappointment, now that I've succeeded not only in intensifying it in her, but in replicating it in me.

Our father has never visited since the night he left,

but for some reason, be it guilt or, more likely, fear of Seraphina's reaction, he's allowed us to stay in this house. There are plenty of bedrooms, but I never use my own, just as Syrena never uses hers. I've no way of knowing where my mother sleeps when I'm away, but as far as I can be sure (because she'd never admit this) she prefers me to stay with her. This is a practice I began soon after my father left, but, whether she knows it or not, it began more for my own sake than for hers.

Seraphina was first taken – under coercion, as I remember – to see Syrena three days after her birth. Stella was asleep, the baby in her lap.

'History repeats,' Seraphina said drily. 'Stella was exactly the same with you, Siena. It seems I'm destined to be irrelevant to you all.'

'You're not irrelevant,' I tell her. 'You're our mother!'

She rolled her eyes. 'This time you'll learn how it feels, Siena.'

'I think Stella's going to love this baby enough for all of you,' said the nurse cheerfully, shaking Stella's shoulder to wake her up. 'What are you going to call her?'

Stella unwillingly tried to pass the baby to Seraphina, at which point Syrena, who had been sleeping soundly with a hand wrapped around Stella's thumb, opened her eyes and began to scream. Seraphina shrank away, at which the noise ceased.

'We decided to call her Serena,' I said. 'Didn't we?'

'Absurd,' Seraphina muttered. 'There's nothing *serene* about this little hurricane.'

'She's peaceable,' said Stella.

'She's a Syren.' Seraphina laughed bitterly. 'And so we'll call her, in the hope that she'll one day direct her destruction at the proper targets.'

'She means *men*,' Stella whispered into Syrena's ear.

Soon after Syrena came home, I woke to hear her crying. She didn't howl like other babies, in piercing wails; she cried like a real person who understood loss. Stella had slept in my bed all her life: apparently scared of losing me in the vastness of the four-poster, she always wound her hand tightly into my hair until it encircled the length of her arm. But when I reached out for her this time, she was gone.

Hearing Seraphina leave her own room, I got up too. But although whispering emanated from Syrena's nursery, I knew even before I looked inside what I'd find.

Why are you here? I thought furiously as I watched Stella rocking a little cuckoo in her crib. *We were a family before you came.*

Something white hot rose and threatened to consume me. They were a pair now, and Syrena needed Stella in the way that Stella had once needed me.

I felt it so keenly that I actually choked.

Stella didn't return to me that night; in fact, she never returned. She shared the nursery until Syrena outgrew her cot, at which point they both slept ever after in Stella's room. I visited only once, to find that Syrena had gathered Stella's abundant hair under her own head as a golden pillow.

From my window I watched Seraphina cross the lawn in her nightgown and bare feet. She was more wraith-like than ever against the red petals of her rose garden, but her frailty was irrelevant as she uprooted stems and pulled off flower heads; as she snapped branches and ripped stalks and tore entire branches from an earth baked hard with frost. She worked as if she didn't feel thorns ripping her fingers; as if she didn't see bloody soil coating her arms, her feet and her face. The nursery lullaby drowned other sounds, but when Seraphina turned her face towards the sky I saw her crying and cursing and perhaps even screaming as she carried out her Armageddon. When the garden was battered like a hurricane, she looked up and stared at me for a long moment. Then she returned to the house as a veteran returning from war.

I fell asleep on the window seat, waking at dawn to see Stella in my mother's place, a white rose amongst the devastation.

'What are you doing?' I asked as I joined her in the garden. Despite having massacred her own, Seraphina had left Stella's white and my pink flowers untouched. Stella was now surrounded by new roses, as yellow as the sun that was starting to break over the horizon.

'I'm planting Syrena's roses,' she said, tipping out a flowerpot into a childishly dug hole. 'She's our sister now.'

'That's not deep enough,' I said, not wanting to laugh at her bucket and spade, which were adequate for rock pools only. Not that Stella had ever been in proximity to a rock pool. 'Let me help.'

She edged a few inches as I crouched beside her. 'Where did you get these?' I asked as we sank yellow roses into the ground.

She looked around furtively. '*He* sent them.'

'You mean . . .' I tailed off, already struggling to remember how to refer to our father.

She nodded. 'They came this morning with a note about yellow roses meaning forgiveness.'

'So they were for Seraphina?'

'Perhaps,' said Stella. 'But I don't think she likes roses anymore. So Syrena will be yellow, here with us.'

'But . . .' I was perturbed that Stella, who had only recently learned to read, should be so decisive. 'What does Syrena have to do with forgiveness?'

'Yellow is beginnings,' Stella said. 'Like the sunrise. And friendship.'

'Are you sure Syrena even belongs in our garden?' I asked, the sweetness of Stella's *our* tasting bitter in my mouth.

'Syrena is our beginning, and our sunrise, and our friend,' said Stella. 'Syrena belongs with us.'

'Where is your ring?' Seraphina asks me now, grasping my hand in a claw-like grip. 'Where is your fiancé?'

I stumble over where to begin. 'It . . . didn't work out.'

'How,' she asks, 'could this have *not worked out*?'

'Jack wants something else,' I say. 'Something other than me.'

It gives me no relief to say these words: the pain is only transferred, like a drop of ice, from somewhere inside me to somewhere before me. It hangs as pendulous and precarious as a pearl drop on a necklace.

'What does he want?' Her face is a mask of disbelief.

'I'm not enough for him. He wants more than just beauty.'

She lets my hand drop, and doesn't speak another word as she stares into the mirror.

'You will help me?' I say when I can't stand the silence any longer.

'Help you?' she asks as if the concept is crazy.

'I'm sorry,' I tell her. 'I don't know how to make it better.'

I make no effort to check the tears that stream down my cheeks. Perhaps I hope she'll react; that for once she'll say the right thing. But how can she, when my failure has broken her too?

Her face is ashen. 'What did I tell you, Siena? Didn't I teach you the consequences of carelessness?'

I open my mouth to tell her that this isn't the end; that there's a life for me beyond tonight. But I can't, because, as I look at her, I don't believe it to be true.

'You . . .' I search for reassurance. 'You do love me? Even if Jack doesn't?'

I wait all night for an answer as we lie side by side, watching the sky change colour outside the open curtains of a prison we created and in which we hold ourselves captive, even though we both must know that these shackles could be destroyed as easily as our rose garden.

Chapter Thirty

Romy

No one leaves school for the Easter holiday, either because it's not long enough to bother doing so or because no one wants to deal with what awaits them beyond the stone walls. I fall into the latter category, even though I'm desperate for a break from Libby and the *#asksiena* rota on which my name appears for the entire weekend. The endlessly regenerating *Which vegetable would you be? . . . Who's your favourite Olsen? . . . Courchevel or Gstaad? . . .* was unappealing, but preferable to the prospect of facing my father.

I change my opinion after the disastrous ball, when I find myself alone in the echoing courtyard to wonder how easily Libby could take me out without anyone noticing. Pride battles my will to survive as I write and delete a text message twenty times before sending my father a post-midnight plea to come and collect me. I'm almost sure he's the least of the evils that await me: I wouldn't even risk returning to my bedroom to pack a case if I didn't need to collect Elisabeth.

I'm waiting on the steps when his Daimler rolls up the drive an hour later. He takes longer than necessary to turn off the engine and undo his seat belt, exiting the car only when there are no more excuses.

'I'm ready to go,' I mutter as I throw my case into the back seat, twisting away as he awkwardly kisses my cheek.

'Good morning to you too,' he says wryly. It's half past one.

'Did I wake you?' I ask. 'I remembered that you often work late, and so . . .'

'I was awake,' he says. 'Although I dislike this habit of collecting you in the middle of the night. Am I to take it that you're fleeing another crisis?'

'Nothing's wrong this time,' I lie. 'I just feel like spending a few days away. It was a last-minute decision.'

With her uncanny knack for finding trouble, Libby appears from the shrubbery when we're halfway down the drive. She's probably taking advantage of the new moon to gather herbs for her cauldron, and she steps out, forcing us to stop.

'You're leaving,' she says sternly. This irks her either because she'll have no one left to blame for everything, or because my absence will mess up the symmetry of the Starlets walking downstairs.

'I have commitments at home,' I say, glancing at my father.

Her expression remains neutral but her voice is acid. 'Jack's gone home tonight too. What a coincidence. He lives near you, doesn't he?'

'I'd have thought that spending time at home would be more important than seeing Jack,' my father rebukes.

221

Resentment boils over in me, even though Libby is watching closely. 'I'm coming home, aren't I?' I snap at him, hating myself for sounding so childish. 'Fully rehabilitated?'

He sighs in embarrassment as he addresses Libby directly. 'I'm glad to see you looking so well, Liberty.'

Libby shows off her scar to its best advantage in the headlights. She smiles as one who has borne intolerable suffering, and then leans towards me while I resist the impulse to raise the window and decapitate her.

'Stay away from Jack,' she mutters as she air-kisses me twice. 'I mean it.'

'Happy Easter to you both,' she says more loudly as she draws back. 'We're so glad to have you safely back in the fold, Romy.'

A frightened expression crosses her face as her phone clangs; she answers within the first ring. 'I have a very good explanation,' she says hurriedly. 'Yes . . . sorry . . . no . . . of course . . .'

'She's very forgiving,' Dad says as we drive away. 'I'm not sure I could be so civil in the same circumstances. You're lucky to have such a good friend.'

Plugging in my headphones, I ignore him for the entire journey back to his house. *Home* hasn't been an accurate description since a confusing chain of events five years ago left me with a stepmother in place of a mother.

Your mother's gone, my father told me when I returned from my last day of the prep school term.

222

She'll be in touch when she's settled, but I'm afraid she won't be back.

Gone? I asked stupidly. *Why?*

It's not your fault, he said hastily.

It wasn't the first time this had happened. Complaining that she found family life *stifling*, she often took extended holidays with no fixed date of return. I waited for her to reappear, believing in her even when the facts became inescapable. She'd left behind the Tarot cards that always told her when to come home. She'd written me a letter reminding me that my name was *Romy*, not *Roma* as my father maintained, and that I'd been named as a symbol of the curtailed wanderlust that she'd always planned to resume once I was old enough to be without her. Finally, Vivienne, previously known to me as a family friend seen only at Christmas parties, took up residence in my mother's place.

How could you? I screamed at my father when he told me of his plans to remarry. *My mother left me because you're in love with someone else!*

No, he maintained stubbornly. *Your mother made her decision long before I did.*

I ignored his explanations, concentrating instead on a phone that never rang and a postman who brought no letters. I hated him as weeks passed with no news. I hated Vivienne as the gaps in our house filled with her belongings until it was as if she'd always lived there. Finally I began to hate my mother for leaving behind her unwanted possessions: clothes that no longer fitted, Tarot cards that no longer amused her, and, least desirable of all, me.

'Where's Vivienne?' I ask now, peering warily down the dark hallway and hiding Elisabeth inside my coat for protection.

'She's in bed,' my father says. 'If you're not too tired, I thought you and I might talk.'

My heart lifts at this entirely unprecedented announcement even as I try to rationalize an involuntary hope that maybe, *maybe*, he's missed me during our time apart. I follow him into my bedroom and then stop short, because I smell my mother's perfume. For a crazy, paralyzing second I believe that she's come back: that I'll see her at the window, or by the bed, packing my bags ready for me to join her on her next trip.

When he steps aside I feel immediately foolish, as well as glad that I didn't have time to articulate this hope. He avoids looking at me as he gestures at a pile of boxes into which my belongings, alongside my mother's, have been neatly packed. My furniture and walls are stripped bare, and the floor is covered with colour charts and carpet samples.

'I'm afraid Vivienne and I need this room,' he says. 'We're having it redecorated.'

'There are other bedrooms in this house,' I point out. 'Why do you need mine?'

He looks awkward. 'This room is next to ours, and we need to be close by.'

The colour charts are all shades of pink and blue, and I notice a flat-pack cot in the place of my bookshelf. 'You're having a baby.'

'Yes.' His tone, cautious and perhaps even fearful, prevents me from feeling any happiness at this news.

'Where will I sleep?' I ask, trying to smile. 'In the stable?'

He shakes his head. 'We'll see you through school, of course, but we'd like you to start using the London flat during your holidays. You won't appreciate a screaming baby when you're revising for your exams, and you'll find it much calmer there.'

I calculate how much waitressing pays; what kind of career I can expect to have without a degree; and how much sooner I'll be out of his debt, and out of the sterile Fulham studio he uses when he's working late in the city, with a Head Girl fee waiver. 'From when?'

'Vivienne thinks it might be better if you moved right away,' he says. 'I'm sure you understand that this is an emotional time for her.'

'This baby will be my brother or sister,' I say. 'I don't mind losing my room, but please don't send me away.'

'This is a big adjustment for us all. Some space will help us gain perspective.'

I swallow hard. 'I don't want to leave. My mother won't know where to find me.'

'How many times?' he says, exasperated. 'She isn't . . . she's not coming back. I'm sorry, but what else can I say?'

I kneel beside one of the boxes and run my hand

over a pile of my mother's scarves. 'Why are all her things here?'

'We've kept them for long enough,' he says. 'I thought you might want to go through them and see if there's anything you want to keep. Let me know if there's anything particularly special to you.'

I open my mouth to ask him how I should decide which of my mother's belongings are *particularly special*, and then close it without making a sound. He hovers outside the doorway as if he has something else to say, and then leaves.

My mother's belongings have been in storage for years, but they're still as familiar to me as my own. I sit cross-legged and sift through clothes, notebooks filled with recipes that she never bothered to make, and books she never got around to reading. Last time I tried one of her dresses it hung off me, but I've evidently filled out in Paris – in certain places at least, despite what Libby says – because the first gown I try fits. It's a black cocktail dress that she once wore to a party, despite complaining that it was too tight and had no pockets. I'm glad to note that I empathize completely as soon as I pull up the zip. I hold my hair off my face until I'm replicating her style and use the dregs of make-up from her vanity case to mimic her eyeshadow and lipstick. My mirror has disappeared, so I open the door and head for the hallway to see how I look.

My dad is carrying a mug upstairs, which he drops onto the cream carpet when I appear. He's staring at me so hard that he doesn't seem to notice that tea has splashed up the wall and onto his trousers.

'Get back in your room,' he whispers furiously, grabbing me by the elbow. 'What do you think you're doing?'

'I want to look in the mirror!' I shake him off, ignoring his gesticulations for me to be quiet, and then it's too late, because Vivienne has opened their bedroom door.

She's wearing a silk nightdress and thick moisturizer, and she recoils at the sight of me. 'What's wrong with you?' she gasps in horror. 'Why would you do this?'

She lays a hand protectively on her stomach and my dad is immediately by her side, his arms wrapped around her. 'She's playing around, dressing up,' he tells her weakly. 'She doesn't know what she's doing.'

'I just wanted to see how it looked,' I explain, realizing that Vivienne, who knew my parents as a couple for years, probably saw my mother in this dress. 'We're the same size now, and . . . I thought it might help me understand what she was thinking, or give me a clue about where she is, or . . .'

Catching sight of the full-length mirror, I touch my hair, my nose and my ears to make sure I'm looking at my reflection and not my mother. The similarity is uncanny, and I smile as I stare at myself in fascination.

'Take it off,' my dad tells me. '*Now.*'

'No,' I say, backing away. 'I won't.'

I shut myself back in my bedroom and stand with my back to the door, listening to them argue. 'You need to be firmer with her,' Vivienne is saying. 'She's violent! She shouldn't be here. Next I suppose you'll be letting her back on that horse.'

I throw open the door. 'What did you say about my horse?'

Neither of them speaks, but my dad casts an annoyed glance at Vivienne.

'He's still here?' I ask. 'You didn't sell him?'

He shakes his head, but I don't wait to hear an explanation. I grab one bag from my room, with nothing in it except Elisabeth, and run down the stairs three at a time. If I weren't wearing a dress and carrying a rabbit I'd have gone straight down the banister, but I still cross the garden and paddock in seconds, falling on Star as I open the stable door.

'You're here, you're here,' I say, grabbing him around his neck and burying my face in his mane. He nuzzles against me, not discernibly excited, and I laugh as he stamps his foot and tries to back out of my embrace.

'Roma!' thunders my dad, sounding closer as he calls a second time.

I prepare to surrender to my next punishment, but then Star throws back his head and snorts, and before I know what I'm doing I've led him out of the back gate. I'm out of practice, barefoot as well as bareback, and clad in a dress that was definitely not designed for horse riding, but I take off as fast as I can into the breaking dawn. I lead Star in the only direction I can think of going; to the place I've fled so many times before.

Chapter Thirty-one

Siena

I remain very aware of my mother's rigid presence beside me. If I sleep, I dream only of her, and of the never-ending circle of our lives. Her eyes are dull but open, and she looks as dazed and estranged as she did on the morning after the rose garden massacre, when I took advantage of Syrena's colic and Paula's distraction to sneak into her room.

That day, the stream of morning sun lit the dust motes like glitter and fired the muslin drapes translucent. She herself appeared no more substantial than they, her skin white and paper-thin, her cheeks concave.

'You're wearing your wedding dress,' I said in surprise, looking at the remains of the display cabinet where it usually hung. She'd smashed the glass door, dragging the dress through glistering shards to freedom. She wore it now, her slight angles half lost in an opulent midsection of silky gauze.

She reached out as I tentatively handed her the glass on her bedside table. Her fingers encircled it like a claw, a stark contrast to the soft pink hands that Stella wrapped around mine, or even Syrena's ferociously dimpled grip. Only as she drank and I saw the bottle on the floor did I understand that it wasn't water. She sat up, her long golden hair tumbling between shoulder blades that jutted like wing buds.

When she spoke, her voice cracked as if she hadn't spoken out loud for some time. 'What do you think of your father?' she asked abruptly.

'He left you,' I said.

She shook her head vehemently. 'No, Siena. He left *us*. You *and* me.'

I swallowed hard. Everything I'd learned about divorce – mainly the pamphlet Sister Eilunedd had given me at Sunday School, *Where Has Daddy Gone?* – had assured me that children were not to blame for their parents' marital strife.

My heart raced as I recalled my more recent offences. Spooning Nutella from the jar and encouraging Stella to do the same. Copying a French translation from my classmate Athena (who lacked linguistic gifts; lesson learned). Pretending not to hear Syrena's baby monitor because Stella would beat me there anyway. 'Was it something I did?'

'No,' she said. 'He left us because of the baby.'

Syrena, well under twenty inches in length, was nevertheless a heavy burden to shoulder. 'They never met,' I pointed out. 'Didn't he want her?'

She picked up her comb and brushed my hair. 'My beautiful daughter. I pity you for the heartbreak that your beauty will bring.'

'Why?' I stared. In my experience, being pretty was

230

only advantageous. I was my teacher's favourite, even though I never worked hard. I was picked first for team sports, even those I disliked. I was a fixture on every little girl's birthday party list, to the extent that no one attended unless I did. Being pretty meant idolization by boys; compliments from strangers; whispers on the rare occasions we took public transport; money and impromptu gifts and promises that I'd break hearts. Never once had my beauty worked against me and I had no reason to think that it ever would.

Her white bedspread was covered in photographs, and she pushed her hands deep into them. 'Can you see how happy I was?' she asked, holding up an image of her wedding day. The dress she wore now was accessorized with a beautiful gold sash, and she was staring at my father in abject adoration. 'How loved I thought I was? How bright I believed my future would be?'

She dropped her hand as if she lacked the strength to hold it up. 'Lies,' she said quietly. 'It was all lies.'

'That won't happen to me,' I said. 'I won't let it. I'll behave like *him* if I want to.'

She focused on me as if a light had gone on in her eyes. 'My little starlet. You have my beauty, but perhaps you have your father's strength.'

'There's a dinner party scheduled for tonight,' I said. 'What should we do?'

Her shoulders drooped, she having evidently forgotten this event, arranged months earlier as an incentive to return to her pre-baby weight in record time. 'Cancel.'

'Parties make you happy. I could attend beside you instead of *him*. I could help you.'

'How old are you, Siena?' she asked.

'Ten.'

She cupped my face in her hands and looked at me closely. Then she picked up her sapphire comb and started to fasten my long hair into a rope.

'Siena!' Stella's panicked voice sounded from downstairs, and I was about to run when my mother placed a hand on my wrist.

'Stella needs me.' I was confused. 'Something might be wrong with the baby.'

Stella called again, and I glanced to the door as my mother leaned towards me and smoothed my hair. 'We need each other more. Don't we?'

When we came downstairs to prepare for the arrival of our guests, Stella was asleep at the half-laid table, her head on a coaster and her hair streaming almost to the ground. Syrena, wrapped in a tea towel in a pewter serving dish, slept too. Stella awoke with a start, staring in confusion between me and our mother.

'Siena?' she said tentatively, as though unsure which of us was which.

Seraphina nodded. 'This is Siena now.'

Syrena stirred, her blue eyes locking with mine. After a moment's consideration she opened her mouth to cry. Stella stood up resignedly, transporting Syrena in her dish as the doorbell rang. And, from that night on, Seraphina's recovery appeared to rest directly on my development.

Elocution lessons taught me the art of saying nothing. *We never explain.*

Gone overnight were my play clothes, replaced by Chantilly lace, silk and tulle. *We're never off-duty.*

Gone were my pigtails and tumbling long curls, replaced by neat French twists and chignons held with the sapphire comb and decorated with gold leaves and flowers and stars. *Loose hair is for little girls.*

And gone were weekends spent at the stables or playing with Stella, replaced by brunches and luncheons and dinners at which my mother talked little and ate less but was watched and admired and sought after like a musical box figurine. *We never chase,* she told me as I learned to discard boys as if they were nothing more than dandelion seeds.

As Stella and Syrena converged and fused, I concentrated on pleasing a mother I'd previously admired only from a distance as she ignored the daughters she'd brought into the world for reasons other than love.

I learned to converse with boys about their schooling and their hobbies and their sports; to position myself in candlelight so that my neck was elongated and light shone upon me brightly and splendidly. I learned to lower my head and stare at boys through my long eyelashes; to hold their attention until there was nowhere else they'd rather be, even though most of the time I didn't speak a word. And I learned to make boys love me until they wanted to love only me for the rest of their lives, even with no hope of me loving them back.

I learned to do these things so that my mother wouldn't forget me again, or revert to the bedridden spectre she'd become. And, although I believed that I was merely playing a role, it was my education, and finally I became my education.

Chapter Thirty-two

Romy

I wake in an unfamiliar bed in a familiar room, but reconciling this information is painful. I put my arm across my face to shut out sunlight and a rush of embarrassment as my memory returns after a few seconds of blessed nothingness.

'How are you feeling?' Jack opens the door and laughs at my hideous state. Despite the cold, he's wearing only shorts. 'Actually, don't answer. You look almost as bad as I do.'

'Where's your top?' I ask him.

'On you,' he says as I glance down to see that I'm wearing his T-shirt.

'I'm sorry.' I struggle into a sitting position. 'I should go.'

'Don't be silly. I said you could come here any time, and I meant it.'

'You were twelve when you said that,' I remind him. 'I'm sure you didn't intend me to abuse your kind offer in the way I have.'

'I have hidden you many times,' he concedes as he sits beside me and hands me a cup of coffee in his favourite WWE mug. 'Every time you have a school uniform fitting . . . or when your grandparents come to stay . . . or when Vivienne makes kedgeree . . . and you always say you're never going back.'

'This time it's true,' I say. 'Although I don't have anything with me except my mother's dress, and that's not exactly day wear.'

He looks shamefaced. 'Actually, your dad already brought over your stuff. I told him you can stay here for as long as you want.'

Jack's house is even bigger than my father's, but there's no Vivienne to keep order. His parents are absent for most of the year on various endeavours – right now his dad is brokering a deal in Shanghai while his mother weaves wicker and feeds chickens in a Devon clinic – and half the rooms are covered in dust sheets, the others decimated by moths. He and Edward share an apartment in the old servants' quarters, which is the only inhabitable wing.

'How did I get into Edward's room?' I ask dubiously. 'What did we drink before I passed out?'

'Half the wine cellar,' Jack says. 'Don't worry about Edward – he's in the correctional facility, but he went voluntarily this time. He's really improved.'

I feel for the scar on my neck where Edward's catapult struck me on my last visit. He behaves like a boy raised by wolves, whirling between acts of evil with the frenzy of a child possessed. But there might be some truth in Jack's statement, because today his bedroom is tidy, with no new fire damage.

'What's happened to improve him?' I ask.

'I'll let you in on his biggest secret.' Jack motions at a bedside table photograph of Siena's little sister Stella, wearing a red dress and matching hair ribbon. The ribbon is tied to the frame along with a handwritten note signed from her in careful copperplate writing, and Edward has drawn an apple, or a misshapen heart, around her face in felt tip.

'Another one bites the dust,' he says as I turn the frame to the wall.

I roll my eyes. 'You do realize that, if you hadn't blown everything, you'd be embarking on a pre-honeymoon with Siena right now, instead of here with me and a hangover? I'm sure she'd have given you a night to remember.'

'That's all we ever do,' he complains. 'There's more to life, you know.'

I laugh. 'Siena is premier league. The idea of not wanting her is, well . . .'

'Go on,' he says. 'What's it like, not to want her?'

I change the subject, peering around apprehensively. 'Did Edward leave a snake in here? Why did you put Elisabeth in a fish tank?'

He crosses the room towards the now-empty tank in which Edward once tried to create a species of fighting goldfish, and pulls out my rabbit. He places her beside me on the pillow where she stretches and quivers as if she's admiring her pink fur. 'No snakes – it was just a precaution. I still can't believe you remembered your rabbit, but forgot your money and phone.'

'Of course I remembered,' I say. 'It's just me and Star and Elisabeth now.'

He wraps an arm around me. 'And me. I gave her to you, don't forget.'

Jack had been encouraged, or bribed, to come and cheer me up after my mother left. He'd interrupted my vigil beside the phone, which I frequently picked up whether it was ringing or not, and, in more desperate moments, dialled random numbers and asked strangers if they knew where she was.

Jack greeted me by pulling a tiny ball of fluff from his pocket and thrusting it at me.

The rabbit was white with dark eyes, and so small that it fitted into the palm of my hand. *Is it mine?* I whispered, looking up at my dad.

It's yours, he said, clearing his throat. *I believe an experiment of Jack's brother has rendered the family with a serious problem, and we're going to do our bit to help.*

We've got rabbits everywhere, even in the bath, Jack confirmed. *They've messed up my mum's medication. She always hallucinates white rabbits after eight pills, so now she can't tell how many she's taken. What are you going to call this one?*

Jack lived in our village, and I'd known him by sight for years. I didn't have much interest in boys, but I was suddenly so taken with his impish expression, his messy black hair, his soft olive skin and his apparent interest in me, that I'd have told him anything.

Elisabeth, I said. *Like my mother.*

Do you know, my dad confided in Jack's dad as Jack grabbed my hand and pulled me away from them, *this is the first time she's smiled in weeks.*

My boarding school future had become a major bone of contention at home since my mother's departure. I'd told my dad, with unfounded conviction, that she wouldn't have sent me away; he maintained that they'd made a mutual agreement. Only later did I see that he'd introduced Jack to my life as a way of settling our disagreement in his favour.

It's no big deal, Jack shrugged when I complained about it to him. *We hardly see our parents anyway. And if you come to the same school as me, we'll have each other.*

Boarding school girls are prissy, I told him. *They only think about their hair.*

We'll face them together, he said. *I never think about my hair.*

We were in his back garden with the ever-increasing rabbit population. Pretending to oil the hinges of a rickety hutch into which Jack had converted his father's bedside table, I tried to sound casual. *You won't forget me as soon as we arrive?*

Jack looked outraged as he abandoned the rosettes with which we were preparing the rabbits for an imaginary show. *Who could be more fun than you?*

Do you swear? I pressed, even though I had no real belief in the value of promises.

He laughed. *I swear. I swear on . . .* He pretended to count the abundant fluffy tails and twitching noses that had decimated the lawn, the flower beds and the vegetable patch. *I swear on Edward's sixty-seven white rabbits.*

On my next visit to Jack's garden, following our first term at Temperley High and the dawn of Jack and Siena's relationship, I was unsurprised to see that all the rabbits had gone.

In Edward's room, Elisabeth hops around the pillow and then stands on her hind legs, completely alert. 'Danger?' Jack asks her, smiling.

'*Terrible* danger,' I confirm as the unmistakable clarion call of Libby sounds on the stairs outside, as loud and menacing as a conquering warrior queen.

Chapter Thirty-three

Siena

Just as the Starlets never eat but are always present at meals, my mother arrives promptly in the breakfast room at eight, the kitchen at one, and the dining room at seven, to sit before menus she's chosen but will barely touch. This morning my sisters flank her in black velveteen dresses with white collars as I take my place opposite her, willing her to refocus on me after our unbearably silent night. Syrena, after all, is doing nothing more diverting than smearing porridge on the tablecloth and dropping melon balls for a cat which rubs decorously against her in hopes of more, and humming as she energetically colours a picture.

Seraphina's attention is trained on Stella, whose china plate is unmarred by food residue. Stella half rises to greet me, but, after glancing at Seraphina, she sinks back into her seat, giving me a polite nod instead of her usual smile and taking a sip of black coffee from a china cup.

'How long will you be staying with us, Siena?' Seraphina asks with the chilly courtesy of a host losing patience with a tiresome house guest.

'A few days?' I say, wondering where I'll go if

this is unacceptable. 'Perhaps I could stay until term begins?'

She's teaching Stella how to appear to enjoy a meal without ingesting anything. It's a trick she taught me when I was younger than Stella, but now, even knowing how valuable it will be to her, I find myself wishing that Stella would copy her little sister in this regard and show interest at the prospect of food, even if she's never allowed to eat any.

In a house devoid of refined sugar, Syrena *Marianne Dreams* herself a birthday tea of cake and roast potatoes and purple Quality Streets in wax crayons.

'Visualization is an effective dietary technique,' Seraphina notes as she takes the drawing from her and pins it to a fridge that holds only green olives and champagne. 'You would do well to remember it on days of temptation such as this.' She pats Syrena's head and blanches at her gap-toothed smile.

I feel an inappropriate urge to laugh as I remember the year that Syrena, refusing to go low-carb, appeared at her birthday party with her face and neck covered in chocolate, pink hair plastered to her scalp. Seraphina could scarcely have been more horrified if Syrena had been spattered in the blood of her first murder victim.

'Paula, what is the meaning of this?' she gasped.

Paula stood firm. 'Syrena is three years old. This is what three-year-olds do.'

Seraphina took a threatening step towards Syrena, but immediately Stella was in front of her little sister

242

like a shield. 'No,' she told Seraphina furiously. 'No.'

Dragging Syrena by her sticky, dripping hand, Stella sat her fully clothed in the shower until the water ran Neapolitan and Syrena was Syrena again.

'Stella has good instincts,' said Paula, behind me. 'I would have done the same, but made the water cold.'

'Where did Syrena find ice cream?' I asked. 'Did she raid a convenience store?'

'Not this time,' said Paula in a low voice. 'She found the ice cream in its usual place, behind the frozen spinach. It is your mother's, for emergencies only.'

In a way that I expect will one day enrage our mother, Syrena is thinner than any of us; but then again, she never stands still. She blazes through the house, shimmering like Tinker Bell, and, no matter how many pairs of shoes she's given, resolutely barefoot.

'There's a dinner party tonight,' Seraphina tells me. 'You may wish to know that Mr Lawrence has declined his invitation.'

I swallow to hide a sinking feeling at the mention of Jack's father. This shouldn't be unexpected, but I feel responsible for denying my mother one of her most valued companions.

'I'll be there anyway.' I make up my mind to throw myself back into my inaugural training ground until I can recommence my role as a daughter she can be proud of. 'We'll invite someone in his place, and I'll do all I can to make it a success.'

Paula has spirited Syrena away to her kitchen domain and I watch through the door as she surveys two piles of presents, rejecting the professionally wrapped Fortnum's rectangles in favour of Paula's chaotic primary colours. I'm wishing that I'd sent Syrena a toy instead of a scarf with a brand name she can't even pronounce when I see their expressions freeze. As quick as a flash, Syrena jumps up and slams the door, but not before I see Paula hide a plate of croissants and brush crumbs hurriedly from Syrena's dress. *They're scared of me*, I realize in horror. *That's how they react to my mother.*

Seraphina hasn't acknowledged my comment, and I follow her gaze as if I'm seeing Stella through her eyes. *She's going to be prettier than both of us.*

Stella at twelve is everything that nature had promised and more. People say she's the image of me; yet I see nothing but differences. Her nose is daintier; her hair is glossier; her lips are fuller. Beside her I am nothing but nature's practice run, and it frightens me in a way I can't explain. It frightens me almost as much as it does to imagine Stella at seventeen.

She's older than I was when I attended my first dinner party, even if I still see her as a French-braided, gingham-clad five-year-old earnestly forcing roses into an unyielding ground. I understand why Seraphina wants to look at Stella today rather than me: because I remind her of herself during an unspeakable time. I'm the ghost of Syrena's birthdays past, significant only as a warning against something that must never happen again.

'I'm going outside,' I mutter as I slide from my chair. I hover for a moment to wait for Stella, who follows me everywhere whether I want her to or not. She looks up at me, and then at Seraphina, and then she takes another sip of coffee. I blush, because Seraphina is watching me with pity, and I leave.

The garden is chilly and clinging to vestiges of winter but I gulp in the air, which at least lacks the sterility of our family meal. Huddling on a bench to keep warm, I glimpse the scene through the window as Seraphina cups Stella's chin in one hand and winds her other into the soft skein of her golden hair.

Chapter Thirty-four

Romy

I've just enough time to pull the duvet over me and the rabbit before Libby enters the room. Jack shoves my mother's dress out of sight and sits in front of me to hide the bump in the bed. I fervently wish that Edward were here doing target practice: Libby would be the perfect kill, and I don't think a single judge would condemn him for it.

'How did you get in here?' Jack asks in bewilderment.

'Your door was unlocked.' She manages to make this sound acceptable.

'Please leave,' he says. 'I'm sure you know how unwelcome you are, but I'll ask politely anyway.'

'I came to talk sense into you,' she says. 'Do you have any idea how many boys are dying to get a ring on Siena's finger?'

He's exasperated. 'Siena isn't even eighteen. She isn't allowed to get married without her mother's permission.'

'We have that in writing already,' Libby counters. 'Why wait? You love each other . . . you'll never do better. There *is* no better. Why risk losing her?'

'I wouldn't have lost her if you hadn't forced the issue. Seriously, what's wrong with you? Why are you so weirdly obsessed with Siena's engagement?'

'I'm her closest friend,' she says defensively. 'I have her best interests at heart.'

'Then why aren't you looking after her now, instead of harassing me? This is about you, not her.'

'About *me*?' she says in outrage. 'I've forfeited a weekend in Nice to stay here and patch things up between the pair of you.'

He laughs. 'I know you better than that, Libby.'

'Is there someone else?' she asks suddenly.

He sighs, but something in his face can't ring true, because she seizes on it. 'Are you sure about that?'

Even I can concede that he sounds guilty. 'There's no one else. Now *please leave*.'

She's suspicious. I hold my breath, losing concentration for long enough to let go of Elisabeth. Before I can grab her, she's made a public bid for freedom, and seconds later Libby is standing over me with the quilt in her hands and a strangely triumphant smirk.

'It's not what you think,' Jack says quietly. He raises an eyebrow for me to help him, but, when I open my mouth to speak, nothing comes out.

'Romy is my oldest friend; you know that,' he says.

'Your oldest *girlfriend*, you mean.' Libby reaches into her bag for her phone. 'Smile for the camera.'

I blink as the light flashes three, four times. I wait for Jack to take it from her and smash the evidence, but he doesn't move. 'Think carefully, Libby,' he says. 'What's

247

this going to achieve? A moment ago all you wanted was to see me and Siena back together.'

'True,' she considers. 'Then I remembered something else I want just as much.'

'Is it worth it?' I ask. 'Is it worth causing Siena this much hurt, just to see me gone?'

Her face flickers with something like humanity, but then reverts to its usual state. 'This time you've well and truly nailed your own coffin.'

She sweeps out, her footsteps clicking down the stairs.

Jack turns to me. 'Why didn't you back me up?'

'What good would it have done?' I say. 'She knew what she wanted to find.'

'Then why won't you tell the truth about last year?' he asks. 'It's cost you everything you had except a rabbit and a horse!'

'At least I'll have transport back to school,' I say.

He shakes his head frustratedly. 'Your dad's kicked you out of home and now your life at school won't be worth living either. Why did you make Libby your enemy?'

'I can deal with it,' I say. 'As long as I'm Head Girl, my life at school will be fine. And with my fees paid, I'll have no need to speak to my dad.'

'When did things get so complicated?' he asks.

'The day you and Siena chose each other over me,' I tell him, even though he doesn't want an answer.

Chapter Thirty-five

Siena

Lacking a more appealing diversion, I sit in the rose garden and attempt to tidy the gaping holes where flowers have been uprooted and used as last night's decorations. I drop my secateurs and hurriedly remove a gardening glove as I hear a noise from behind me.

'What's happened here?' gasps a familiar voice as I look down at myself in panic. My clothes are muddy and torn. My hair is messily tied into a ribbon and my face is bare. This isn't the kind of state in which I ever spend time on my own, let alone in public view.

'Hello, Libby,' I say reluctantly. She's immaculate, as if she's made a special effort to show me up. 'What are you doing here?'

Stella emerges from her hiding place behind Libby's voluminous handbag and hops nervously from one foot to the other. 'I called her.'

Libby pats her on the head. 'She did the right thing. It looks as if I got here in the nick of time.'

'For what?' I say hopelessly. 'Everything's already over.'

'That's what people thought about stack heels, remember?'

'This is worse,' I say. 'It's not the end of a fashion

revolution; it's the end of my life. What am I supposed to do now?'

Tears are falling down my cheeks and I suddenly lack the energy to stand. I start to crumple, but within seconds I'm supported by a tiny blonde bookend as Stella puts her arms around me and lets me hide my face in her hair.

Libby opens the day planner as if it's a hymn sheet. 'You have two options, as far as I can see. You can get over Jack . . .'

'Our mother would never allow that,' says Stella decisively. 'And she'd *never* forgive the person who suggested it.'

Libby blanches and scribbles vigorously. 'You have *one* option. You can win Jack back.'

Stella wrinkles her perfect nose. 'Why would she want him back after what he did?'

Libby is flailing in the face of her cool opposition. 'You said . . . you just said that my other option was impossible! What do *you* suggest we do?'

Stella rolls her eyes. 'We make *him* want *her* back, of course.'

'And . . . might you have any ideas on that subject?'

'Isn't that your job?' Stella asks icily.

Syrena barrels over, stopping short at the sight of Libby. 'Oh, it's you.'

'Don't be rude, Syrena,' I say, because Libby looks mortally offended.

'Sorry,' says Syrena with gleeful insincerity. 'But

Paula said you had a friend here and I thought it might be . . .' She tails off into a whisper. '*Romy.*'

Libby is thunderstruck. 'Has Romy been in this house?'

'Of course not,' I say, because Libby should never know about Romy's past visits here. Inviting her without the knowledge of the other Starlets may have been an error of judgement on my part, but she was accepting of a feral sibling and an unusual mother as others were not. 'Syrena's never even met her.'

'I have,' contests Syrena. 'I've met Romy *and* her rabbit.'

Stella takes in the situation and steers Syrena away, a hand on her forehead. 'You feel hot. Maybe it's typhoid again.'

'I had measles, not typhoid,' Syrena says crossly.

Libby stares after them. 'Why doesn't she like me? What is it about Romy that people like so much?'

'She's delirious,' I say. 'Let's go inside.'

Libby looks so sad that I'm glad she'll never know about the month Syrena once spent dressed in curtains and oversized high heels to play Libby in a high-octane world of tea parties, shopping for shoes she couldn't walk in, and chasing boys who were always running at top speed in the opposite direction.

Libby walks around my mother's room, frowning critically. Seraphina always closes the curtains at dawn, and Libby twitches them now, letting in an

251

unwelcome shaft of sunlight, and runs her finger across the dressing table, blowing away the dust. I wonder if my mother ever allows Paula in here while I'm away.

'Look at yourself,' she instructs, pushing me in front of the mirror.

I flinch at the dark circles that dominate my face, my sharp cheekbones and collarbone, and my translucent skin. I've cut myself on the roses, and blood stains my cheek like tears. I look as if I'm already dead.

My mother floats in, as ethereal as if she's been blown on the wind. Libby is taken aback to see her at such close quarters and her mouth drops open before she recovers herself. 'M-Miss Hamilton?' she says, holding out her hand. 'I'm here to help Siena.'

'How did you plan to help her?' Seraphina asks with little interest.

'I have lots of ideas, and an excellent success rate.' Despite her fear, Libby injects a note of pride at this.

'I assume the non-proposal took place on your watch?' Seraphina asks.

Libby falters, but she's come through worse than this. 'If Jack's going to be Head Boy, then Siena should be Head Girl,' she says bravely.

Turning to my mother I'm unsurprised to see my distaste mirrored on her face.

'Wait,' Libby says quickly. 'Siena becoming Head Girl will show Jack that she has the depth he's looking for. It'll prove that she's the one for him.'

'What does the process involve?' sighs Seraphina. 'A party, I presume? Low lighting? A formal dress code?'

'I don't remember a dress code,' I say. 'And the lighting in the hall is terrible.'

'Then this sounds very unsuitable,' says Seraphina. 'Thank you for your work, Liberty.' Her voice manages to convey both that the conversation is over, and that this is the last piece of work Libby will ever undertake. 'Perhaps you'd like to spend the remainder of your holiday with Liberty, Siena, as we have nothing left to discuss. Now, where is Stella?'

Libby taps her foot desperately. 'We'll have an election campaign, so everyone in the school can support Siena. At the Elevation ceremony, people will throw rose petals at her and cheer as she and Jack are crowned. He'll realize that she's the most perfect girl in the world, and the year will end exactly as we planned.'

'I don't see how,' I say. 'We planned to end the year with the party to end all parties.'

Libby opens her bag and takes out a pile of books, magazines, collages and samples of white fabric. She scatters them across the carpet as Seraphina and I look over wedding venues, all of them white and gauzy and featuring exclusively attractive guests.

'This was for your engagement party, but now we'll use it for Elevation,' she says. 'It won't be an assembly; it will be a ball, and everyone shall go!'

'Bibbibi bobbidi boo,' sings Syrena helpfully from outside the door.

'Can I take it that you won't make any more catastrophic wardrobe decisions, Liberty?' Seraphina asks. 'That pink abomination has blocked the furnace.'

'Absolutely,' Libby says. 'She'll wear . . . We'll find her something perfect to wear, as soon as we appoint a new designer and have the current postholder killed.'

Seraphina, sighing with the air of one who has to do everything, plucks her wedding dress from its hanger. 'Siena shall wear this. We're leaving nothing else to the fates.'

'It's beautiful,' Libby breathes, reaching out for it even as Seraphina whisks it away. 'Siena, you'll look like an angel.'

'This will be an appropriate addition to a victorious Head Girl's outfit, no?' Seraphina holds up her gold sash to the light.

'Of course,' Libby says excitedly. 'It'll be like a pageant!'

Seraphina turns to me, mollified. 'You may stay for tonight's party after all, Siena. Perhaps I have neglected you and should take some part of the blame.'

She leaves the room following this generous admission, and Libby relaxes visibly. 'You're welcome,' she beams. 'Everything is back on track.'

'Except that I have to become *Head Girl*?' I mutter. 'How does that work?'

She waves dismissively. 'It's a figurehead position.

Your committee will do all the work. Don't you see? This covers all bases.'

'Such as? Sealing my social suicide?'

She ticks off on her fingers. 'It gives you a new focus now the wedding is postponed. It shows Jack your serious, responsible side. It totally shows Romy the door. And did you know there are Prefect positions for all of us on the Council? You won't be on your own!'

'The Starlets on the Student Council?' I say in disbelief. 'The *Starlets* joining the least glamorous committee in world history?'

'That's in the past. Starting from now, the Head Girl position is *Miss Temperley High*. Jack will be fighting to get you down the aisle.' She places a veil on my head.

'Romy really wants this.'

Expecting Libby to launch once again into her tragic ladder rendition, I stop listening as she reaches into her bag, imagining instead the Starlet table without Romy on it. Free of conflict, free of judgement, free of tension, this would restore us to our former equilibrium.

And it would make life immeasurably dull.

'Look!' Libby interrupts, pushing her phone right up to my face.

I hold the picture upright, upside down, close up and far away. A dull pain in the pit of my stomach intensifies like cramp, and I'm unable to take my eyes off the image of Romy in bed wearing Jack's T-shirt,

255

with Jack beside her. Her hair is tousled in the way mine always is following particular activities, and make-up – which she never wears – is smeared right across her face as if she's slept in it. But the worst thing is her expression, contrasting with Jack's guilty fear, somehow scared and aggressive and triumphant all at the same time. She's staring into the camera as if she's looking directly at me.

'How did you get this?' I grip the arm of my chair to keep me upright, because, once I start falling, I might never stop.

Libby sighs. 'If you must know, I went to visit Jack today, thinking only of you. I didn't want to have to show you this, but I can't live with you believing that Romy is your friend. We have to get rid of her. Now are you in?'

'I'm in,' I say numbly.

Libby smiles. 'Then Romy's out. In more ways than you could *ever* imagine.'

Chapter Thirty-six

Romy

I dawdle outside the cafeteria on the first evening of the summer term. Twice I turn to leave, but extreme, un-Starlet-like hunger propels me inside. Speeding to the hatch, I recklessly throw an assortment of forbidden carbohydrates onto my tray. I swipe my card and hide behind some Fifth Formers as I prepare to scurry back to safety.

'Romy!' Phoebe's voice stops me in my tracks. 'Where do you think you're going?'

Before I can try and beat her to the doorway, Mrs Denbigh steps into my way. 'I expect you were about to join Phoebe?' she says. 'Our agreement still stands this term, you know.'

'Of course,' I mutter, trudging towards the Starlet table. Siena and Libby are missing and I look around agitatedly in case they're ready to take pot shots.

'Why do you look so frightened, Romy?' Cassidy asks with supreme innocence.

Phoebe looks equally guileless. Only Madison, drooping and pale, avoids my eyes.

'No reason,' I say carefully. It's impossible to tell whether they've seen the picture of me and Jack. 'What's going on?'

'We're just catching up,' says Cassidy. 'So much has happened since last week.'

'I hope Siena comes in soon so we can see the ring,' says Phoebe impatiently. 'She hasn't replied to a single message since the ball, and I haven't even seen a picture.'

'What ring?' I ask, and they all stare at me.

'Um, Siena's engagement ring?' Cassidy says.

It seems inconceivable that anyone could think that the ball ended successfully for Siena or Jack, but that's without taking into account Libby's talent for spinning events to suit her purposes. For reasons I'm sure I'm about to uncover, the Starlets have heard a very different version.

Everyone's eyes are trained on Siena's left hand when she and Libby arrive. Such is the contagious anticipation that even I find myself expecting to see a diamond on her ring finger. Siena lifts her chin before she speaks, as if daring us to disagree with her, and the Starlets look at her bare hand in confusion. Only Libby is unmoved, and she watches her like a prompt from the wings.

'I have an announcement to make,' Siena says. 'It concerns Jack.'

'Does the engagement ring have to be resized?' Cassidy asks sweetly. 'Is that why you aren't wearing it?'

'Did you already elope?' says Phoebe. 'Is that what you were doing today? Getting married in Capri?'

'Today Siena went to Harvey Nichols,' Libby reminds her. 'She was only gone for a few hours.'

Phoebe mutters something about the time

difference, which everyone is kind enough to ignore.

'It's something else,' Siena says. 'Jack and I aren't engaged.'

She sits back as the Starlets disintegrate into shock and distress.

'W-why?' stammers Madison. 'I don't understand. Did he . . . ?' She can't continue but she mouths the words she daren't speak aloud.

Siena bristles in indignation. 'Did he *break up* with me? What do you mean by that?'

'Nothing!' Madison says quickly. 'I'm just trying to understand . . .'

'Then you shouldn't be so *insulting*,' Siena says. 'Especially considering your current instability in this group.'

'Didn't you know that weddings are completely passé, Madison?' asks Libby pityingly.

Madison is confused. 'Siena said this year was about *weddings, and weddings alone.*'

'I never said that,' hisses Siena. 'Are you *trying* to be deposed, Mads?'

'How's Jack?' interjects Cassidy. 'Is he upset?'

'Devastated.' Siena smiles brightly. 'He's practically bedridden. He threatened to jump off the tower. Some of the Stripes had to talk him off the ledge, and . . .'

The Starlets' attention has wavered somewhat and I twist around to see that they're all watching the Stripes' triumphant entry to the cafeteria. They've evidently won something, as their cheering and back-slapping and mutual admiration is even more metrosexual than usual. At the centre, Jack is grinning widely, and I see Siena flush. Libby fans her cheeks with a napkin while attention is diverted.

'He looks much better,' Cassidy says encouragingly. 'Perhaps he can be taken off suicide watch now.'

'Bravado,' Siena rallies. 'He's crying a river on the inside, but you know he's a great sufferer in silence. He'll want to stay strong for his teammates, because they're very sensitive.'

Jack rakes a hand through his hair and glances reluctantly around the room. Siena waves, although I notice that Libby practically performs the action for her by lifting and shaking her elbow, and that her smile is more of a snarl. Finally she beckons him over, an impulse which she appears to regret almost immediately.

'What are you doing?' Libby mutters. 'You aren't ready for this.'

Seeing me watching, she affects a smile almost as uninviting as Siena's. '*Jack* isn't ready for this,' she corrects herself. '*Jack* has only just come off hunger strike.'

Jack walks towards us with the enthusiasm of someone approaching the gallows, while Siena upholds her rictus grin. 'Siena?' he says uncertainly.

'Jack,' she trills, air-kissing him four times. 'How wonderful to see you!'

'Um . . .' He looks around for help. 'It's good to see you too. How have you been?'

She shakes her head impatiently. 'The important question is, how have *you* been? You look much better.'

Jack takes her hand and tries to address her without Libby interrupting. 'We need to talk. I've been trying to reach you for days. Are we breaking up because I don't want to get married? I still love you – I don't want this to be the end for us.'

I know she's wavering, because she doesn't pull her hand away as he takes a cautious step closer.

Then Libby slams between them. 'How was hospital, Jack? The rest and relaxation have obviously done you a power of good.'

'What is this bullshit?' he says as he shakes her off. 'What's wrong with you, Libby? Why can't you tell the truth?'

'What truth?' Libby says. 'The truth that Siena broke your heart?'

Her tone is quietly dangerous and I expect Jack to surrender, but he turns away from her as the whole cafeteria goes quiet. 'The real reason we broke up is that *Libby*—'

Libby drowns him out. 'Romy split them up.' She whips out her phone and taps it triumphantly. 'She slept with Jack!'

Jack starts to argue, but before he can say anything coherent I hear phones all around the room ping and beep and chirrup, and I don't have to be able to see their screens to know that they're looking at a picture

261

of me lying half dressed and dishevelled in bed with Jack beside me.

A gasp seems to echo around the whole room.

'How could you, Romy?' asks Phoebe. 'After the kindness we've shown you?'

'I have an official statement,' Libby announces, and the room hushes again. *'Siena regrets this gross betrayal, especially in view of her generosity towards Romy – sometimes at my expense – but she wishes them well in their future endeavours.'*

'Do you really, Siena?' says Cassidy. 'You're so nice!'

'Siena is *very* nice,' Libby confirms. 'She understands that Jack was on the rebound, and vulnerable prey to an aggressor who'd been circling him for several years. However, she has concerns regarding his evident . . . emotional difficulties.'

'Are you suggesting that anyone who likes me must have *emotional difficulties*?' I ask.

'I'm afraid so,' Libby says soberly. 'What's more, anyone who'd make an error as *cataclysmic* as stealing Jack obviously has a serious lack of moral compass. And that's why we're ruling you unfit to be Head Girl.'

'You can't do that,' I say. 'Who's going to take my place? Siena, I suppose?'

I mean this as a joke, but she and Siena both nod.

'She can't!' I raise my voice even though the whole room is staring at me.

Libby smiles widely. 'But, you see, she can.'

Chapter Thirty-seven

Siena

'Are you sure that was the right course of action?' I ask uneasily as we take our seats. The cafeteria has erupted around us, and Romy, after a final glance at me, has left the room at speed.

'What choice did I have?' asks Libby. 'Jack was about to make a calamitous announcement. I'm not sure even I could have saved your reputation from the insinuation that you aggressively pursued a proposal from him against his will.'

'I suppose you're right,' I wince. 'I just . . . maybe we were wrong about Romy and Jack, and now we'll never know for sure.'

'They didn't deny it. They're as guilty as sin. Why are you even thinking about that?'

'Jack told me he didn't want us to break up. Maybe I should have heard him out.'

'Remember what you're fighting for,' she whispers. 'You owe this to your mother, and you owe it to yourself. If Jack respects you, he'll propose, and you shouldn't accept anything less. If he loves you as he says he does, what's he waiting for?'

The noise in the room suddenly dies away, and I look up to see that Jack is beside me again. 'What do you want?' Libby asks frostily.

'I want to talk to Siena,' he says. '*Alone*.'

I stare at the table, because I'll buckle if I meet his eyes. 'No.'

He sits down. 'Then I'll tell you right here what a mistake you're making.'

'*You* were Siena's only mistake,' Libby says.

'No,' he says. 'Siena, please think carefully about who you surround yourself with.'

'Libby is my best friend,' I say.

'She's not a friend; she's a yes man. Instead of running from everyone who disagrees with you, why don't you stop and consider whether those people might be right?'

'I thought you wanted me to better myself,' I say.

'Not like this. You don't need to launch yourself into some Student Council coup. Leave the Head Girl position to Romy, where it belongs.'

'Don't you believe I'm capable of being Head Girl?' I'm not sure why this bothers me when only a week ago I'd have been horrified at the mere concept.

'I think you're capable of a million and one things,' he says. 'But misplaced revenge shouldn't be one of them. I hope you realize that before it's too late.'

'How dare he?' Libby says as he walks away.

'He's wrong, isn't he?' I ask. 'This will work, won't it?'

'Of course,' Cassidy says stalwartly. 'If you're going to be Head Girl – and we support *all* your decisions, even unexpected ones – you'll be the best we've ever had.'

Phoebe and Madison exchange a glance and then nod. 'We're on board,' Phoebe announces. 'You don't have to explain yourself to us: we have blind faith.'

'Not that it matters what *Mads* thinks,' says Libby. 'I'll note for the minutes that she's lost her right to an opinion.'

'Mads has been punished enough,' says Cassidy. 'She missed the ball.'

'She hasn't been punished for giving Siena's dress to Romy,' Libby counters.

'Technically it's my dress,' argues Madison. 'I made it.'

'You made it for me,' I say, 'which makes it *my* dress.'

'You said it was the most hideous thing you'd ever seen,' she protests. 'You said the pattern looked like a disease from Jack's Biology textbook.'

'That's not the point. If Kate Middleton turns down a dress, it doesn't get given away to the person standing closest.'

'You aren't Kate Middleton,' she says. 'You don't have a castle, and the one time you danced near Prince William in Boujis, he didn't seem to notice you.'

I move on with dignity. 'I don't see how we're going to make this happen, blind faith or not. No one outside the Council cares about the Head Girl position.'

'People might not care yet,' says Libby. 'But they

265

will, once we have the right marketing strategy.'

'Marketing strategy?' I'm annoyed. 'What are you suggesting?'

'Everything needs to be advertised,' Phoebe agrees. 'Even products that people already love. Otherwise how would we make choices? We'd never be able to buy anything; we'd die of starvation and exposure and indecision.'

'More important than marketing *you* is marketing the *campaign*.' Libby drowns out Phoebe. 'You're thinking backwards. You're worrying that you don't fit the Head Girl position, but all we need to do is rebrand it so that *it* fits *you*.'

'That sounds impossible,' I say.

Libby smiles and the others follow, evidently understanding before I do. 'Think about the role you were supposed to play this term, and transpose it onto the Elevation ceremony.'

'So I'm a Head Girl – Bride hybrid?' I ask. 'Are you crazy?'

'Crazy . . . brilliant . . .' Libby considers. 'There's no need to decide right away.'

'But the plan will fall apart if Jack thinks I'm in this for the wrong reasons.'

'He'll only know what we want him to know,' says Libby. 'And right now, that's nothing at all. So let me worry about the details.'

Chapter Thirty-eight

Romy

I hear the noise a whole staircase away, but I imagine it's coming from somewhere else until I open the door to find the hitherto tidy Council room in chaos. The School Rules have been pushed from tables to the floor, to be replaced with streamers, magazine cuttings and sequins, and the Council members themselves have been displaced from their usual seats, crowding at the far end while the Starlets spread themselves across the head of the table.

'Am I interrupting something?' I ask as I slam down my books.

'No,' says Siena with a big smile as she moves a pile of magazines one inch to the left and then back again, giving me precisely no more space.

'What on earth are you doing?' I stare at the posters, felt-tip pens and glitter festooning the table top. I haven't seen the Starlets so into arts and crafts since we were thirteen, and they spent a month making a papier mâché model of Tom Cruise for a *Cosmo* competition. They all took managerial positions as my direct supervisors, making it doubly unfair when it transpired that there were only five places on the winners' trip to the Dolby Theatre. Not to mention that their conception of papier mâche involved sealing Eric inside a newspaper, where he nearly suffocated.

'We're getting started on the election campaign.' Cassidy happily affixes a silver star to her forehead. 'Do you want to help?'

'Of course Romy doesn't want to help!' Phoebe tells her. 'She's on the opposing side, Cassidy. That's like asking *Wales* for help.'

'Whose election campaign?' I ask.

Phoebe sighs in annoyance as Cassidy continues. '*Siena's* election campaign. We're working on posters and slogans. What do you think of this: *A vote for Siena is a vote for yourself.*'

'I think it's dreadful,' I say frankly.

'Why?' Cassidy puzzles. 'Should it be *oneself*?'

'Never mind,' I say. 'Why is Siena having an election campaign?'

'Don't you know?' asks Libby. 'I thought you were the bright one.'

'I suppose I am, even considering the stiff competition –' I watch Phoebe glue her elbow to her knee – 'but that doesn't explain what's going on, or why you're so excited about it. Student politics has nothing in common with high-end fashion, you know.'

'We've never exactly loved the sound of student politics,' Phoebe understates clangingly. 'It's so . . . dusty.' She sends a stray copy of the School Rules hurtling like a missile so that it chips the skirting board. 'But Siena's going to change all that.'

'How is she, when my rabbit is more politically aware than she is?'

'For a start, I'm Siena's campaign manager,' Libby explains. 'I'll add professionalism to proceedings.'

'That's ridiculous,' I say. 'She doesn't need a campaign manager!'

'Of course she does,' Libby argues. 'Do you expect her to print her own posters?'

'Schedule her own interviews?' says Phoebe.

'Style herself?' Madison flicks through a *Vogue* feature on *First Lady Fashions*. 'She needs a campaign manager and a glam squad.'

'The glam squad won't include you, Mads,' Libby mutters with a gimlet stare.

I raise my voice. 'The Council nominates the Head Girl, and they nominated me.'

'We think that's very undemocratic,' says Libby. 'Why should the Council choose? What did they do that no one else did? What qualifies them for the job?'

'What did they *do*?' I ask furiously. 'How about sitting in this fusty room for hours on end, year after year, working on budgets and petitions and student rights, just to make your lives better?'

'Apart from that, what did they do?' asks Phoebe placidly.

'The position is under-utilized,' Libby explains. 'The Head Girl should be making crucial decisions that affect us all, like school uniform design and party plans, and how many free afternoons we're allowed, and curfew time. Then people would care enough to vote, and the election would be exciting and relevant to us all, like a royal wedding.'

'How dare you pretend to care about democracy?' I ask. 'The Starlets are the least democratic institution imaginable. You're elitist, malicious, superficial . . . you're a force only for evil.'

'That's untrue. We're literally the opposite of that.' Cassidy holds up a poster of Siena dressed as an angel. 'See?'

'What's in it for you?' I ask. 'Don't tell me you're doing this out of the goodness of your hearts. You don't even have hearts; just pulsating selfishness.'

Phoebe smiles. 'We're going to be Prefects, of course. These will be our seats.'

'Do you even know what that involves?' I ask.

'Not exactly,' she says vaguely. 'I expect Mrs Denbigh will explain it to us.'

'You have to attend meetings with Dr Tringle and the governors, and vote on school policies, and manage a budget, and one of you will have to write minutes, which will be difficult, as none of you knows how to write . . .'

'We could get these matching outfits to meet the governors!' Cassidy jabs excitedly at a picture of the Kennedys.

'I can't believe we never considered a political career before,' says Phoebe, examining it closely. 'Now we finally have a good excuse to buy pink Chanel suits.'

'You're a genius,' Cassidy tells Siena as they all nod. 'I already can't imagine life without this campaign.'

Siena smiles helplessly at me. 'What can I do? They love me unconditionally.'

'I don't know why we're even having this discussion,' I mutter. 'You don't have the power to change the School Rules, no matter how many copies you destroy. The Council chose me as their candidate, and only they can alter that decision.'

Libby stops crayoning Siena's halo. 'It's funny you should mention that. You see . . .'

She gazes at the end of the table, where Avery and Ambrose are blushing furiously.

'No way,' I say, shaking my head. 'You wouldn't.'

'The Council stands for democracy and choice,' falters Avery. 'It's better for everyone if there's more than one candidate.'

'We're also a little concerned about your commitment,' says Ambrose. 'We took you back as Head Girl-elect on the proviso that you'd make up for your lost year. But instead of convincing us that you'd grown during your time away, you organized a very expensive ball.'

Avery nods. 'We lost a great deal of money that night, Romy. Lots of the hired materials were broken. We need a way to recoup our losses, and a high-profile election campaign sounds like a good method. The Starlets bring publicity wherever they go.'

'I'm sorry about the ball,' I say. 'Even though it

271

wasn't my fault. But haven't I done enough to convince you of my sound character? Aside from one incident, for which I was soundly punished, I've always displayed good morals.'

Libby whips out her phone, and everyone receives a meme featuring an image of Siena that blurs and melts into an image of me. Siena is angelic in her pink Cinderella dress, her hair pale and glimmering beneath a golden halo. Beside her, an injured student casts off his crutch as she watches benignly. I'm in bed with Jack, wearing a screwed-up T-shirt and superimposed devil horns. Elisabeth has been transformed into a spitting serpent, and the wall behind me is papered with the Devil Tarot card. *Good Morals, Bad Morals*, is the swirly headline.

'Don't you see what you've done?' I ask Avery. 'You've let the Starlets take over the one thing in this school they didn't already dominate.'

'Siena seems very serious about it,' Bethany says. 'Look at the effort she's making.'

We turn to see her don a sugar-paper crown.

'It's been non-stop work for us all,' agrees Phoebe. 'Look at my cuticles. You'd think I'd been washing dishes. With my *hands*.'

'Siena should definitely have a crown,' murmurs Libby. 'I'll have Tristan design one.'

'Why are you so *angry* about this?' Bethany asks me. 'You're still allowed to compete, and, if you're the best candidate, you'll win.'

'Siena's only doing it so Jack will think she's marriageable,' I say exasperatedly

'And why are you doing it?'

'For all the right reasons!' I say. 'Honour, and integrity, and . . .'

'Jack?' prompts Avery.

Chapter Thirty-nine

Siena

'Where is Jack, anyway?' Phoebe asks. 'Shouldn't he be here?'

'He doesn't need to be,' Libby explains. 'He's the only candidate. Actually, we should probably call him *consort*. I don't think we've explained to Romy the change in protocol this year. Like the fact that from now on, all candidates will run in teams of four. Head Girl, Head Boy, and two campaign managers.'

'That's not fair!' argues Romy. 'What if candidates can't find a team?'

Libby looks unsympathetic. 'We can't be held responsible for people so clueless that they can't find even three friends. We've been propping up inadequates for far too long.'

'Jack and Siena weren't even on speaking terms the last time I checked,' Romy says. 'What makes you think Jack will want to be her teammate?'

'Jack wants to be a success,' shrugs Libby. 'It's time the students had a real role model.'

I'm half listening and half concentrating on my hair. 'That's right,' I say as Phoebe touches up my mascara. 'A real role model.'

Romy sighs and turns her attention to the campaign

posters. 'There's something funny about these. Why are you wearing a wedding dress in all the pictures?'

'It's not a wedding dress,' I say. 'It's a white dress suitable for a variety of occasions, including an election.'

'Why are you and Jack standing at an altar?'

'It's not an altar,' I say. 'It's a lectern suitable for any kind of ceremony, including Elevation.'

'Why's Jack putting a wedding ring on your finger?'

'Who says it's a wedding ring?' I ask. 'It's a generic prototype symbol of victory.'

'Why is Libby dressed as a vicar, marrying you?'

'Clergywear is huge for autumn.' I lick my index finger as I turn the pages of *Vanity Fair*. 'Libby is always ahead of the curve.'

'Siena, why don't you just admit it?' she snaps.

I turn the pages at speed until I reach the end of the magazine, at which point I start again; she snatches it from my hands, throwing it against the wall.

'Admit what?' I say, devoid of distractions. 'You've given me a paper cut.'

'Admit that this so-called campaign is bogus. All you've done is swap *bride* for *Head Girl*, and *engagement* for *Elevation*. Everyone's going to see through you and . . .'

'What are they going to do? As far as I can see, everyone's very happy about their lives actually being glamorous for once.'

'You're wrong,' she says. 'Everyone has more sense.'

She realizes her error as I gesture around the room. It's typical of her to be so unobservant, but her eyes widen as she takes in the Council members' glossy hair; their stylish outfits; their cutting-edge make-up (girls) and shapely eyebrows (boys). We're all proud, because taking on such unprepossessing subjects was something of a reputational risk.

'You've given the Council a makeover?' she gasps. 'What were you thinking?'

'We were *thinking*,' I explain with dignity, 'that we couldn't be expected to spend time in a room with so much body hair. It could make us asthmatic.'

'You're a disgrace,' I tell the room at large.

'You have no idea of the strings we had to pull,' boasts Phoebe. 'Who knew Miu Miu even made clothes in these sizes?'

'You don't condone this?' Romy appeals to Avery. 'You see that it's madness?'

Avery smoothes her highlighted hair and blushes beneath a layer of La Prairie foundation. 'We have to be presentable, Romy. We're the public face of the school.'

'Ambrose?' she says desperately.

Ambrose pushes his new D&G glasses up his nose and taps his YSL loafer. 'We've lived in the shadows for too long. We'll be publicizing the election as much as possible, starting with a Speech Day where each candidate will present their manifesto to the school.'

'Those things are just propaganda,' she says. 'They pressure people to make promises they won't keep, and undermine the integrity of the whole system.'

I'm not keen on a Speech Day either, to say the least, but I'm pleased to have found a weak spot in her. 'What a wonderful idea,' I say warmly. 'I have an unrivalled stage presence, as I'm sure you know.'

'Siena is a five-time winner of the Best Actress TEMPA,' confirms Libby, producing a photograph of me accepting my statuette at the last ceremony. 'I can play you her showreel. The *Tribune* described her Juliet as 'breathtakingly moving, and—'

'It's not supposed to be acting,' Romy says. 'You're supposed to give a cerebral speech about what you can offer the school.'

'Whatever Siena does on Speech Day, she'll win,' says Libby. 'We're throwing everything we have at this campaign, and our straw poll proved that Siena's fans want to see her in Head Girl chic. We've even abandoned our bikini car wash in aid of the white rhino.'

'You had no more interest in the white rhino than you do in politics,' Romy says.

'I had much interest in it,' I correct her. 'White is very easy to accessorize.'

'White rhinos aren't white, you moron!' she explodes. 'What do you think they look like?'

'Do they have a horn?' I ask Libby, who nods. 'A bit

like unicorns, I suppose. Next year we should support unicorns instead. Unicorns are definitely white, aren't they?'

I look to Romy for confirmation, but, instead of replying, she slumps into her chair as if she can no longer hold herself up. Libby high-fives me, and then Phoebe on her other side, and I smile at Romy as we await her inevitable resignation.

Chapter Forty

Romy

Siena might be the most talented in our Art class, but she takes pains to share her disdain for the department. Even today, when she's supposed to be soliciting support from potential voters ahead of tomorrow's Speech Day, she wrinkles her nose as she flounces to her desk. 'Motley crew,' she mutters to the room at large.

'We're in an art studio,' I say. 'Do you expect people to wear Prada?'

'Yes. Whereas no doubt you consider a messy room an excuse for everyone to go to sartorial hell in . . . in some kind of *backpack*.'

She glances conceitedly at her pink pencil skirt and white jacket before wincing at my pebble-dashed overalls. She's showcasing an even higher-octane wardrobe this term, and she seems to go out of her way to look perfect in here, as if she wants the rest of us to benefit from her example.

'Mr Kidd,' she pleads, raising her hand. 'I'd like a new partner. Romy's outfit is inhumanely ugly, and could even be a carrier of infection.'

Mr Kidd is bearded and grandfatherly; he usually, like all men, lets Siena have her way, and I prepare to gather my belongings and move seats.

'I'm sorry to hear that,' he says blandly. 'But it's too late. You should already be well under way with your project, and today I'm asking some of you to present your work to the class. As you don't like sitting so close to Romy, why don't you start us off?'

She opens her mouth incredulously, but he's already introducing her.

Siena hasn't the slightest interest in discovering my inspirations, and has spent every lesson so far staring into space and using art tools as beauty products. 'I expect you haven't even started, have you?' I ask.

She bats her eyelashes at Mr Kidd, and I'm looking forward to her ridiculous excuse for having nothing to exhibit when she moves to stand in front of my dust-sheet-covered painting.

'I'm flattered to be asked to present first,' she says sincerely. 'But I'd like to share some of the limelight with someone who lives mostly in gloom. Romy, please come up and tell us all about your wonderful work!'

She removes the dust sheet with a flourish and starts an applause that the other students half-heartedly continue.

'I really, really hate you,' I mutter as I take her place at the front of the room, wondering where to start and wishing I'd listened harder when Siena explained her inspiration in such detail that there should be no excuse for getting it wrong.

'Our brief is *Inspiration*,' I say laconically as I gesture at my giant portrait of Siena wearing a white dress. 'As you can see, Siena's inspiration is *Siena*.'

Siena whips her head around as someone sniggers. I'm surprised at this overt rebellion, but then the Art crowd are a law unto themselves. They've never fitted into any circle of popularity, and tend to ignore Siena in a way most students would never dare. Her attitude certainly doesn't stand up against their own inspirations, which include Frida Kahlo, Harriet Tubman and a decorated war veteran.

'Does anyone have any questions for Romy?' asks Mr Kidd. 'Remember that her job is to convince you of the worth of her project.'

Christopher raises his hand. His face is serious but his lip twitches as if he's holding back a smile. 'How does Siena inspire people?'

'She invented the Starlets, of course,' I explain, remembering her briefing notes. 'Everyone wants to be a Starlet.'

'I don't want to be a Starlet,' Christopher says. As more students laugh, I remember Libby encouraging everyone to make fun of his goatee beard until he shaved it off.

'Me neither,' says Christopher's partner Angus. I remember that Phoebe once tripped him up into a wet ochre canvas, and that he didn't get a new blazer for almost a year. 'What else?'

I muster the strength to continue, quoting directly from her brief. 'Everyone copies Siena's hair, her

281

clothes and her attitude. Everyone wants to look like her. Everyone wants to *be* her. She's Temperley High's ultimate brand.'

'When's the last time Siena helped anyone?' puts in Annabelle, an erstwhile Starlet wannabe. Libby told her she headed a waiting list that didn't exist, encouraging her to trail them ever more desperately until my conscience pricked me enough to tell her the truth.

Seconds tick by before Siena prompts me by pointing at her feet. 'She helped Phoebe choose her shoes this morning. Phoebe thought she wanted to wear nude pumps, but it turned out that pink courts better complement her calf muscles.'

Annabelle has also noticed Siena's shoes. 'So it wasn't because Siena wanted to wear Phoebe's nude pumps today?'

Siena stands up in annoyance. 'This is slander.'

'I've only given answers from our interview,' I protest. 'How can it be slander when I'm quoting you directly?'

'You're quoting me *selectively*,' she says. 'You've completely disregarded my charitable work.'

I sigh. 'Classmates, Siena spent last term preparing to strip to a bikini in order to protect the unicorn from extinction.'

Christopher laughs and raises his hand again, addressing Siena directly. 'What will people say about you when you're dead?'

'People will say the *nicest* things,' she says. 'And my

influence will ensure that the mourners at my funeral are appropriately stylish.'

Mr Kidd clears his throat. 'Perhaps we could stop planning funerals and return to the lesson. Siena, give us your opinion on Romy's interpretation.'

'Romy hasn't fulfilled the brief,' she says. 'It's unimaginative. You told us to find out details about each other, like the best and worst moments of our lives, so that we could render *Inspiration* in a new and interesting way.'

Mr Kidd nods encouragingly. 'Tell us, then. What was the worst day of your life?'

'The day my baby sister was born,' she says, and then blushes furiously.

'You see?' I appeal. 'My painting shows her in a better light than she deserves. And at least I'm trying! When's she going to give some thought to my *Inspiration*?'

'You're a photographer,' she says. 'That's not even art. Anyone with opposable thumbs could do it, so I only need to allow myself five minutes to rustle something up.'

Mr Kidd has lost patience. 'We'll revisit this next lesson. I hope you're taking it more seriously than you appear to be, Siena.'

I'm too angry with her to let this pass. 'You *bitch*,' I say as soon as he's gone. I dip a paintbrush in the emulsion with which Hattie is coating her clay panda and flick it at her. Black spatters her white Balmain jacket.

'Look what you've done!' she says, holding up her sleeve. 'You can pay for that.'

I shrug as I ruin her other sleeve with a second flick. 'I don't think so. How many times have you been warned about wearing appropriate clothes around paint?'

She picks up a can with which Tristan is lovingly depicting the Royal Standard. I dodge, but, instead of throwing the contents over me, she tosses it right over her portrait. Red paint runs down the length of the canvas, obscuring her face, her neck and her white dress, until the image of her is completely gone.

Mr Kidd emerges from the supply cupboard and stops short. 'What happened?' he splutters in disbelief. 'Who did this?'

I open my mouth to tell him that Siena has destroyed my work out of pure spite. But all I see is red paint.

'Weeks of work,' he says to me. 'What will you do now?'

My mother taught me to read people using their facial expressions; their reactions to exploratory questions; their involuntary desire to feed helpful details. Siena is immune to those tricks. I've tried to ignore my inability to guess at her future, but, as paint covers her lovely features until they might never have existed on the canvas, I feel something I've never felt; something that makes me shake involuntarily and turn towards her to check that she's still there.

Mr Kidd looks from one of us to the other. 'I don't know what's going on, but I suggest you remedy it while you still can,' he says quietly.

'How could you do that to me?' I ask her when he's gone.

She seems a little stunned. 'I'll paint you another one. Our styles are similar enough that he'll never know.'

'I don't need your help,' I say. 'But if you think I'm going to give you an easy ride from now on, you can think again.'

'I don't want an easy ride,' she says. 'We both know who the final curtain belongs to, and you're just complicating the inevitable.'

She ducks through the dust sheets by the door. But the stark image of red on a white dress, white curtains, a white moonlight, hasn't dissipated by the time my vision clears several minutes later.

Chapter Forty-one

Siena

'Cut.' Madison sighs patiently as I stare at the script Libby has provided for Speech Day, trying to memorize it. *Romy is dangerous* is the upshot, but there are so many adjectives that it won't stay in my head.

'Don't cut again!' groans Phoebe as Cassidy claps the board. 'I can't bear it.'

'I had no choice,' Madison says. 'What take are we on now?'

Cassidy erases 43 and chalks 44, then tries to hide the evidence. 'Only about seven,' she lies. 'Hardly any at all.'

'I need a time out with my client,' says Libby. 'Where's the stand-in?'

Bethany rushes onto my mark as I exit the stage, sitting on my canvas chair as Nicole drapes a dressing gown over my shoulders.

'Must you be quite so *wooden*?' says Madison.

'I'm not wooden!' I modulate my words into an interesting tonal sequence. 'My Best Actress TEMPAs speak for themselves.'

'If you can play Olga, and Éponine, and Ophelia, then why are you so bad at playing yourself?'

'I don't know,' I frown. 'Maybe I need more time to go method.'

'You've had seventeen years to go method. You know that you *are* yourself, right?'

'We only have an hour left.' Cassidy offers a can of Diet Coke with a straw in it so I don't smudge my lip gloss. 'We don't have time to explore any other techniques.'

Libby is scowling. 'It's disastrous. You promised you had everything in hand, Siena, but you're not even trying. And what happened to your *Inspiration* portrait? You were supposed to deliver your speech in front of it.'

'My artwork has since taken another direction,' I say. 'It isn't a problem. I have this in the bag.'

'Why are you so sure?' asks Madison. 'Romy is a good actress too. She usually gets the Best Supporting Actress TEMPA, and people say that character parts are more challenging, especially as we never include them in the costume budget.'

'Character parts are *not* more challenging,' I correct her. 'They're a theatrical meal ticket for unattractive people.'

'You haven't learned Libby's speech,' says Madison. 'What are you going to do?'

'Speeches are for the undecorative,' I say. 'I'll use my slot to stand onstage and have people look at me.'

I'm not sure,' she frowns. 'You might look lightweight without *anything* to say.'

'Everyone's on my side,' I shrug, hoping they never find out about the Art class's dissent. 'I'm a pro.'

'Not everyone's on your side,' ventures Cassidy.

'The Council have changed allegiance and are supporting Romy.'

'*What?*' asks Libby. 'Why didn't you mention this before?'

Cassidy shrinks into her chair. 'It only just happened. Apparently Romy called a meeting this morning and promised to make them all Prefects if she was elected.'

'*We* promised to make them Prefects too!' Phoebe says in outrage. 'We reassured them *at length* that their positions were safe and that we'd treat them with the same respect as Romy would.'

'We were lying,' Cassidy reminds her. 'Romy revealed our plans to eradicate the Council and hold Prefects' meetings in Soho House. Apparently they were upset to hear that we've got planning permission to convert their meeting room into a hot yoga studio.'

Libby glares at Bethany with such ferocity that I fear for her safety. 'Stand-in, you're fired,' she barks as Bethany flees. 'You'll never work in this school again.'

'After we were kind enough to give them all makeovers?' Phoebe whips off my dressing-gown cord and flexes it until Nicole also backs out of the hall. 'And *makeover* is a total understatement for the hard labour we put in. *Major renovation* is more like it. Does bribery count for nothing?'

'The Council are irrelevant.' I wish I felt as confident as I sound. 'No one cares what they do, so we have everyone that matters on our side.'

288

Chapter Forty-two

Romy

'Is that right?' I assume an unconcerned smile as the Starlets swing around to face me. 'Have you actually *asked* any of the students if they're on your side?'

'Don't be so foolish,' Siena says. 'We don't speak to them directly.'

'Students will vote for someone they can relate to, who will represent their views and understand them,' I tell her. 'It's the *underdog* that people will support, not the spoiled princess. Jane Eyre, not Estella Havisham.'

'I hardly think that the students would choose someone gloomy and northern over the most aspirational heroine in literature,' she argues.

'You're missing the point,' I say. 'How can you be relevant to students when you only socialize with each other?'

'We socialize with many people,' contests Phoebe. 'We maintain a constant dialogue with the Stripes, for example.'

She gestures proudly at the group of Stripes, minus Jack, that Libby has gathered together as Siena's test audience. They've been alternately falling asleep and muttering to each other, but return to wakefulness as Phoebe blows them a kiss.

'The Stripes don't count, because you don't really *talk* to them,' I say. 'You order them around and periodically hook up with them. You can't even tell them apart.'

'That's not true,' Siena bristles as some of the Stripes look hurt. 'They all have their own distinct personalities, and each one of them is a very valued friend.'

'Name them,' I suggest.

'They don't need me to do that,' she says, smiling at them warmly. Most of them look slightly hypnotized, but one – Sam, not that she'd know – stands up. I remember that Phoebe kissed him recently and has since avoided his calls.

He addresses Phoebe directly, but she stares without recognition. 'Romy's right. If you want our votes, show that you care about us as more than serfs.'

'We must know them all,' Phoebe murmurs to Siena. 'Even if it's just by osmosis.'

'They're familiar, of course,' Siena muses. 'But collectively they blend into a soup of quiffs and aftershave. It's easier to refer to them by number.'

She stands in front of them. 'Sam,' she says correctly, moving down the line at speed. 'Harry. Fergus. Miles. James. Spencer. Taylor. Evan. That's everyone.'

'You missed two,' I interrupt. 'And you got some wrong.'

'Amadeo,' she says with a fresh burst of inspiration. 'And Gaston.'

'Aren't they from the *Eligible Young Royals* list you

keep under your pillow?' I ask. 'And who the hell is Evan?'

'That one!' She points at Steven. 'Mads went out with him.'

'I did not,' Madison says hotly. 'I went out with Eight.'

'You went out with Three,' corrects Phoebe. 'Cassidy dated Eight.'

'Wasn't he called *Ewan*?' Cassidy frowns.

'How dare you!' squeaks Four – *James* – as the others nod in outrage. 'We'd never disrespect you like this.'

Other students enter the hall, and I take advantage of the extended audience. 'If you don't know the Stripes, you definitely don't know anyone else. Why should anyone vote for you when you can't be bothered to learn their names?'

The Stripes emerge, empowered, from a brief team huddle. 'We're voting for Romy,' announces Sam. 'She hasn't dated any of us and not returned our calls, and she knows all our names.'

'Thanks, guys,' I say gratefully. 'I promise I'll always value your human qualities, and not your six-packs.'

Spencer, a powerhouse of bulk and protein shakes, is visibly touched. 'I never thought I'd hear a girl say that. It's not easy to be judged on looks alone. There's so much more to us, and we're individuals, as well as a team.'

'You lost us the Stripes!' Libby says in outrage. 'How *dare* you encourage them to think independently?'

'We need them tonight,' Phoebe says. 'They're our ushers!'

The Stripes form another huddle, in which I distinctly hear them debate the merits of regular hook-ups versus self-worth, and then they throw a pile of suits at Phoebe. 'Do it yourself,' says James as they stalk away. 'We deserve better.'

Mrs Denbigh steps between Libby and me. 'Seats, girls,' she says pleasantly.

'I'm sitting with Siena on stage,' Libby tells her. 'I'm her campaign manager.'

'However many times you say it, a campaign manager will never be a real thing,' I say. 'Notice that Jack and I don't have one.'

Mrs Denbigh nods. 'You can sit in the wings, if you like, Libby. We could use somebody to open and close the curtains.'

'We need you down here, Libby,' whines Phoebe as she, Madison and Cassidy stoically don top hats and oversized blazers. 'We can't control the crowds without you.'

'I need to be close to Siena,' Libby decides.

'Thanks a lot,' mutters Madison as she picks up a giant box of pink *Siena* rosettes and starts to stick them to chairs.

I pause before following Siena to the stage. 'Do you really think this is the best thing for her?'

Madison looks around furtively. 'No. I wish she'd give it up.'

'So will you help me to win instead?'

She shakes her head violently. 'Don't include me in this.'

'They're treating you horribly,' I remind her. 'They're marginalizing you. You might as well have some principles.'

Libby shouts at her to *stop slacking*, and she slowly nods her head. 'Fine. I suppose there's nothing left to lose.'

Chapter Forty-three

Siena

'Happy now?' I ask as Romy joins me on stage. 'Or will you be stirring up more trouble?'

'No,' she says innocently. 'I'm just musing on the fact that this is all sort of ironic.'

I want to ignore her, but she's reeled me in. 'What's ironic?'

'You've done such a good job of making the Starlets do your bidding that you've qualified them for a future without you. You're a vacuum that they plough their talents into.'

'That's not true, *or* ironic,' I say.

She fixes her emerald eyes on me. 'The irony is that you're merely the embodiment of Cassidy's vanity case, and Madison's mood boards, and Phoebe's attitude, and Libby's organization. Once they fly the coop – and they will, as soon as they discover a world beyond your face – you won't exist. And most ironic is that, although they spend every waking hour catering to your every need, the only person who knows you at all is me.'

'You're wrong,' I say, although it doesn't help my case that, right now, Phoebe, Cassidy and Madison are busily showing students to their seats wearing men's suits.

'What are they *doing*?' she asks.

'They're ushers,' I say, 'but I'm not exactly sure what that entails.'

'I think ushers show the wedding party to the bride or the groom's side of the church,' she says. 'They're splitting the audience according to whom they're supporting.'

'Your side will be a bit sparse, then,' I say, ignoring the fact that the Council have taken their seats on Romy's side alongside the newly activist Stripes. I exhale in silent relief when the lights go up to reveal the crowd, showing my side still notably fuller than hers.

'Your chairs have pink rosettes and mine have . . . screwed-up newspaper,' she says. 'How lovely.'

As the only male candidate, Jack isn't giving a speech, but he sits between us anyway. Folding my arms and staring ahead, I force a smile as Dr Tringle, and then Avery and Ambrose, discuss the importance of the Head Girl position at interminable length before introducing Romy.

She's wearing her usual jeans and vest top, her unbrushed hair cascading down her back. I feel irritated that she moves so easily in her ballet shoes while I limp in heels; that she runs her hand through her hair without trapping it in adornments; that she eats what she likes without considering the fit of custom-made clothes. I imagine for a moment how this must feel, and then I dismiss it.

Her supporters cheer while I wait for her to fall on her face with an ill-judged remark about the teachers, making Jack see that I was born to be Head Girl (and, by extension, his wife), thus fully restoring equilibrium. I almost want to alert my mother to the good news right now, and I'm so cheered that I start to plan our reconciliation: Jack's reintroduction at our next dinner party, and an exciting Upper Sixth with him by my side.

But when I sneak a glance at him, those things seem irrelevant, and I meander into distractions like his citrus smell when he comes out of the shower, the tickle of his hair on my cheek when he kisses my collarbone, and the feeling I get when we sit in the courtyard listening to the clock without saying a word because it's nice just to watch time pass, storing our memories and anticipating the unreleased seconds and minutes ahead of us.

'Classmates,' Romy says easily, taking the lectern with both hands. It hasn't occurred to me until this moment how much support she might be able to gather, but perhaps it should have, because the Starlets have always had what we call *critical friends*, and they're a resolute presence on her side of the hall. Nor has it occurred to me how well matched she and Jack really are, and how much more he has in common with her than with me. *Of course he likes her.* I hunch over my shoes and search my mind for something – anything – that will count as a speech to make him respect me as he respects her.

'I don't believe in organized politics,' she says, and some of the more liberal students transfer from my side to hers. 'But then I realized that, while I can't address most of the world's problems – I mean, everyone recycles and has an adopted Cambodian goat, but do these things really make a difference? – I can do something to help right here.'

A conglomerate of slackers lazily unwind themselves from their seats on my side – where it occurs to me they may only have sat because it was closest – and join Romy's. Our support is now even.

'I care about this school,' she continues. 'I cared enough to come back after I got kicked out. I cared enough to give this speech. I cared enough to stand for Head Girl when no one else wanted the job and there were no associated benefits, and I prepared for it with four years on the Student Council.

'I also did something else to prepare, which, let's face it, took a lot of self-sacrifice. Does anyone know what that was?'

'Trying to murder Libby?' someone shouts. Laughter erupts, and not, I feel, at Romy's expense. A group of girls who've experienced the rough edge of Libby on a couple of occasions deliberately join Romy's side, putting her in the lead.

'Not quite,' she says. 'I joined the Starlets.'

The crowd is silent and I shift back my chair so I don't have to look directly at Libby.

'You'll have noticed that I don't fit in with them,' she says candidly. 'I've asked myself many times why they made me a member. My best guess is that, what they don't understand, they take over and crush.

'So when you cast your vote, you should consider what you stand for, and who you want to stand for *you*. Because I know from personal experience that everything brought under the control of the Starlets ends up like *this* – frightened and completely absurd.'

With that she pulls out a quivering pink rabbit from her pocket and places it on the lectern, to thunderous applause.

Chapter Forty-four

Romy

'What the hell was that?' Siena leans across Jack towards me as I return to my seat. I expected anger, but she seems bewildered. 'You betrayed us!'

'I betrayed *you*?'

'We made you popular,' she says. 'It's not our fault if you're unhappy. We made your life easier than it would have otherwise been.'

'*Easier*? You've ruined everything! It's impossible to be Head Girl and a Starlet at the same time.'

'You couldn't be more wrong,' she says. 'It's perfectly possible to be both.'

'Prove it,' I say. 'Prove right now that you're capable of saying something sensible.'

Jack looks worried as her name is called. 'Siena, I'm not sure that you should do this. There are plenty of things you're good at, but I'm not sure that politics . . .'

She shakes him off, throwing back one last defiant glance as she takes to the lectern.

'This should be good,' I mutter, and then I'm cut off from the audience as Libby powers the curtain so that Siena appears to be the only presence on stage.

'It doesn't matter what you do,' I hiss at her. 'Hiding me doesn't give Siena a brain.'

Then I fall silent, because Siena isn't behaving as if she's at a party, or at London Fashion Week, or on a yacht; she's behaving exactly as if she's giving a campaign speech suitable for teachers and students alike. The audience is silent, not because they're flattered that she's addressing them, but because she finally has something to say. Judging by the speed at which chairs are scraping, I sense that her support is growing with every word.

I'm here to explain why I'm the best, and indeed the only, person to fulfil this role.

'She didn't write this,' I tell Jack.

'Credit where it's due,' he says. 'She might have wasted potential.'

'She's running an *engagement* campaign, not an *election* campaign.'

'She's over that,' he says. 'I'm sure she sees it as a moment of madness.'

I promise to give the same dedication to the post of Head Girl as I've given to every other activity I've participated in at Temperley High.

'She doesn't,' I insist as more chairs scrape. 'She thinks that reinventing herself will make you fall in love with her again. It's all calculated.'

'Siena needs time to work out what she wants without stupid considerations like marriage. It's the last thing on her mind.'

'The audience is a wedding congregation!' I look for something to back me up. Siena has left her bag under her chair, and I kick it so that a pile of campaign leaflets fall out.

'Look properly at these,' I say urgently. 'They were going to be your engagement party invitations. You can see the old writing underneath!'

He looks closely at a poster of him and Siena at a mocked-up Elevation ceremony, and his face darkens. *Join us to celebrate this joyous occasion . . .*

'Soon these will be all over school, and Elevation will be your engagement party,' I say hurriedly. 'She's backing you into a corner.'

'This is . . . crazy,' he says, shaking his head. 'To say the least.'

'She could win this,' I say. 'She only needs your endorsement, and then she has the whole election in the bag.'

'So if I endorse you instead . . .'

'I'm back in the game. Just because you chose her once doesn't mean you have to again. This time you could choose me.'

'How do I choose you?' he asks. 'For all we know, she's already won.'

He hesitates as I lean towards him. 'You know this is for her own good,' I say. 'Choose me, and she'll throw the speech.'

When Siena glances at us, I kiss him. He doesn't resist, and I focus on the movement of his lips against mine. But we break apart to two jarring sounds: a screech as she drops her microphone, and a whirring as

Libby whizzes open the curtain and exposes us to the room.

The audience is silent, the two sides equally populated, but as Siena stands mute before her fallen microphone, my supporters start to shift, clique by clique, until her side is full and mine deserted. The Council who promised me so faithfully; the Stripes who wanted to be treated as individuals; everyone stands in silent support of her alleged love for Jack as silent tears spill down her cheeks.

Libby joins her in the centre of the stage, but she shakes her off. 'Why did you do that? How could you?'

Libby is open-mouthed in shock. 'I exposed Romy! I won this for you!'

Siena shakes her head. 'You humiliated us all. Jack and I aren't together, and he has a right to be with whomever he wants.'

'He does not,' Libby says emphatically. 'He's going to marry you!'

'How?' she asks. 'Will you handcuff him and force him down the aisle?'

'If that's what it takes,' says Libby. 'You mustn't give up now.'

'Jack deserves to be happy,' she says as she walks away from her standing ovation. 'What makes him happy is no longer up to me.'

Chapter Forty-five

Siena

I'm sleeping, or as sure as I can be of that fact, when bony fingers shake me hard. 'Get up,' hisses a familiar voice. 'We don't have much time.'

'No bell, no foul,' I mutter.

The shaking continues until I throw back my duvet and snap on my lamp. 'Go away,' I tell Libby. 'You too,' I add to Phoebe, who's standing behind her.

'What on earth are you wearing?' Phoebe giggles as she takes in my outfit. 'Is that what passes as a nightdress these days?'

I fold my arms across my chest and scowl at her. 'I told you to go away.'

'I thought you were a morning person.' Phoebe flicks through a copy of my manifesto, reading aloud in a poor imitation of my voice. '*I love summer sunrise, and can often be found outside meditating, doing a spot of surprise gardening for an elderly neighbour, or simply watching the horizon and wondering what blessings the day will bring . . .*'

'You're responsible for that drivel, I presume?' I ask Libby. 'Even though I've never seen this time of day before?'

'That's not true,' Phoebe says. 'Last week we spent

a beautiful sunrise by the boating lake.'

'It doesn't count if you've been up all night,' I say. 'Now, please leave and we'll put this down to temporary insanity.'

'This is important.' Libby throws something furry at me. 'Get up and put this on.'

'She's wide awake,' Phoebe mutters. 'We've missed our window to overpower her.'

'We haven't,' Libby asserts as if I can't hear. 'We still have the element of surprise. Siena, *put that on*.'

'That yeti outfit?' I ask, kicking the fur.

'It's a rabbit costume,' she corrects, as if this is better. 'Your final campaign task is an Easter egg hunt for the Shells. There's a sack of eggs outside; you just have to scatter them.'

'Easter was months ago,' I protest.

'In which case there's no time to lose,' says Libby triumphantly.

'I can't.' I'm almost crying as they push me into a pair of fake fluffy feet and zip me into a mound of fur. 'Don't make me. Anything but this.'

'You have to be strong,' says Phoebe.

My hair is loose down my back, and I reach to tie it up, but as I do so Libby shoves my arms into furry sleeves complete with paws. 'No time for that,' she says breathlessly. 'Once you start on your hair we'll be here all day.'

She twists my hair into limp submission and shoves handfuls of it into the hood.

'I'm claustrophobic,' I say as she looms over me. 'What if I die in here?'

'No one ever died inside a rabbit costume,' Phoebe says.

'How do you know?' I moan.

She takes my hands, hidden somewhere inside giant furry paws, and squeezes them hard. 'It'll be over soon. It's an hour of your life, tops.'

'But the humiliation,' I sob. 'Libby, do something.'

'We have no choice,' Libby says. 'Your Speech Day victory was helpful, but not all students will vote for crying alone. We have to convert those who want a fun Head Girl. Romy is all about the fun.'

'This isn't fun. Fun is holidaying on Necker, or shopping at Dior, or losing weight, or . . .'

'It's not supposed to be fun for *you*,' she clarifies. 'You're creating fun for others.'

'I do that constantly,' I begin, but then Phoebe shoves an elasticated rabbit nose and whiskers onto my face before pulling my hood back up.

'How will she rope in Jack?' she asks Libby. 'She shouldn't handle him directly.'

'What does Jack have to do with this?' I ask. 'Don't tell me . . .'

Libby gestures to a second rabbit costume on the floor. 'You won't regret this. Elevation night is going to be our greatest ever two-birds-with-one-stone feat. We'll soon be running the school, and you'll be back with Jack.'

'Don't you mean *three* birds?' asks Phoebe.

'Why three?' I ask. It's uncomfortable to be slower than Phoebe.

'Getting rid of Romy? Restoring the natural order? She can't possibly come back next year after such a humiliating defeat.'

'Yes, of course,' I say quickly. 'I counted wrongly.'

Phoebe can relate to this, and I allow myself three seconds to consider the oddly dismal prospect of another Romy-less year. Then I dismiss it, because next year will be a new era entirely, in which I'll be too busy even to remember her.

Jack's room is in darkness, and I curse as I knock something with my stupid fake feet and send it crashing.

'What the hell?' Jack snaps on the light and sits up, looking utterly confused.

I tug at my rabbit whiskers. 'It's me.'

'I can see that.' Despite his confusion, he's actually smiling; my heart leaps as I realize how painfully I've missed that smile. 'Have you been at the diazepam? Or have I?'

I feel my rictus grin relax. 'I thought this would be fun. It's a surprise Easter egg hunt for the Shells.'

'It's not Easter,' he says. 'And you think the Shells are a nuisance.'

'That's why it's a big surprise,' I say. 'And I don't think they're a nuisance. I just haven't had the

306

opportunity to get to know them.'

'How do I fit into this?' he asks as I throw his costume at him. 'As if I couldn't guess.'

'You hardly have to do anything. And it'll give you a great sense of wellbeing.'

He gets out of bed, running his hand through his messy hair and stretching before he pulls the costume over his boxer shorts. I deliberately avert my eyes from his bare chest, but not soon enough; he sees me watching, and we both blush.

'Come on.' He snaps on his whiskers and drapes an arm casually around me as we leave the room. 'Who made these costumes, anyway?'

'Mads, of course.'

'Mads?' he says in surprise. 'So she's really on your side? You're playing a very dangerous game, you know. If they find out . . .'

I'm not sure what he means, but I feel sufficiently ashamed of my recent treatment of Madison to change the subject. 'Do you like the costumes?'

'Very much,' he says drily. 'Whose idea was this?'

'Mine,' I say untruthfully. 'I love spontaneous good deeds.'

I point at our sack of eggs as we walk outside. 'Pick that up.'

He laughs. 'You sound exactly like . . . I mean, nice impression.'

Still confused, I raise an eyebrow until he laughs again. 'Let me carry that for you,' he says with a note of sarcasm, throwing it over his shoulder.

Libby has promised to follow us at a distance, taking supposedly unauthorized photographs that we can publish later to publicize my random act of kindness. The images will be clear enough to identify me, but nothing more; that's the deal.

But when the sack is empty, Jack puts two fingers to his mouth and whistles. I wince in horror as the Shells start to gather at their dormitory windows, giggling and pointing.

'Anyone for chocolate?' he calls nonchalantly, holding up an egg.

They disappear, and, moments later, stream towards us. Close up, they're little and childlike in regulation dressing gowns, and it strikes me how young they are to be living away from their families.

'It's hard to believe we were once this small, isn't it?' he asks, echoing my thoughts as I imagine Stella being here; Stella, who has never played games like this in her life. I'm suddenly grateful that her home existence, her ever-clean clothes and hushed hallways and no carbs and sterilized indoor activities and vetted friends, will soon be replaced by these rough-and-tumble children who giggle and crawl into undergrowth and cram chocolate into their mouths as if it won't make them fat. I'm so occupied by these thoughts that, when the Shells approach to thank me, I make up my mind to encourage Stella to befriend girls like this instead of debutantes who have been formed and moulded so that they're beautiful above all else. I make up my mind to be a sister that Stella will feel proud of; a sister who leads and assists rather than one who floats and preens.

We step back as the Shells' housemistress, Miss Finch, appears to take them inside. Libby has fallen into step with her, explaining and negotiating until Miss Finch, worn down by sheer force of personality, shrugs in assent.

Jack's face darkens at the sight of her. 'What's Libby doing here?'

'She needs to take some pictures to make sure we're credited.'

'Credited?' he asks. 'I thought we were doing a good deed.'

'Of course,' I agree. 'A good deed and a vote winner rolled into one.'

'What are you talking about?' His bewilderment intensifies as Romy appears on her way out of Woodlands. He looks from me, to Romy, and back again.

'You tricked me into spending time with you, *Siena*.' His voice is suddenly harsh.

'*Tricked* you?' I ask. 'I don't understand . . .' Then his confusing comments fall into place. 'You thought I was Romy?'

He laughs. 'You knew that's what I'd think! Why else would you wear a disguise?'

'It's a rabbit costume!' I raise my voice. 'I didn't

want anyone to know it was me.'

Libby undermines this statement somewhat as she runs around, trying to photograph our best angles. 'Take off your whiskers,' she shouts. 'Put your arms around each other!'

I'm too ashamed for Jack to see me undisguised. We stand deadlocked as the bell rings and Sixth Formers swarm out to join us.

'I want to go inside,' I tell Libby, but I can't get away before Romy confronts us.

'What's going on?' she asks angrily.

'Siena doesn't want anyone to know it's her under there,' Jack explains. 'Including me, apparently.'

'I'm not surprised,' Romy says. 'She stole those costumes.'

'*Stole* them?' I ask. 'Mads made these costumes.'

'Mads made them for *my* Easter egg hunt. This is low even for you, Siena.'

Madison pushes her way towards us, looking uncertainly between me and Romy.

'Mads, Romy is under the impression that you made these costumes for her,' Libby says, her tone fakely casual. 'That would mean you were helping her beat Siena in the election. I expect you can explain this massive misunderstanding.'

Madison looks scared; Romy waits with an expression of resignation.

'Mads?' I say uncertainly. 'Did you make these costumes for Romy's campaign?'

'Tell the truth, Mads,' says Libby sweetly. 'Do you want Romy to win? Are you renouncing your Starlet membership? Because you should know that Siena has no more need of you as a designer. She's using a different fashion house for her Elevation dress.'

'Not because I don't trust you,' I say. 'I just didn't . . . tell you.'

'Romy misunderstood,' whispers Madison in the least convincing lie I've ever seen. 'I'm on your side, Siena.'

She's trembling as she waits to be told that I forgive her. Seeing her so fearful of a group who pretend to be her friends, yet will ruin her with the slightest excuse, horrifies me even as I witness the ease with which my behaviour can sway votes. I search for the real connections I've formed with my peers, and I can't identify a single one.

My costume is so claustrophobic that I can't bear it for another second. I unzip the fur and step out of it, kicking it away and remembering too late that my pyjamas comprise Jack's spare football kit, complete with his name and number.

His derisive expression flickers, just for a second. 'You've gained a few votes, I'd say.'

'That's not why I . . .' I break off.

'I know why you did it,' he says dismissively. 'And yet . . .'

'Yet what?' It strikes me as odd that once I had all the time in the world to listen to him, and I listened only to the thoughts in my head. Now, as I absorb every word he speaks, there are ever fewer to cling to.

'Yet . . . maybe, before it's too late, you might show me who you really are.'

Before I can ask him what he means, he's gone.

Chapter Forty-six

Romy

After my sixth Election Day phone call from Libby, I'm ready to push her off something higher than a clock tower, and a knock on my bedroom door heralds the limit of my patience.

'*What?*' I snap as I throw it open.

'Sorry,' Jack says penitently. 'Actually, I'm not sorry. You need to come with me.'

'I haven't had time to get ready,' I argue. 'Libby keeps phoning me about bunting.'

He shrugs at my shorts and vest. 'You look the same as ever.'

'Thanks a lot,' I mutter as I push my feet into flip-flops and follow him down the corridor.

'You're welcome,' he says. 'I like the way you look. Sometimes Siena takes so long to get ready that it's barely worth going out at all.'

He imbues this criticism with such long-suffering affection that I stop short. 'What's this about?' I ask suspiciously. 'Where are we going?'

He doesn't say any more, but leads me across the courtyard to the Art studio. 'Is this an elaborate plan to drown me in paint?' I ask, hanging back.

'I'm not that organized,' he says as we reach the darkroom.

'We can't go in there,' I say. 'We might destroy a masterpiece.'

'We won't,' he says as he unlocks the door. 'I have permission.'

With no time for photography until my replacement painting is finished, I haven't been in here for a while, and today it's a hundred years away from my last visit. A huge project is in progress, and hanging from the ceiling, propped up against the walls, and covering every work surface, are images that are at once painfully familiar and utterly extraordinary.

'Did you know about this?' I stammer as I step inside.

'Not until this morning, when Siena brought me the key. It's your *Inspiration*.'

I stare around open-mouthed. There's nothing here that links directly to Siena, and yet her influence is everywhere. The photographs appear at first to depict Temperley High students through the years, but on closer glance are something else entirely. I see the Council, and the Stripes, and the Starlets, and students who have never fitted into any clique or club, but none of this giant collage makes sense.

Eric stands fearlessly with his rocks beside Madison showcasing spring-summer espadrilles beneath Avery receiving a place at Oxford above the Stripes celebrating a win overlapping with the Council planting trees in Argentina. Ambrose wears protective goggles beside

314

a smoking test tube as Phoebe pouts in a mermaid costume watching Jack score a winning goal as Bethany is flanked by friends and Cassidy makes snow angels with me.

A Starlet becomes a Stripe as a Council emblem merges with a TEMPA trophy. Cassidy's make-up pallets become Eric's fossils while Siena's hair is an icy torrent leading the canoeing team to safety. We sit as Fifths with last year's Shells; as Sixth Formers with thirteen-year-old Stripes; as Fourths with today's Council; and we're jagged pieces of ourselves and each other as time flows backwards and forwards and sideways and up and down, the walls a seemingly random map to innumerable outcomes as every student in the school is woven into a sea of possibilities, all of them Head Girls and Boys and scientists and beauty queens and graduates and star performers and politicians and brides and grooms.

'I can't believe she did this,' I whisper. 'I didn't think she cared about me at all.'

'I'm pretty sure it's the best thing she's ever done for anyone,' he says. 'Why did she choose this as your *Inspiration*?'

'I have no idea,' I say. 'This kind of possibility; of choosing our own futures? She knows I don't believe in that.'

'You don't believe that we decide our own futures?'

'Rather than repeating our parents' errors?' I ask. 'Siena doesn't believe that any more than I do. She let me into the Starlets because I could tell fortunes. She convinced Libby that they needed me to keep them on the right track.'

'I remember that,' he laughs as I regress to the moment that changed my life forever; the moment when Libby first anointed girls with earrings that glinted and sparked and danced as the rest of us watched in silent frenzy, even without knowing what they meant.

After Phoebe had accepted this membership symbol that was as platinum-sharp as her triumphant smile, Libby and Siena conferred in a heated whisper. I scanned the room for the likely final recipient, but, before Libby could make her announcement, Siena stood up.

'You,' she said in a voice as cool as water.

And Siena wanted me.

'I hear you tell fortunes?' Libby's eyes were narrowed in barely disguised disapproval at this unexpected situation as I stood before them.

Siena was smiling. 'She gave my sister a reading yesterday.'

I remembered Stella; the Star.

Libby was waiting. 'Go on then; impress us.'

I reluctantly shuffled my Tarot cards, hoping for inspiration as I held them out to Phoebe. Libby laughed at her choice as Phoebe scowled at the Fool.

'That seems about right,' Siena conceded. 'Now Libby.'

Libby picked the High Priestess with a grudging

smile, before Siena raised an eyebrow at her Tower card.

'It means you'll reach dizzy heights,' I improvised. 'Higher than anyone else.'

Having momentarily diverted every girl's gaze from Siena's silvery perfection, I'd never been more aware of my untreated hair or my chipped nail polish, let alone my laddered tights.

Why you? came in waves of disbelief as everyone ignored Mrs Denbigh's introductory assembly about *loyalty, integrity and a sense of fun*; as Siena looked into her mirror and Libby looked at Siena and the other Starlets looked as if they couldn't believe their luck and everyone looked at me as if they couldn't believe mine.

'Siena has some fascinating ideas about deterministic chaos,' Jack muses, his eyes lighting up as I imagine Siena laughing at this in-depth analysis. 'See how she's illustrated her theories on the butterfly effect with actual butterfly images . . .'

'Saved by the bell,' I interrupt as I look at my ringing phone, freezing in shock as I see who's calling.

'Romy?' my dad says. 'I've come to visit you, if you have time.'

'You called me *Romy*,' I say incredulously.

Chapter Forty-seven

Siena

I sit on Seraphina's velvet chair before the three light-bulb-surrounded mirrors from her days as a model. The reflections show off my full triptych of apathy as she tries out new hairstyles, twisting and weaving and tightening curls as if I'm a doll. I stare at my faces, then at hers, so that we blur into each other and out again, and I see not only myself but my sisters as they grow old enough to sit in my place, bored and beautiful mannequins who think only of calories and popularity and status.

That won't happen to them, I remind myself. *Stella's life at Temperley High will be different to mine. We just have to make it that far.*

'I'm not sure about this,' I venture as we regard the wedding dress hanging against the door. 'Perhaps I should wear something else tonight.'

'*Perhaps* you could have mentioned that earlier,' she rebukes me as I remember the hours I've spent here having the dress moulded around me, gripping me from all angles like skeleton fingers.

'I'm sorry,' I say. 'It's so *tight*.'

'Do I take it that you are not going to win this . . . election?' she says.

We both know that she means something entirely different when she says *election*, and that I lack the courage to follow this conversation through.

'What if I don't want to win?' I whisper.

She releases my hair so that it crashes to my waist. For a second I look exactly like Stella, and I know what she's thinking.

'You're not my only child,' she says. 'So you may do as you wish. In turn, I may invite whom *I* like to your victory dinner party tonight.'

'Not Stella,' I stammer in panic. 'You can't invite Stella!'

'Jealousy is a most unattractive trait,' she says, a smile playing across her lips.

'I'm not jealous,' I say. 'I just don't want her attending dinner parties at her age.'

'You did.'

'I was different. I want her left alone. I don't want anyone looking at her.'

'So you are jealous,' she says triumphantly.

I answer her by crossing the room, removing my dressing gown and putting on the dress, wincing as it pinches and bruises my ribs. But this is endurable, because as long as my mother has me, and as long as I can be what she wants, she has no need of Stella.

'*I* am your only child,' I say. 'In every way that counts. I'll wear this dress, and win everything you want me to win.'

I watch the dress in the lights of the mirror. I don't look like myself at all, and I remember that Seraphina was the same age I am now when she last looked like this.

Chapter Forty-eight

Romy

My dad is in the stables with his back to me, awkwardly feeding Star a carrot. He motions me onto a bale of straw as formally as if it's a boardroom chair, sitting opposite and clearing his throat.

'You have a baby brother,' he announces, pride creeping into his voice despite his attempt to remain businesslike. 'He was born last night.'

'Wow.' I try to process this. 'A brother! Is Vivienne okay?'

'She's fine now,' he frowns, ruefully rubbing his arm where a handprint of bruises is visible. 'Whatever our differences – we wanted to tell you as soon as we could.'

'I appreciate that,' I nod. *A baby brother*.

'I behaved badly after your mother left,' he says after a moment's silence. 'But I want you to know, Romy, that it was her choice to leave, and hers alone. There was no affair.'

'She must have seen it in her Tarot cards,' I say. 'Even if you and Vivienne hadn't started anything, she must have seen it happen. She knew she couldn't escape it.'

He shakes his head vehemently. 'Romy, she didn't see it happen; she *made* it happen. Her decision to leave wasn't imposed on her.'

'She wouldn't have gone unless she had to,' I insist. 'Why would she leave me?'

'I wish I had a better answer for you,' he says. 'She was unhappy living in one place, and I didn't want to travel. We were incompatible, and I'm afraid you were the casualty.'

'But you moved on immediately,' I remind him. 'She hadn't been gone a month before Vivienne moved in.'

'I was wrong,' he admits. 'As crazy as it sounds, I thought I was doing the best for you. I didn't know how to handle you, and I wanted you to have a mother.'

'You sent *me* away too.' I'm crying, even though it's pointless. 'You didn't want her, and you don't want me either. No wonder she left, when you don't care about either of us.'

'That's not true,' he says, looking stricken. 'I never stopped caring about your mother, and I'll never stop caring about you. I think . . . you're so much like her, it's been hard for me to be near you. Perhaps I punished you because I couldn't punish her.'

'You're still punishing me,' I say. 'Last year you blamed me without even listening. You were happy to have an excuse to get rid of me.'

'There's a lot I haven't listened to,' he says. 'But I'd like to get to know you, if you'll let me.'

Confusing anger flares inside me, and, perhaps for the first time in years, begins to subside. 'Can you forgive me?' he asks.

'I don't know. Are you still throwing me out?'

He looks around as if fearful that Vivienne is listening. 'I wish things were different for us. Maybe in the future . . .'

'In the future, who knows?' I say as something inside me realigns like a river changing course, breaking and speeding and separating as the possibilities of my future swell and multiply until they are too many to conceive. 'Maybe no one can decide that but us.'

He hugs me as he gets up to leave. 'Good luck in your election tonight.'

'Who told you about the election? Was it Mrs Denbigh?'

'No,' he says. 'It was one of your friends – she sent me something . . .'

'I won't win,' I say as he reaches into his pocket. 'I can confidently predict that.'

'I don't care who wins.' He hands me a photograph of me taken at Speech Day. It's been doctored in the style of a yearbook picture, but instead of my *Best Felon* sash, I'm encased in the words *Most Loyal*. I wonder for a moment who taught Siena to Photoshop.

'I understand that your old friends have forgiven you,' he says. 'Mrs Denbigh tells me you're doing very well.'

'I suppose I'm making progress,' I concede.

'I'll collect you at the end of term, shall I?' he asks as he steps away. 'We'll see where the river takes us.'

Chapter Forty-nine

Siena

Stella and Syrena arrive to witness this final fitting, dressed as neatly as bridesmaids, Syrena's ice lolly confiscated in case we all end up stained with blackberry.

'Do you think one day we'll go to a party together?' Stella asks, modelling her dress.

'Of course,' I tell her, although I never want her exposed to a world of sticky floors and men who objectify her and girls who toss drinks at her because she represents something they believe they want. I don't want to imagine a Stella beyond this little girl, although perhaps I can't see a life beyond this one for any of us.

'What will you be when you grow up, Syrena?' I ask, hoping to be convinced otherwise.

'A circus master,' she says indistinctly, twirling at high speed so that her dress spins out wide.

'Good girl,' says Seraphina, believing her response to be metaphorical.

'And you, Stella?' I ask.

'I want to be you,' Stella says.

'Who am I?'

She doesn't answer, and I wonder if this is because

I'm nothing more than a beacon shining before her and beyond her, always out of reach and because of that – only because of that – impossible for her to relinquish.

'What do you see in your future?' Seraphina asks me.

'I want to go to Oxford,' I say, surprising myself with this answer.

'Why? Where will that lead you?'

I lead myself, as a recent Art project has taught me, into an infinite set of possibilities that, however unlikely, might form my future. I'm a university student, cycling to a lecture down an ancient cobbled street. I'm in the catacombs on a research trip in Rome. I'm one of hundreds in an echoing theatre, weighed down by a mortar board and white fur collar, as my sisters witness a ceremony of which I'm truly proud to be part.

Then it's not alien, or bad, to imagine myself dressed for an office, walking through revolving doors with a briefcase, enduring team outings and communal kitchens and six weeks' annual leave. In none of these images is there a husband by my side, and nor do I mourn his absence.

Seraphina speaks weightily, as if she can read my thoughts. 'I'm considering taking you out of school, Siena. I don't care for its teachings, and I no longer feel that I can trust you to follow mine.'

Panic rises in me at the prospect of being kept

here in the state she wishes me to remain. While my classmates have careers and babies and families, as their youth metamorphoses into crow's feet that remind them of sadness and happiness and loss and gain, I remain here with a mother who doesn't age and doesn't move and doesn't love. It's a gilded prison in which we don't alter or improve or achieve; but, in fear of ageing, and thickening, and wrinkling, find it preferable to live like stone. And I wonder if the reason my father left was this: because my mother never really lived with him even when she did.

As my sisters circle me like handmaidens and throw gold lace at me like confetti, I remember a time just months ago when it seemed that nothing mattered but this, and there was no achievement greater than a wedding, because if my mother never needed more than that, then why should I?

Chapter Fifty

Romy

Jack is still in the darkroom when I return, no doubt formulating ever more complex analyses of Siena's newly discovered genius.

'I need your help,' I say as I begin to tug at the installation. 'We need to move this out of here.'

'What are you . . . ?' he asks. 'Are you sure about this?'

'Surer than I've ever been about anything.' I carry the first set of photographs out of the room and gesture for him to follow me with the next.

'Put your back into it!' Libby is screaming as Cassidy and Madison, both close to tears, struggle with a giant bin of confetti. They've been in the hall since sunrise, and it looks like a cross between the *Gatsby* curtain scene and snow blindness, complete with Siena-decorated bunting and an Aston Martin waiting outside with balloons tied to the bumper.

'Good grief.' Jack stumbles at the sight of the white chairs, carpet, table decorations, lectern-cum-altar, and wall-length posters of him and Siena captured in their most romantic moments. 'Is this where bridegrooms come to die?'

'What are you doing here?' asks Libby in panic. 'It's

bad luck. You aren't supposed to see the room until the—'

'*Wedding*?' he asks. 'Is that where you were heading?'

'Of course not,' she says feebly. '*Election* is what I meant.'

'Well, it's a good thing I came, because I didn't approve this décor.'

'You said we could take charge,' says Phoebe indignantly. 'You said you'd rather die than look at any more colour charts.'

'That was before I found my style . . . pizzazz,' he says. 'As Head Boy-elect, I have a say in this, and I've brought my own decorations.'

He steps aside to reveal the Stripes, who are each carrying a section of Siena's photography.

'You can't come in.' Libby is always a happy believer that she can get the outcome she wants simply by being loudest. 'What is this atrocity?'

'This *atrocity* is our lives,' I say as the Stripes pile in more images. 'Whether you like it or not.'

'None of these moments happened!' protests Libby. 'Everything's mutated. Is it the result of a virus?'

'All these things happened,' whispers Cassidy.

'Not like this!' Libby argues. 'They happened separately, and the ones we didn't see might as well not have happened at all. This is all distorted.'

'It's beautiful,' Cassidy says. 'And it all sort of happened . . . or could've happened.'

'It needs to be removed,' says Libby. 'It makes no

sense – it's the opposite of our aesthetic. It suggests that anyone can be anything . . . that the future is random . . . that we should live communally . . . God, it actually suggests that we're all the *same*.'

She takes a break to glare at me. 'I'm sure I don't have to ask who's responsible?'

'Siena is,' I say with deep satisfaction.

'You're suggesting that *Siena* did this?' She's horrified. 'This isn't Siena's mission statement! There's no order, or status, or reason. Why would she do this?'

'I don't think it matters *why*,' says Madison. 'Just that she did.'

Libby turns on her furiously. 'Why are you talking? Why are you *here*? Siena has yet to decide if you can even remain a Starlet.'

'Don't you see?' says Madison recklessly. 'Siena *has* decided. There are no Starlets anymore, or anything else. We're all just *people*.'

Chapter Fifty-one

Siena

As babies, infants and schoolgirls, my sisters and I strike identical poses in a mass of photographs as though we're separated only by flimsy metal frames, rather than time or age. For months Stella conscientiously followed Syrena's wriggling baby form with our father's old camera, recapturing the poses she and I had struck apparently spontaneously at the same age. Shifting our pictures across the table top to make room, she wedged Syrena cuckooishly between us.

'There isn't space,' I objected once, shoving Syrena's face out of sight.

'She belongs here.' Stella pulled her back.

'It's not symmetrical,' I said feebly.

The next time I saw the display, symmetry had been restored, but a closer glance showed that Stella had made herself the casualty. I pulled her back into place, making my own face invisible instead, and instigating an unspoken tug of war.

'I've never seen this before.' Stella stares at a new photograph of our parents' wedding day. 'Mother, I thought you wore a sash?'

All Seraphina's wedding photographs depict her

wearing a gold sash over her wedding dress; the sash I'll wear if crowned tonight. This image is sashless, and I wonder why it makes such a difference to her appearance. Then my corset, which has needed surprisingly extensive alterations, pinches me more painfully than ever and I flinch.

'I'm finished with you,' Seraphina tells Stella. 'Take the other one with you.'

Stella leads Syrena by the hand, turning a confused look towards me before leaving.

'He married you because you were pregnant,' I blurt out, running dates through my mind as I stare at this image; the only picture in which she appears relaxed. She's facing rigidly forward in her other photographs, but here, turned towards my father and with one hand protectively placed on her swelling stomach, there's no doubt. 'You were pregnant at your wedding.'

'He'd discovered my condition, yes,' she says guardedly. 'He agreed to support me.'

'You blame Syrena for him leaving, but were we all mistakes to him?'

'He'd never expressed a wish for children,' she says, for once not flinching away from the subject. 'But he was aware of his responsibilities. For a time.'

'You only had us to make him marry you, and then to stay with you.'

'That's a cynical view of our relationship.'

'It's the truth,' I say. 'Did he love you?'

'Look at me! How could he not?'

331

She's thin and crumbling and frail. 'People don't fall in love with a face,' I tell her. 'I've believed that he was wrong for leaving us, but *all* this is wrong. You let me blame Syrena, and you made me believe that getting engaged was my only path.'

'Am I to take it that your priorities have changed?' she asks. 'Because, if you no longer care for our values, or the significance of this dress, I'll find someone else who will benefit from them.'

I shake my head violently. 'I promise to use this dress for its intended purpose, if you promise me in turn that you'll let me stay in school, and decide what's best for Stella.'

'Very well,' she shrugs, but she pulls the sapphire comb from my head; the comb she gave me after Syrena was born. 'I'll keep this in case it's needed.'

'Please don't give it to Stella,' I beg her.

I walk to the balcony and watch Syrena digging holes in the lawn with a long spade. Where the ground is particularly hard, she swaps her spade for a sabre-toothed fork. The white dress into which she's been bribed and coaxed and finally forced is covered in muddy handprints, and she's ripped off the bottom six inches and tied it like a bandanna to keep her hair off her face. Her refusal to wear shoes has annoyed me for years, but now, as she stands in the rose garden and digs her little feet into the soil, it's not so hard to see her as the changeling I once feared, who has never been able to sever her roots.

'Paula . . .' says Seraphina quietly, and Paula is beside us in a second. 'Retrieve the pickaxe from Syrena, *por favor*. She's known to be incautious with weaponry.'

Edward is showing Syrena how to strike the earth for the best impact whilst hanging from a tree by his knees, his face red with pride and rush of blood and the effort of calling out to Stella. She looks towards him occasionally, shielding her eyes from the sun and nodding politely as he risks life and limb to impress her.

I've sometimes wondered if Jack and Edward are the wrong way around; that is, that feckless, daredevil Edward would be a better match for me, and that careful, hardworking Jack would be good for Stella. But perhaps it's the balance that matters; perhaps Edward and I would kill each other, and Jack and Stella bore each other to death. It occurs to me to hope that Edward and Syrena never get better acquainted.

'What don't you want for her?' Seraphina asks. 'Everywhere she goes, people will notice her. They will envy her, and desire her, and adore her.'

'They'll hate her too,' I say with a certainty I've never understood before. 'They'll hate her as they hate us.'

She looks at me in amusement. 'What does that matter, if the end result is the same?'

She gestures at Edward, who's performing a one-armed, death-defying feat that Stella has tired of watching. 'She'll have everything she wants in him alone.'

I hope that Syrena achieves her own ambition, because taming lions and jumping through fires and swinging on trapezes surely pose less threat than this household.

In a departure from normal behaviour, and possibly with some idea of rebellion, I hold out my arms to my sisters as I say goodbye. Entwined and intermingled, we're a blur of fair hair and lacy tulle and golden flowers; and, flanked by their baby chests, I feel their hearts beat with mine. This is how they hold each other.

Waiting for Stella to smile requires time. It doesn't occur to me until now that our father, with his busy schedule, and his limited patience, and his reticence to listen or see or hear, probably never once saw that smile.

Stella is summoned away while Syrena hangs back. She wiggles her toes in the grass, which for the first time makes me not irritated but envious. 'Are you bringing any friends tonight?'

'Only Jack,' I say. 'The girls will be busy.'

'Even Libby?' she says impatiently. 'What are we paying her for? She's no good.'

'You've got your wires crossed,' I say. 'We don't *pay* Libby.'

She nods her head emphatically. '*Yes, Miss Hamilton. No, Miss Hamilton. I promise she'll win, Miss*

Hamilton. Of course that will make Jack propose. Don't fire me! Wow, a bonus? For me?'

Her voice is squeaky and seven years old but I let it merge into Libby's imperious tone. As she puts her hands over her heart and flutters her eyelashes, I see Libby's face so vividly that I know she's telling the truth.

'Who else knows about this?' I ask, lowering my voice. 'Does Stella know?'

'No, they always make sure Stella isn't around.' She tugs my hand. 'Can I get paid to be someone's friend? Weapons don't grow on trees.'

I stumble away, but turn as she calls after me. 'I don't think we'd have to pay Romy,' she says, her face illuminated in excitement at her good idea. 'She'd be your friend for free.'

Chapter Fifty-two

Romy

Siena doesn't reappear all afternoon, by which time rumours have begun that she's left Temperley High for a Swiss finishing school, and the Starlets have degenerated into brief panic before recuperating with the help of a team-building swimming trip with the Stripes.

She joins me in the Art studio an hour before Elevation is due to begin. The hall is locked, so she's as yet unaware of the success of her project. 'You look very pretty,' I tell her.

'Of course I look pretty.'

I roll my eyes. 'Modest much?'

'Modesty has nothing to do with it,' she says honestly. 'People tell me I'm pretty as if . . . as if they're accusing me of something awful.'

'You make yourself as beautiful as you can be,' I say. 'You wear it like a weapon.'

'It's not a weapon; it's armour. I don't know what I'd be without it. And it makes me scared of what Stella will become. Of what that face will make her.'

'Her face isn't *her*, any more than your face is *you*,' I say. 'What do you want for her?'

'I want her to cut off all that hair and run around

barefoot,' she says. 'Walk the Inca Trail. Fall in love with someone who loves her for *her*.'

She rattles the darkroom door, and, finding it locked, flops restlessly onto a chair beside me. 'Don't tell me you actually want to get in there?' I ask her.

She tries to work out what I know, but I keep my expression bland until she gives up. 'Of course not. You'll be lucky if I bother to take a single photograph for you.'

She stares at my replacement *Inspiration* painting, copied from a photograph of her family on a boat trip. 'Where did you get this?'

'Jack gave it to me,' I say. 'Don't tell me it's wrong *again*? You've written on the back that it was the best day of your life.'

We stare at this image of Siena looking great on a boat despite high winds, with baby sisters who adore the ground she walks on, that might be anyone's perfect day.

'It *was* the best day of my life,' she says. 'Stella nearly drowned that day.'

I pause in disbelief. 'Siena, every time I think you've changed . . .'

She picks up a paintbrush and describes, in words that match her even strokes, sunbathing on a Capri beach until Syrena screams. *Stella's gone.*

Siena runs into the sea, choking as waves crash over her head and the current pulls her under. She's tipped up and down and tossed back and forth as her eyes and ears fill with water. Then she sees a shock of golden hair.

Back on the shore, Siena pounds Stella's chest and screams her name until Stella opens her eyes, and Siena promises her, as she twists Stella's hair around her arm like ivy that will destroy a building before it can be uprooted, that she'll never lose her again.

And Siena adds something into the painting that's not visible in the photograph – a hideous stuffed rabbit with red eyes and buck teeth.

'Oh God,' I say. 'Syrena had lost that rabbit in the sea, hadn't she? Stella was fetching it for her.'

Siena nods. 'It washed up later, unfortunately, missing a paw.'

'This was your *best day*?' I ask doubtfully. 'It doesn't sound like a lot of fun.'

'It wasn't fun at the time,' she says. 'Stella and Syrena had always been such a unit that I thought they didn't need me. That was the first time I felt we all needed each other. I'd never known before that day that we only make sense as a three.'

We turn at a knock on the door. Jack is outside, and Siena gets up to leave. 'Syrena did one more thing that wasn't so terrible after all,' she tells me. 'She introduced me to you.'

Chapter Fifty-three

Siena

Under the arbour of apple trees where Jack and I first kissed, he takes out Edward's Swiss Army knife and carves into the tree: *Jack Lawrence + Siena Hamilton.*

'What's that for?' I ask. 'I don't think we'll be soon forgotten.'

'That depends on what you want your legacy to be. Perhaps you want to be remembered as Head Girl.'

'And you as Head Boy,' I say.

'In some ways,' he acknowledges. 'But mostly I want to be remembered for things I'm proud of. And the thing I'm most proud of is right in front of me.'

Leaning forward, I kiss his jaw, feeling him shiver. He kisses the edge of my mouth. Then my back is pressing hard against the tree and he's holding my hands.

'Is this what you wanted?' he asks.

'Something like this,' I hear myself say.

Running his hands over my dress, he circles my hip bones in a sensation of hot and cold and light and dark and strength and weakness and silence and noise. I watch his pupils dilate as I gently rake my fingernails up and down the insides of his wrists.

'I missed you,' he says right into my ear, but I turn

away as he twists his arm into mine.

'I should never have kissed you that day,' I say. 'Because you were with Romy and I knew that . . .'

I wonder at his insensitivity as he impatiently shakes his head. 'Have you tortured yourself with that for all these years?'

'You said when we got together that it ruined the possibility of a beautiful relationship,' I remind him. 'Because Romy has always been in love with you.'

'Listen to me,' he says slowly and clearly. 'I'm not keeping this secret any longer. Romy is in love with *you.*'

Romy is in love with me. I begin to tell him that he's wrong, but then I remember the way Romy looks at me and Jack, with longing and regret. I see the way she's protected me, and jeopardized her school career for me, and I see that my betrayal did break her heart, but not for the reason I've always understood.

'So I was your first?' I ask.

'You were my first and only.' He pulls me close. 'Last term I asked if you really loved me, aside from weddings and expectations and everything else that isn't us.'

I open my mouth to tell him *yes,* but the word is inadequate, because I'd also use it to say *yes* I like that dress or *yes* I want to win the election or *yes* I'd like to fire Libby from a cannon. Instead I kiss him as I always have, except that now we play each other not like toys but like strings, as if it doesn't matter that our connection grew from at best desire and at worst deceit, as long as it's grown until it's bigger than either of us. And that maybe, if all these feelings co-exist like pearl drops on a necklace, our feelings for each other can be infinite, and that this infinity can mean as much, or even be the same, as love.

Chapter Fifty-four

Romy

I leave the Art studio as the clock strikes eight, looking up at the clock tower as Siena drops her usual calling card: a golden leaf that flutters to the ground and lands by my feet.

When I join her in the tower, only a few minutes since we sat and painted together, something has changed. I'm certain – even without knowing how – what Jack has just told her, but, though I've spent five years protecting this secret, I find that I no longer mind.

'You know, don't you?' I ask as I climb out of the window to sit beside her. 'I can tell, because I've been here for three seconds and you haven't tried to pick a fight yet.'

'That can change in an instant,' she says. 'But I'd rather not risk it when we're sitting on such a narrow ledge. Especially with your track record.'

'I didn't push Libby.' It's a relief to say this now that Libby has nothing to threaten me with.

Siena's suddenly crying for a friendship that never existed. 'You found out that she's on my mother's payroll.'

Siena's mother is paying you to make Jack propose? I asked Libby that evening. I'd noticed that she became

342

wealthier when Jack and Siena were happy. She took a lot of telephone calls that made her very scared. Her obsession with Siena and Jack overstepped the boundaries of normal friendship. But it wasn't until I asked the question that I knew for sure. We were the last to climb down the ladder, and I held her arm to stop her from leaving.

I receive an allowance, she said stiffly. *For necessary expenses.*

Siena's mother pays your school fees, I said. *She buys you handbags and presents. Your chauffeur really belongs to her. You wouldn't be in this school without Siena.*

It's important that Siena follows the right path. Libby was absolutely serious. *I'd appreciate it if you didn't interfere.*

You can't expect me to keep this from her, I protested.

She took a step away from me, keeping one foot on solid ground while the other hovered in space. *Think carefully about that in light of the secret you're hiding.*

What secret? I asked, vainly hoping that she was bluffing.

Back in control, her expression was triumphant. *You love Siena.*

You can't prove that. You can't prove anything at all.

The way you look at her is proof enough, she said. *I'm surprised the whole school doesn't know. Not to mention the fact that your relationship with Jack was completely fake.*

How can you be sure? I asked lamely. *And why would that stop me telling Siena that her mother pays you?*

She rolled her eyes. *Please. You're terrified of Siena finding out about your feelings for her. You think it'll ruin your friendship, and you're right. But, just to make sure, let's call this insurance.*

With an ear-splitting scream, she fell backwards through the trapdoor.

'Why did you say that Jack was your boyfriend?' Siena asks me now. 'That first day, in the rain?'

'I didn't want to lose my best friend. My *only* friend. I knew as soon as he saw you that he'd no longer need me. Pretending he was my boyfriend was my only chance of keeping him.'

'But it made me want him more,' she smiles. 'It made me jealous.'

'How do you think I convinced him to go along with it?' I ask her drily.

'I'm sorry I stole him,' she says. 'Friend, boyfriend; I know now that it's just as bad.'

'Why do you come up here so much?' I ask her. 'It's dark, and dank, and dusty . . . it's the kind of place that you usually run a mile from.'

'I feel safe here,' she says.

I look at the decrepit room behind us; the drop before us. 'There's no way out!'

'But, you see, there is.' Before I know what she's doing, she's reached into my bag and pulled out the

344

Tarot cards that I've hidden from her for a year.

'Why did you convince the Starlets that I could tell fortunes?' I ask as she shuffles the cards. 'Why did you want them to accept me? Was it just to get close to Jack?'

She shakes her head. 'Maybe I wanted to rebel against my mother even then. Syrena liked you, and maybe I didn't despise her as much as I thought I did. Or maybe . . .'

She leans her head back against the wall. 'Maybe I just liked you. With no agenda.'

'That's the most unexpected thing you've ever said,' I tell her. 'So you never believed I was psychic?'

She laughs. 'No one can tell the future. Most of us can't even see the present.'

She holds the cards to her chest, and I almost tell her that I don't believe it either. I've waited long enough for a gift that shows no sign of materializing. But then she stretches out her arms, letting the cards fall between her fingers, and flings the whole pack into the sky. For a moment we're surrounded by our collapsing destinies, as the Empress and the Fool and the Moon and the Tower jostle for topmost position. And, as they catch on the breeze and float away, I see that my mother was right.

You'll just know.

I've believed that Siena is impossible to read because she surrenders nothing. But now I see another possibility: that the swirling, swooping darkness I see in place of her future means that, for reasons I can't consider, she doesn't have one.

'Don't come up here anymore,' I say, my heart beating hard. 'That's not a prediction, it's a . . . a *cri de coeur*.'

Her face is close to mine; her eyes are so blue that, even when I close my own, I still see cornflower. 'Come on,' she says, pulling me inside. 'I want to swap dresses with you.'

'What are you talking about?' I look at the yellow dress that I've borrowed from Madison to ensure that it gets a proper outing. 'You're wearing your dream gown. And yellow gives you a conniption fit.'

'My dress hurts,' she says breathlessly as she wriggles out of the corset.

'I don't want to wear something painful,' I protest as she imprisons me inside layers of chiffon and ties a sash around my waist.

'It'll do you good to learn how to stand correctly,' she says as she pulls on the yellow dress. 'And it'll do *me* good to wear something I can breathe in unassisted for once.'

'I thought we were the same size,' I wince, pushing my feet into her unyielding glass-heeled shoes. 'These are tiny. They must cripple you.'

She pulls her hair loose, letting long waves crash around her face and to her hips. Shaking herself free of adornments, she weaves gold into my own hair until a burning glow fills my head like fireflies.

'I'm not wearing shoes tonight,' she says in satisfaction. Her legs are long and brown against the floating yellow fabric, and, barefoot, she looks like a flower fairy. She takes from her bag a swirlingly multi-coloured rose and smiles as she pushes it into her hair.

I try to memorize the way she looks right now, because she'll never look this way again, and because I no longer have to hide it.

'You had a boyfriend in Paris,' she remembers.

'Max,' I tell her, 'is short for Maxine.'

'How long have you known?' she asks. 'That you were...'

'Since the first time I saw you,' I tell her, and I don't know what makes me say it out loud except that perhaps I believe this is the last chance I'll ever have.

Chapter Fifty-five

Siena

Jack and I walk towards Elevation when there are no more excuses. I drag my feet, dreading the anachronistic wedding-themed hall, but he pulls me onwards at top speed.

'You're very enthusiastic,' I tell him. 'Especially as you hate formal events.'

'You're going to enjoy this one,' he says as he holds open the door.

At first I think I've walked into a weird parallel universe where I enter one door and exit in another location entirely. But we're not in the darkroom, where I've spent so many solitary hours memorizing faces I've never bothered to speak to; learning about perspective and tone and composition; placing and shaping and working students into a semblance of unity and free will that doesn't heed popularity or status or money. We're in the hall, surrounded not only by my photographs, but by their human forms.

'You did this?' I ask Jack incredulously.

He kisses me on the forehead. 'You did it, Siena. I was just a witness.'

Cameras flash endlessly as we pass through the crowd. Usually I make for the centre of the room,

348

because no one worth knowing congregates anywhere else. Divisions are usually as obvious as if people are in containers. But tonight I can't find the Starlets, or the Stripes, or the Council, because the dance floor is as unified as the pictures on the walls. I don't even stand out. People whirl around us in an odd time lapse of today and yesterday as if we'll always exist here in every guise we've ever taken, and as if we don't exist at all.

'You did it!' squeaks Cassidy. 'You're back together, and you're winning!'

'I haven't done anything yet. People are still voting.'

'It's just a formality,' Phoebe says. 'Your entrance with Jack is the moment everyone was waiting for.'

'So I'm not getting elected for my intellect?' I ask wryly.

'No,' she says with a flash of honesty. 'But you've got a whole year of being Head Girl ahead of you. No one will underestimate you after that.'

Madison is crying, but I think this time with happiness. 'You're wearing my dress. It looks as beautiful as I knew it would, if you just gave yellow a chance.'

Libby elbows her out of the way. 'Something's happened,' she says anxiously. 'I know you so well, Siena. I can always tell when something's wrong.'

'Of course you do,' I agree. 'After all, you're paid to know.'

Colour drains from her face. 'I . . .' she manages. 'Give me a moment to explain.'

'I'm not interested in your motivations. But please tell me why my mother considered this necessary. Was it a complete lack of faith in me?'

'No.' For a moment she sounds as if she cares. 'She worried that your compassion would obstruct her – *your* – ambition. I was a means of keeping you distant.'

'Like an exhibit?' I ask. 'Pinned into shape behind glass?'

'Exactly. And, obviously, to keep you on the straight and narrow, away from corrupting influences. I failed on that front.'

'I believed you were my Fairy Godmother,' I say. 'But all this time it was Syrena.'

'That child,' mutters Libby. 'The sooner she's in military school, the better.'

'She's not so bad.' I smile despite myself. 'You just have to get to know her.'

'Next you'll be saying that Romy isn't so bad either. You know I'd be as loyal to you without any payment. Whereas *she* . . .'

'Libby, I know *everything*,' I say. 'Including how you fell down the ladder. This means the end of the Starlets.'

'It doesn't have to,' she protests. 'Even if you don't want to continue, I could . . .'

Romy laughs loud and long as Libby explains ways in which the Starlets could succeed with me in a less prominent role. Her voice fades as Jack and I are propelled to the stage.

Chapter Fifty-six

Romy

Siena's life snaps into alignment as she takes her place beside Jack, accepting her title but refusing her crown. The Starlets and Stripes surround her in a circle that pulses and jumps and screams, and she lets Jack raise her hand above their heads and punch the air as they take in a victory that rains star-shaped confetti. Somehow she's transformed Temperley High, but not, as it always seemed she would, for worse.

More people join them onstage and push and jostle and kiss her and shake his hand until finally, *finally*, Jack wraps both his arms tightly around her, so tightly that I know she can believe no one else is there.

'I need my dress back,' she says as she hurries off the stage. She pulls me into an alcove where we swap clothes once again, and she arranges her hair into its usual order and dons the crown and sash.

'I need an official photograph,' she explains. 'Then we can change back.'

'Don't worry; I have nothing better to do than endlessly swap outfits with you,' I say, but she's already beckoning Jack and gesturing at Libby.

'Can you fetch Tristan?' she asks Libby. 'He takes a very soft-focus shot.'

'He's dancing with Sam.' Libby glares at Jack as he laughs. '*Only* because he doesn't like to lead. I'm tonight's photographer.'

Libby frowns as Siena twirls and smiles. 'You look too happy.'

'It's hard not to look happy tonight,' Siena says. She arranges herself and Jack into a formal embrace, carefully holding his right hand with her left so that her fingers are obscured. 'You need to send this to my mother as soon as possible.'

Libby looks stricken. 'I already sent your mother a picture of your winning moment. Was I not supposed to?'

'You sent her mother a picture of the *other dress*?' Siena asks. 'The yellow dress?'

'She ordered me to,' says Libby feebly. 'She wanted a picture at the *instant* you won.'

'We have to go home.' Siena pushes Libby away. 'Right now.'

'Don't,' I say hurriedly, although I don't know why. 'Stay here.'

She looks amused, despite her evident worry. 'I'm coming straight back.'

She blows a kiss, and I watch her, framed underneath a time-lapsed arch that depicts her as a cheerleader, a fairy, a schoolgirl, a hockey champion, a ragged orphan and a pink Cinderella. Light frames her like a halo in which all her past selves seem not to have been cast off, but absorbed.

Chapter Fifty-seven

Siena

I lean forward in my seat. A beat of anticipation about finally having something substantial to share with Stella is overtaken by the possibility that she may no longer be interested in hearing it.

I lead Jack to the back of the house, where he holds me against the wall and kisses me, and I laugh because his eyes are blazing with an intensity that frightens me, and I don't know how else to make it dissipate.

'Wait for me here.' I run up the stairs and push open the door where Stella and Syrena should be sleeping like sisters who share everything and want for nothing, because they have each other, and know that, even in sleep.

Syrena's head is resting on her hand, her face lit by the spinning stars of her constellation lamp. But she's alone, and she doesn't stir as I touch her softly rounded cheek.

'How could I have thought that any of this was your fault?' I whisper. 'And, if it were, how could I have thought that mattered?'

I return to Jack after checking the other bedrooms. 'I can't find Stella.'

He pulls a face. 'Don't make me go into the party,'

he says as we walk to the front door. 'My dad's going to ask me about my exams.'

'He'll be pleased with you,' I remind him. 'We've achieved something tonight.'

'You could at least have brought Syrena as protection,' he says. 'Does she still have the heretic's fork Edward gave her for Christmas?'

I laugh, and the murmur of voices in the dining room immediately hushes.

As I push open the doors and take in the enormous white cake with its elegant figurines of me and Jack on a towering top tier, the silver stars dusting the table, and the confetti covering the plates as though Elevation is at once my wedding day and my funeral and my salvation and my ruination, I'm too late to save this little girl who would have listened to anything I told her and copied any example I set her. As the example I set was one of lies and detachment and an inability to love, this is what she's become.

Stella sits in my place, wearing a white dress that obscures every bit of the child she was this afternoon. She's no longer that child, because she's beautiful in a way that will make people watch and covet and love and despise her without ever caring why. Her beauty has the power to strip away everything that makes her worth knowing.

Every time I've greeted Stella since she could walk, she's reached me as fast as she can travel. But tonight she can't move, any more than I can. We're deadlocked, and trapped, and condemned. I see too late that the detachment I've strived for has kept me from the people who value me for what I am, and moulded me into a symbol of thwarted ambition.

'You deceived me,' Seraphina tells me with a flick of her mobile phone on which I see a girl in a yellow dress, barefoot and loose-haired and incandescent with undignified happiness that's entirely at odds with her plans. 'Now you see that you're replaceable.'

Jack's face is sweet and inherently trusting. 'I can't see you anymore,' I tell him in a voice steady and cold enough for him to believe me, because he must have a chance of avoiding the damage that I'll otherwise cause him, no matter how hard I fight against it.

'I love you,' he tells me.

'That's why I have to let you go,' I say, even though my lips are numb and I can hardly speak through the pain tightening across my chest.

Jack's father pushes him out of the door and I flinch away as he reaches for my hand. I argue with Seraphina through a pulse of panic and guilt, and I stare past her to Stella, frozen in her seat, her enormous eyes dark and frightened. I run outside, thinking of nothing but ridding myself of beauty and vanity so that she can see me once without this gilding.

I pick up a lighter and wrench off my sash and dress, so that I'm just wearing my slip. Throwing down the dress, I hold back the sash as I set the dress on fire. There's a dull roar in the airless humidity as flames tear through silk and dupion and chiffon, because the dress, despite having held me in its thrall like iron bars, is substanceless and snuffed out in seconds.

Stella has followed me outside. She reaches for the sash that hid such deception for so many years, and I snatch it back. 'Stay away from this.'

Pulling out her hateful sapphire comb, I watch golden waves of life-saving hair tumble to her waist. 'Always wear your hair like this,' I tell her, 'and don't listen to anyone who tells you differently.'

She's crying. 'Where are you going?'

I put my hand to her cheek. 'There's something I have to do.'

'Don't leave me.' Her voice is the last thing I hear as I close the car door behind me.

At school, Elevation is still in full swing, the fireworks due just before midnight. I try to stay on course, but before entering the tower I turn to see the Starlets dancing under a spotlight. It occurs to me how complete they are without me and how little they need me, even if I've believed myself to be their cornerstone. Without me they have Libby, and without Libby they have Phoebe, and it continues in ever-changing circles as they change and fight and regenerate and endure, whether I'm there or not.

I run up the stairs and climb the ladder, and I stand amongst detritus and discarded splendour and doom. And, as I have a hundred times before, I climb out of the window and stand on the ledge.

Chapter Fifty-eight

Romy

I stay at Elevation for the sake of appearances, taking advantage of the distraction as my phone rings to leave the pounding dance floor.

'What's up?' I ask Jack, smiling. 'Trouble with the mother-in-law?'

The urgency of his voice makes me move immediately. 'I need you to find Siena.'

Woodlands is deserted, and Siena's room unlocked and unoccupied.

'Where else would she go?' he asks as I run back outside. 'The tower?'

'No,' I say with certainty. 'I asked her not to go back there, and I'm sure she was listening.'

'She's there,' he says. 'Look, I just know. Please.'

He's right, because on the bottom step of the spiral staircase I see her shoe, its glass heel sparkling in the dim light.

'Are you coming?' I ask him. 'I can't do this alone.'

'I'll be there as soon as I can,' he says. 'Just make her stay.'

Chapter Fifty-nine

Siena

How long will you love me? I often asked Jack.

Usually he told me *forever*, or *for infinity*, or quoted an incomprehensible sci-fi line, but on one occasion he paused. It was a warm day and we were sitting in a grassy corner of the courtyard, and he pointed up at the tower. *Until the clock stops ticking.*

I was offended, because a ticking clock seemed so impermanent and transient in relation to his usual responses. But he explained, more fully than I considered necessary, that the clock hadn't missed a single beat since the school was built, and that there was a back-up generator to ensure that nothing like a power cut could affect it; and that there was in fact only one way to stop the clock.

We can be confident that that will never happen, he said. *So it's the same as loving you to infinity. And beyond.*

I remove my binding sash, letting the frills of my lace slip swirl and dance, and I wind it around the centre of the clock as tightly and as many times as I can. I hear shouts from below as students call my name; and eventually the sounds settle into a chant that rises on the windless air and surrounds me.

The clock doesn't want to stop. The ticking continues after the hands have stalled, straining as I tighten the tourniquet and stifle it with all my weight.

Chapter Sixty

Romy

I phone Mrs Denbigh. I phone Libby. I phone Security. I vainly input call after call as I climb the stairs, my lungs burning as I push myself onwards.

'You promised me you'd stay away from here,' I say when I reach her. She's standing on the window ledge, unsteady in one shoe, and she looks at me without really seeing anything.

'Jack said he'd love me until the clock stopped,' she says. 'What else can I do?'

'It was a metaphor,' I say. 'He didn't mean it literally. You're not the same as your mother, Siena. You can still help your sisters.'

Her face is pale and lovely in the moonlight. 'You see it now, don't you?' she says, and her voice strums with a million tears unshed. 'You were right. There's no freedom from this cycle. It's already all decided.'

I shake my head vehemently. 'The cycle *is* freedom. You showed me that.'

My phone buzzes. *I'm on my way*, Jack says. It's almost twenty to twelve.

'He's coming. If you think stopping the clock will stop him loving you, you're wrong.'

She winds her hand into the sash as she reaches

361

down to remove her remaining shoe, and I look away for a second as my phone buzzes again.

Tell her I will love her until the clock stops ticking.

She doesn't make a sound, and yet sound is what I notice because what happens is the opposite of sound, as the sash pulls taut and the clock stops ticking. The silence is deafening as she falls, a flaming star of golden hair and golden skin and a spirit that I never got close to touching.

Much later I read the message from Jack that she'll never see.

And for one hundred years more.

Chapter Sixty-one

Siena

I grip the concrete ledge with my toes, closing my eyes and surrendering to the breeze. I tighten my grip in the sash, using my other hand to pull out pins and flowers and gold leaves until my hair falls to my waist and I shed everything I've become; everything I've been made; everything that's distanced me from those I love.

When I open my eyes I don't see the clock beside me. I don't see the courtyard below. I see only the night sky and its millions of stars, surrounding me until there's nothing else. I'm nowhere, and I'm everywhere, and I see everyone I need to see even as they fade away.

I'm with Stella as she hides her own photographs to make room for mine; I'm with Syrena as I paint her toenails ice-cream colours; we're all together as we lie half drowned on a beach, Syrena twisting my long hair around her baby arm as Stella's is wrapped around mine.

Instead of falling, I float like a butterfly towards a garden in which Syrena has wound shoots and stems and sprays around me and Stella until our roots are intermingled and our thorns are blunt and our petals

363

are multi-coloured Neapolitan swirls that encapsulate us all. I see a pastel safety net, pale and slight, yet resolute and as unstoppable as Stella fracturing a frozen ground and Syrena cartwheeling barefoot on a dewy lawn; and I unwind in a golden rope of aerial silk as I am brought to land and moored amongst the sweetly blooming roses that are my sisters.

Chapter Sixty-two

Romy

I trudge up the sweeping driveway, wishing I could camouflage myself in the undergrowth. I run through conversation points, which include the memorial plaque and pink rose garden that will stand at the point she fell. *Beloved sister, daughter and friend* is the word order I fought for, and won. *Siena was a sister first.*

I can tell them that she'd have been a great Head Girl; that the whole school will attend her funeral; and that, instead of the white rhino, a donation will be made in her name to a rabbit protection society. Hard to find, but easier than one protecting unicorns.

I can tell them that the school exists in a kind of petrifaction as people try to make sense of the past and present and future; that her artwork will be dismantled at the end of the school year so that each student can take a piece of her with them.

I can't tell them about the sounds that rose from the courtyard when she was found, contrasting violently with the pillowy silence of her fall; the sirens screaming up the drive; the howls that seemed to come from me as I fell the length of the ladder on my way back to earth. I can't tell them about Jack, for whom nothing in life will ever matter more than the night he was too late; about the Starlets, who stood outside all night like mice at an abandoned feast, wrung with supranatural sleeplessness; with pervading panic; with directionless despair.

I'm undecided about whether to tell them what everyone reported, despite the impossibility of it: that when she fell, a shooting star lit the school white, and, for that one moment, eradicated all other colours like a supernova.

I'm hoping to bypass the enormous front door, but it swings open as I approach.

'Quick,' whispers Syrena, hanging off the door handle. 'No one should see you.'

'Why not?' I ask as I climb the steps.

'No one's been cleaning,' she says as I take in the cluttered hallway, dusty surfaces and general gloom.

Syrena puts her finger to her lips as we pass a dining room covered with debris. The table is laid for a party, complete with white tablecloth and cake, but the room has only one inhabitant, motionless at the head of the table in a long white dress.

'My mother never leaves that room,' Syrena whispers.

My feet are rooted to the spot as Siena's mother turns towards me, her eyes dark in her pale face, her expression uncomprehending. Then I jerk away, stumbling after Syrena up the staircase.

'I told you,' Syrena says matter-of-factly, and I stumble again.

In their bedroom, Stella stands before a full-length mirror, her long hair falling around her like a veil. She's deep in concentration, reaching for pins to hem her white dress. It's so big, I realize, because it belonged to Siena.

'Stella, listen to me,' I say as Syrena looks at me imploringly.

Stella sits down obediently. Her hands are clasped in her lap, her ankles neatly swung to one side. I prepare to tell her that she doesn't have to start at Temperley High this year; that she has a choice about where she takes her life. And then I realize from her expression of polite disinterest that I'm not her first visitor.

'Has Libby been here?' I ask. 'What did she tell you?'

Stella speaks as dispassionately and rhythmically as a ticking clock. 'Siena loved Temperley High. She loved Jack. She loved her friends. Her life was perfect.'

'Stella . . .' I'm already floundering.

'She didn't finish it,' she interrupts. 'She wanted to finish it.'

'You can't finish it for her,' I say. 'You have your own path.'

She turns her head away, and I wonder if she's hiding tears.

'Will you do something for me?' I press. When she doesn't reply, I crouch in front of her. 'Will you promise that you'll consider starting a different school this year?'

She turns back, her eyes clear. 'Why?'

367

I try to tell her what Siena wanted for her: a life that will take her in unexpected and untrodden and messy and wrong directions, with no burdensome legacy of expectation. But a phone rings out before I can speak, and she's on her feet towards it.

'Stella has a PA now,' Syrena whispers. 'She won't tell me who it is, but . . .'

Stella is a miniature silhouette against the window as she pouts and postures and tosses her hair through a conversation about table settings that she can't possibly understand.

'I already know about difficult decisions,' she says, looking directly at me as she steps towards the door. 'When acquiring any venture, redundancies are inevitable.'

She slams the door behind her, and, by the time I follow, she's disappeared.

'Stella will get better,' I tell Syrena as we walk downstairs. 'She just needs time to learn who she's going to be.'

'She won't get better,' Syrena says. 'She already knows who she's going to be.'

She reaches for my hand. 'Promise me you'll stay at Temperley High and help her. Promise me you'll find a way to talk to her.'

'How? Do I make an appointment with her PA?'

She shakes her head, 'She'll listen at the funeral. She can't answer her phone there, or leave the room. At the funeral you can tell the truth.'

'I promise,' I tell her, and we break apart to the sound of shattering glass from the dining room.

I look back once at the end of the drive, fully expecting to see three identical faces watching me through the windows of a house spellbound by loss. But, rather than three faces, I see four. They watch me through curtains on balconies and drawing rooms and hallways and bedrooms, and, no matter how long I stare, I have no way of knowing which face is which, or whether they are living or dead.

The same faces sit in a church heavy with the scent of lilies, and I watch them as Stella becomes Siena and Syrena becomes Stella and their mother remains static in a world collapsing around her.

I watch them as Jack, ashen and faltering, places a single rose – the only pink rose present at this cere- mony – atop her white coffin and then stands paralysed before their pew, staring at each of them in turn as if some permutation of them can restore her to him.

I watch them as the Starlets recount memories of heroism and hedonism and happiness that bear no relation to the girl Siena died to become. I watch them endure this service that holds nothing of Siena, now everything that mattered has been swept away and replaced with the anodyne chasm of propaganda that she seemed for most of her life to be. The room itself is as sterile as the intended Elevation ball, white and gauzy and filled, not with Siena's collage or even her oil paintings, but with the affected pageantry of an existence in which nothing mattered but window-dressing. Jack, in the midst of it, puts his head into his hands as if the images are closing in on him.

I break my gaze to focus on Syrena as she turns towards me, her teeth denting her bottom lip as she reminds me of my responsibilities. *You promised to tell the truth.*

Mrs Denbigh lays her hand on mine. 'We can't let you speak.'

'Why?' The final hymn begins and my opportunity is lost.

'See how this looks,' she says. 'Two girls fall from the tower. One says you pushed her, and the other will never speak again.'

'Libby fell on purpose. And Siena . . .'

Her face is set. 'This isn't my choice. But perhaps the school's decision is best for *you*.'

'What decision?'

'You can't come back to Temperley High next year,' she says over the sound of the organ, which dies away before she moderates her volume. 'I'm sorry.'

Siena's mother winds Stella's hair around her fingers until it's coiled and neatly sprung, using it as a shackle to pull her closer. Syrena doesn't take her eyes off me as she clambers onto her seat. Her despairing scream cuts across everything, silencing the congregation even as Stella sways and tumbles onto the flags with a finality that makes me envy her unconsciousness. Her mother lets her fall, her face turning from triumph to something sourer as Stella's Rapunzel hair unwinds from her hands in a braid of aerial silk that breaks her stone landing.

Syrena is forgotten in the furore, and I take advantage of the disruption to follow her as she streaks past. Out in the graveyard I find her curled, cat-like, against a crumbling tombstone, her eyes too large in her head and too blue for her pale skin.

'We're all the same,' she shivers as I sit beside her.

Syrena is Siena, whose boundless radiance, unimaginably aborted, will lie beneath us as cold as marble, her eyes shut to the sunlight filtering through these horse chestnut trees above her; the spiky frost and veil of snow pillowing a resting place that needs no air; the hedgerows regenerating endlessly while underground she turns to dust.

And Siena is Stella, who wears her beauty like something stolen and who sleeps on a stone floor as chaos erupts around her, finding nothing in the tangible world that can bring her home.

Alive, they stood as slender and fragile as a trio of roses, righting themselves against each other in a dance that gave them air and warmth and nourishment. Cast asunder, the remaining pair may grow beyond Siena, surpassing her interrupted existence with identities of their own, or they may remain with her, absorbing her qualities as they interwreathe into a quiescently peaceful golden halo.

Epilogue

Romy

This morning feels in some ways like any other as I stare around the cafeteria at the inevitable regression that's taken place since the unity of Elevation. The Starlets, with Libby at their head, are restored as the centrepiece. The Stripes, without Jack, are beside us. The Council are on the broken benches at the back. Yet it's not like any morning that's come before it, because it will be my last.

'I wanted to give Stella a choice,' I tell the Starlets, in case any vestige of sanity remains amongst them. 'I wanted her to start a different school. As herself.'

'History shows that she'll be safer following my lead than yours,' says Libby. 'Siena died on your watch. Stella will not die on mine.'

'Are you still working for Siena's mother?' I ask disbelievingly.

'My contract has been extended,' she admits. 'I have a new client now, and we have a responsibility to lay the foundations for a clique-in-waiting. Our job is to inspire and coach the next generation until we're ready to step aside.'

'*Our* job?' Everyone stares at the table instead of meeting my eyes. 'You, Cassidy? Even you, Mads?'

372

'Stella's upbringing is of the upmost importance,' murmurs Madison as Cassidy nods beside her. 'We'll give her the best possible start.'

'Siena dissolved the Starlets before she died,' I protest. 'You can't indoctrinate Stella into believing that Siena wanted this.'

'Siena would have wished me to show Stella the right path,' Libby says. 'We're contractually bound to help her.'

She's wearing her new Head Girl badge, awarded for services to the school in leading students through a time of intense grief, and she's sitting in Siena's engraved place.

They accuse me of hating them and of knowing more than I'm letting on; they discuss, endlessly, how Siena must have felt as she died. The conversation degenerates as the new Shells start to arrive.

'I'm leaving today,' I say. 'Does it mean nothing to you that I was Siena's friend?'

Phoebe stares me out. 'Stop feeling sorry for yourself. We aren't fooled. We all know *exactly* how you felt about Siena. How you feel about us all, for that matter.'

I tip back my head as if it will stop my tears from falling, looking beyond the Starlets and beyond the little girl entering the cafeteria. My chair crashes backwards as I leave it, clawing the curtain and stumbling through the French windows towards a fleeting, disappearing image. It's an image that no longer exists in this world, but that captivates me long enough for a sea change to occur in the cafeteria behind me.

Redundancies are inevitable, Stella said with the assurance of a managing director. And her entrance from the wings has introduced a new balance, displacing the Starlets who now huddle, shell-shocked, in the doorway.

'What happened?' I ask as I rejoin them, frowning at the new group sitting around the hallowed Starlet table.

'Nothing happened,' says Libby stiffly. 'We're . . . having a team meeting.'

'Were you *fired*?' I ask in disbelief.

'I'm not sure what happened . . .' Phoebe says dreamily. 'One minute we were sitting there, and then . . .'

She waves towards the table, where six little Shells match six star-pointed initials. They toss their hair and sip coffee as if they've been there all their lives, the only clue to their newness in the way that five of them watch and copy the girl in Siena's place.

'I thought you were going to inspire and coach the new generation until they were ready to take over?' I ask.

'The next generation are ready now,' says Cassidy.

Stella is talking closely with a brown-haired girl who looks as if she can't believe her luck. They are the image of Siena and Libby. Around them, I count a straw-haired fashionista, a red-haired little misfit, a baby-blonde fluff ball and a brunette in a leather jacket identical to mine.

'Even their initials match ours. We each have a little doppelgänger. Mine's Mary-Ann.' I sense a note of pride as Madison gestures to the gangly girl with straw-coloured hair.

'Mine's Penny,' says Phoebe, looking maternally at the tiny white-blonde girl. 'There's a Lila, and a Katrina. I expect someone beginning with C will join them later, Cassidy. I wonder which of them will get kicked out to make way for her.'

Libby laughs mirthlessly. '*Ruby*, of course. Guess who she matches?'

'You, Romy,' she adds when I don't reply. 'She matches you.'

'Don't you understand that the Starlets are no more?' I ask. 'That *you* are no more?'

'They're only playing,' says Libby. 'They don't have the authority, or the expertise, to overthrow us.'

'Are you sure about that?' I ask. 'You shared a lot of information with Stella, and now she's become the master. You've walked into a trap.'

The little girls pile their hands rapidly on top of each other as everyone turns to watch. The other new girls, awkward in too-big uniforms and unflattering boaters, watch Stella with expressions veering between envy and sheer longing; the boys, notably a serious blond boy who's already wearing a Stripes kit, don't take their eyes off her. Edward, unnaturally neat in his blazer and combed hair, is openly mesmerized. The five of us, huddled beneath an exit sign, might as well no longer exist.

'*I'm* the master,' protests Libby.

'Stars aligned,' chorus the little girls, lifting their hands above their heads.

As their place is cemented in the centre of the school's consciousness, and their rights to the table acknowledged beyond doubt, Stella looks at Libby, purpose like regicide blazing in her eyes, and then she turns to the open door.

The Daimler stands to my left, my belongings packed ready to be transported to Bedales, or Roedean, or wherever else I'll endure another school year. My father occupies the front seat, his shoulders sagging under a weight he can never shed.

I take one step forward before looking to my right, where the stables stand before open countryside. My fortune may lie beyond the next corner, or in a distant field, but, as I lead my horse from his stable, I can do no more than follow Siena's untrodden path of freedom as I ride barefoot and bareback into the infinite peace of a celestial cornflower sky.